Stepchild

To Marie
I hope you
enjoy.

Erskine Havili

Stepchild

Erskine Hawkins Jr.

MOUNTAIN ARBOR
PRESS

Mountain Arbor
Press
Alpharetta, GA

ISBN: 978-1-63183-010-5

This ISBN is the property of Mountain Arbor Press for the express purpose of sales and distribution of this title. The content of this book is the property of the copyright holder only. Mountain Arbor Press does not hold any ownership of the content of this book and is not liable in any way for the materials contained within. The views and opinions expressed in this book are the property of the Author/Copyright holder, and do not necessarily reflect those of Mountain Arbor Press.

Library of Congress Control Number: 2016917102

10 9 8 7 6 5 4 3 2   011717

Printed in the United States of America

∞This paper meets the requirements of ANSI/NISO Z39.48-1992 (Permanence of Paper)

Scripture quotations marked "KJV" are taken from the Holy Bible, King James Version (Public Domain).

For Erston,
my baby brother who fell in the reaping.
You are missed.

To fling my arms wide
In some place of the sun,
To whirl and to dance
Till the white day is done.
Then rest at cool evening
Beneath a tall tree
While night comes on gently,
Dark like me—
That is my dream!

To fling my arms wide
In the face of the sun,
Dance! Whirl! Whirl!
Till the quick day is done.
Rest at pale evening . . .
A tall, slim tree . . .
Night coming tenderly
Black like me.

—Langston Hughes, "Dream Variations"

Contents

Acknowledgments

I would like to thank my wife, Yvette, for listening to me bellow all these years about a solution. Job would be jealous of your patience. I would like to thank Melody Foster for reading and rereading and critiquing this work until I had something I could be happy with. Thanks to my dear friend Min Brown for the great suggestions and insight. Mary McBeth, whose invaluable advice showed me there's a book in there somewhere. The staff at BookLogix for helping me to walk the last mile to publication. And finally I'd like to thank my father for all of his advice and support.

Part I

Chapter 1

Sarah

Josh pulled on his cigarette, enjoying the feel of the nicotine rush surging through his mind as War's "The World Is a Ghetto" played on his radio. Three o'clock in the afternoon found him starting his third pack of the day. He'd have to remember to pick up a carton. He absentmindedly reached for the box of breath mints lying on the passenger seat and popped two pieces of candy into his mouth. All that smoke had dried his throat out.

He swung into a parking space as he gulped down the remnants of his riding partner, the quart of malt liquor sitting between his legs. He put the car in park and cut it off. He took another drag, got out, and walked across the parking lot and up the steps to his apartment.

Sarah had asked him once why he lived upstairs. He had told her he knew from his days in the moving business that it was a lot harder to move somebody if they lived upstairs. She'd looked puzzled and asked why he would want to make it harder to bring his stuff out when he decided to move. He'd laughed, explaining that the movers he worked with always came in unannounced, preferably when no one was at home.

He thought about that girl he and Slim had moved twice in one week. Pat told him about how after the first lick, the girl rented a TV to replace the one they'd taken from her ground-floor apartment. He shook his head and said, "Damn, niggers ain't shit. And I bet she works hard for her stuff, too." He and Slim couldn't resist. They went back in through the same bedroom window the next night. She'd locked it again, not realizing all they had to do was take a butter knife and tap it on the window to spring that cheap-assed lock builders loved to use in Atlanta. Slim cracked that the builders must have been planning to come back to hit a lick someday.

His back door opened into his kitchen. Nobody ever came through the front door in these apartments because the parking was in the back of each building. Next to his favorite space was the one where Sarah had parked religiously up until six months ago, when she moved out.

He'd made a couple of half-assed efforts to get her to give him another chance, something they both knew she didn't need to do. He tried showing up at her new place, which was of course upstairs, pleading with her to take him back. Eventually she cracked, agreeing to meet him for lunch, to talk things over. His failure to show up had not gone over too well, but, for reasons he could not begin to fathom, what really seemed to upset her was the fact that he hadn't bothered to call and say he wasn't going to show up.

After Faith met Sarah for the first time, she told Josh, "That girl's in love with you." Regina, his mother, had said the same thing. He didn't believe it then, and he had a hard time accepting it now. He could understand why anybody would love her; Sarah was smart, funny, and fine as hell. Anyone who could love her would, same as he did. What he never could get was why she loved *him*. Maybe that was why he kept pushing her away.

He opened the refrigerator. Eight pony-sized bottles of beer sat on the top shelf. He reached for one before changing his mind. He thought about the week ahead. Three new people to meet, something he hated to do. Genna wanted him to talk to that damned Morehouse professor, Faith had a new client she wanted him to talk to, and Lynn had invited him to lunch to meet his new partner.

Everybody wanted his opinion on somebody, or so it seemed. Lynn would be easy. With Faith, he never knew what to expect. He was afraid she was trying to hook him up. Underneath her gruff exterior, she was good people. She felt like it was time for him to move on from Sarah. Genna, on the other hand, was business, and he wasn't feeling it at this moment.

He was feeling Sarah, or feeling bad about tearing his ass with Sarah. He walked over to the phone on the wall and picked it up off its cradle. His chest tightened. He dialed her number as fast as he could before he lost his nerve and put the phone down. Maybe she wouldn't be there. Maybe she was somewhere with Felton. One, two rings, and all of a sudden, on the other end of the line, he heard:

"Hello?"

"Hello, Sarah Smith, what's up?"

"Josh?"

"Yeah, it's me. What, you don't know my voice anymore?" he teased her.

"It's not that, I just wasn't expecting to hear from you."

"I've been thinking about you—a lot," he said. "I just really needed to hear your voice."

She laughed and said, "A-B-C-D-E-F-G."

He cracked up. A turning point in their relationship had been one Saturday morning about three a.m. He hadn't been able to get her out of his mind. For once, he had overcome his worries—about how she would feel about him waking her up so early, or if she might have somebody lying there beside her—and picked up the phone and dialed. She had answered in a sleepy, concerned kind of voice, and he'd told her he just really needed to hear her voice. He'd said, "You don't have to talk, just say your ABCs or count to one hundred or something." And she had laughed and played along, reciting *A-B-C-D-E-F-G* in a voice that got deeper and sexier with every letter. Then they'd stayed on the phone until ten in the morning, forgetting the sunrise, talking about anything and everything.

"I really wanted to be the first person to tell you happy New Year," he said.

"Thank you," she said. "You and Genna going to see your mom today?"

"I'm supposed to meet Genna around five. She told me you called her."

"Yeah, I wanted to wish her a merry Christmas."

"You didn't call me," he said in a teasing tone.

"I didn't think you'd answer." He could hear a faint touch of anger in her voice. "Anything else you want? I'm expecting company."

"Tell Felton to hold up," he said.

He could hear her giggle at being busted. She always said he was clairvoyant with the way he could figure things out.

"You tell that sorry-ass nigger if I hadn't fu—messed up, he wouldn't stand a chance." He knew how she hated him cursing, and he wanted to make her feel good today. He owed her that. "You tell him he's lucky, 'cause you're special, and if I wasn't so stupid we'd be together."

"Josh, we've been through this." Her voice quivered slightly. "I just can't trust you. Not anymore."

He started to ask what she meant, but knew better. He still hoped one day . . .

He felt better than he had in a long time. He was glad to be on speaking terms with her again. He was prepared to wall her away in a special section of his heart called "Sarah," but he was able to see now that he might not have to after all.

"Sarah Smith, I'm not going to hold you." Now his voice was starting to shake with emotion. *You'll always have a special place in my heart. I want you to know that. I want you to know that I want you. Period. I want you to know I love you, Sarah Smith. I always have; I always will. I love you so much. I know you deserve better than me. I know you always say that's not my decision, but you mean so much to me; I can't mistreat you anymore. I hope you trip and fall and hit your head and never remember you knew a Josh Gibson, so when one day I'm ready to treat you the way I always wanted, I can sneak back into your life and you won't remember the bad things I did, and maybe you can fall in love with me and we can live happily ever after, like those people in the fairytales we used to read when we were kids, 'cause you're in my heart and you own my heart and you are my heart, so I can't hold you anymore, 'cause I can't hurt you, 'cause it hurts me and I know you don't see that, so I want you to know that and I gotta go.* He thought all this but said, "I know you're busy, but I wanted you to know you're on my mind . . ." His voice trailed off.

There was silence on the line. He was afraid she was ready to hang up.

"Josh?"

"Uh-huh."

"Happy New Year."

"Thanks."

"I'm glad you called."

"Okay."

"Josh, I hope you know I mean that."

They chitchatted a few more minutes. He told her about Genna maybe finding a solution to their problem with some of the parents over their promotion of what he liked to call "The Primacy of Black Culture." They both laughed when she mentioned the "scared Negro" look on the faces of some of the people in the room when he'd made that comment. She'd been there to support the cause. She always was there to support him. "Black woman's burden," she called it, fooling with Josh.

Naturally, Genna had already run it by her. She thought it was a good idea. "Worth a try, at least," was how she put it. He asked why she was so sure. She told him Genna had told her about the professor's ideas. They were good.

He asked how her mom was doing. She told him she was doing well and that she was planning on going home in the spring to spend a week with her. She told him how she missed Regina. She asked if he was doing anything special for New Year's Eve—or "amateur night," as she called it. They both laughed. She told him to wish Genna a happy New Year. They agreed they'd get together and have lunch together one day soon.

Chapter 2

Faith

Josh decided to have that beer, relieved how the conversation with Sarah had gone. He missed her. He grabbed a Pony out of the eight pack. He twisted off the top and downed the tiny bottle in one big gulp. He promised himself he would stop drinking so much. That'd be his New Year's resolution. He took one more pull on his cigarette and used the butt to light another one.

He picked up the phone again and dialed Faith's number, figuring he could wish her a happy New Year and get a little business done at the same time.

She answered, happy to hear his voice. "What's up, Mr. Gibson?"

"I was just calling to see if Friday works for you."

"For you? Anything."

"Stop with your bullshit," Josh replied.

She laughed and asked, "What you doing with yourself tonight? Still headed over to Genna's?"

"Yeah, I'm going over there," he said, irritated by the question. He could tell she was making sure he wasn't going to wind up somewhere ringing in the new year with a glass pipe in his mouth. "Now, who's this you want me to meet and why, again?"

"Sarah Smith, I'm building her a deck."

"Fuck you."

They both got a big laugh out of her comment. "Now, I can call her and set something up if you want me to."

"I just got through talking to her."

"Josh, you ain't shit."

"Why you say that, Faith?"

"Why I say that! Did you ask her to go out with you tonight?"

"She already had a date."

"She told you that and I bet you didn't make one effort to get her to change her mind."

"Nah, why would I do that?"

"Because she wanted you to, Josh. It's why she told you she already had a date; so you would try to stop her from seeing him."

"Come on, Faith, I mean, it's the first thing she told me when we got on the phone, after she said hello. 'Uh, I got a date,'" he said in a mocking tone.

Faith sighed. "Josh, a woman wants to feel like a man sees her as special, somebody worth fighting for, somebody who's important to you. Besides, you haven't talked to her in forever. She had to let you know other people find her interesting. That you can't just pop up any ole time and find her sitting there waiting on you."

"So you saying she would have went out with me tonight?"

"You know, Josh, Sarah is so crazy about you she might have, but see, that was always her problem with you. She's too forgiving, too understanding of your bullshit. Nah, she shouldn't have, I hope she wouldn't have, but she sure would have been open to maybe getting together with you, oh, say, next week. She doesn't want that nigger."

"How you know that?"

"Boy, I know 'cause I'm a woman, and men like you have a way of getting under a woman's skin and moving in on your heart. I can *hear* her thinking, 'I can fix him.' And you don't help with your bullshit, calling her up on New Year's Eve even though you know she probably has a date. What'd you tell her, something like, 'I just wanted to hear the sound of your voice'?"

"Hey, man, get off me."

"See! You a jive motherfucker. You said that to the girl, didn't you? See, that's what I'm talking about. You playing with her, and that ain't right."

"I ain't playing with that girl. Genna told me she called her. So, I figured I'd give her a call to see how she's doing."

"Uh-huh, you tell the devil that when you sitting in the ninth circle of hell suffering through eternity 'cause of your bullshit. Course the devil will love your jive ass. And that damn Sarah will be telling Saint Peter, 'Nah, you don't understand, I got to go get Josh. Please let me bring him up here. He just made a few mistakes. I can fix him.'"

They cracked up again.

"Josh, seriously. Leave her alone. Let her get over you. She can't do that if every time she starts to, you pop back up in her life."

"What if I don't want to leave her alone?"

He could feel Faith hesitating on the other end of the line. He knew she was getting ready to play the God card. The trick was for her to finesse it enough so he wouldn't boil over. He pretty much could hold the coming conversation by himself.

He knew she was going to tell him he had to give Sarah to God, accept the idea God knew, better than he did, the path his life needed to take. She'd talk real soft, plead with him, and tell him he needed to quit fighting the will of God, reminding him God had seen him through some other troubles. Ones that would have caused even Sarah to turn her back on him.

Faith was his dead boy Slim's aunt, and she loved her some Josh Gibson. They understood each other. She was a bisexual former streetwalker, that old cliché come to life about a hooker with a heart of gold. She'd done ten years for killing her pimp, a cat with the well-deserved street name of T. Cold Blood.

Tyrell—she called him by his Christian name—had been her heart, until the morning she came in off the stroll ten dollars short. He stripped Faith naked, tied her to a tree, and gave her a wet-towel whipping. Faith had explained to him Tyrell loved this particular brand of punishment because it hurt like hell but didn't leave a mark.

She humped her ass off that night, making sure to come back paid. She wanted Mr. Tyrell Cold Blood to know he had made his mark on her mind. After she gave him the count, she cooked him bacon and eggs, cooing, "Ooh, Daddy, you ain't still mad at Faith," as she served him breakfast. She rubbed his ear, knowing he wouldn't like the familiarity, yet he was pimp enough to keep her on her toes by waiting for the proper moment to lash out.

This gave her the jump she was looking for. She pulled out a straight razor and cut off that ear. She didn't stop cutting until he was dead and gone. She did her time for manslaughter, coming out of prison a reformed sinner. Six feet tall with a brick-red, short 'fro, she must have been quite the looker in her day. She ran though men and women like they were going out of style.

She owned a contracting business Josh worked for on weekends. She'd have run through him too, but Josh was uneasy about going there with Faith, sure it would lead to trouble. Besides, she took too much pleasure in talking about that ear.

For this, and other reasons, she didn't like Sarah. Sarah had been where she wanted to go. This was a chance for her to drive a wedge between him and his feelings for the esteemed Miss Smith. He decided he'd play along so she would leave him alone. Faith was cool, she was like an aunt or a big sister to him, but she was wrong about the God thing—and wrong about Sarah.

So he spoke up before she could start in on him. "You know maybe I *should* just leave her alone. What does that old Chinese proverb say? 'If you love something, let it go, and if it comes back, it truly belongs to you'?"

"Josh, you're full of it. I know you're just trying to play me off. You keep on. I'm not going to say anything else, but you keep clinging to the past, you gonna look right over the blessing sitting right ahead in your future."

"Damn, I know why your mama named you Faith."

"Boy, what I am gonna do with you?"

He took another drag on his cigarette. He was glad to have Faith to talk to; right about now Genna would be getting mighty disturbed about his comments. Faith knew they were his way of expressing his dismay at the prospect of losing Sarah.

"Josh, you ever read a story called 'The Most Dangerous Game' when you were little?"

"Yeah, the story about the guy who hunts people because he's bored by how easy it is to kill animals and starts getting bored with hunting people until he meets his match. What about it?"

"You're that hunter," she said. "Except you don't really mean your victims any harm. You don't run around with a lot of women, you're as nice as you can be, you'll spend your money like there's no tomorrow, but you just not right. You're frustrating, 'cause you look like somebody any woman would want, but you just too damn crazy. And it's in a different kind of way a woman can't prepare for, 'cause she's never seen anything like you before."

"I try to be."

"It works, too, but what we need is a woman like that guy in the story, somebody who can deal with your mess. You'll be better off for it."

"And you got just the one, don't you?"

"No, I don't, Josh. I wish I did for your sake."

"Somebody who can change me for the better?"

"Nah, Josh, somebody who makes you want to be better. That's what you need. You good people, Josh, you a real good man, but you could be a lot better if you didn't smoke like a chimney, drink like a fish, and we ain't even gonna get into the dope."

"Point well taken."

"Well, Mr. Gibson, I have to go. You be good. I'm gonna call Genna to make sure you get there in one piece."

"Both y'all need to quit."

"You tell Genna and your mom I said hello."

"I will, Faith." He hung up.

Chapter 3

To Gina's House

Josh looked at the clock on the kitchen wall. It was almost three thirty. He wandered back to his bedroom, figuring he would watch a little television to kill some time before he went to Regina's. He clicked the On button and took a seat at the foot of the bed. *General Hospital* was on.

His mind drifted, settling on a day five years ago when he happened into the Kroger down by Greenbrier Mall, or "Treasure Island," as the fellas used to call it, because it was always stocked with goodies there for the taking. He was minding his own business, contemplating what to get for dinner, when a flash of jeans caught his eye. All full of fat ass and thick, the kind that made you want to touch them thighs. The owner of the jeans strode past him, stopped in front of the soup, and bent down to look at something on the bottom shelf. He muttered to himself, "Thank God for chicken and rice."

He'd never been the kind to strike up conversations with strangers, so he took a good look, thinking, *It sure would be nice to know her.* She stood up, glanced his way, and moved on toward the meat section. She was paper-sack brown and one nice-looking young lady. He could never get over how many different ways black women could be good looking. His sister, Genna, and his mom,

Regina, looked like twin Hershey bars. His Grandma Gibson was high yellow with long, dark hair down her back. Etched in the features of this girl's face was the story of a long-ago night of passion between a slave and a Seminole. *Oh well*, he thought and meandered through the store, picking up items, until he found himself in the checkout line.

He saw her coming, hoping she would choose his line. He looked at her; she smiled, said "hi," and it was on. She wound up pulling the I'll-take-your-number-and-call-you trick on him after five minutes of conversation that started with him making some really lame comment about this being his lucky day.

He didn't expect to hear from her, but two days later his phone rang at work, the only place he knew she could call and have any chance of him picking up the receiver. They laughed when she said she'd called because she knew he needed help with an opening line like the one he used on her. She cracked it was a sister's duty to help a brother who was so obviously rap challenged. Plus, it was near Christmas, and she was in a charitable mood.

Yeah, she was his heart. And all he had done was make her miserable.

He lit a cigarette. His favorite character Luke was bumbling through some conversation with his girl Laura on the television. Normally he enjoyed watching them together, but today he wasn't feeling it. He belched. The combination of malt liquor and beer in his stomach popped up to his mouth for a visit, depositing a foul-tasting souvenir on his tongue before sliding back down his throat. *Fuck the Ponies, time for another quart*, he thought.

He debated putting on his coat, thinking about the time he put her out of his car. He decided against the coat. He could hear Genna screaming at him a few months ago. "Josh, that's so high school."

He retorted, "I went back and got her."

"That's not the point," Genna replied.

He told her, "Man, she was all over me, talking shit. What was I supposed to do?"

"What were you supposed to do? You were supposed to act like an adult. What was she complaining about? How you get high all the time?"

He had answered, "I don't get high all the time."

Genna shook her head and said quietly, "Big brother, the only person you're lying to is you."

Sarah couldn't believe he would actually dump her on the side of the road. When he came back and picked her up, she sobbed for a few moments before going silent on him. He pleaded with her to forgive him as he rode along, but he could tell he'd broken something in their relationship that afternoon. Sarah's girl Cynthia introduced her to Felton not too long afterward. If he didn't love her so much, he would have felt relieved she'd found someone who would treat her right.

Regina always told him Sarah wasn't the one for him. They argued about it all the time. He'd ask, "Why you say that?" and she'd answer, "'Cause I know you. She lets you get away with too much."

He sure wished she'd let him get away with it one last time. And of course, after she wavered, he stood her up. They hadn't talked for a long time, but now he felt like she was opening up to him again. He smiled at the thought.

He walked back through the apartment and out his kitchen door, then got in his car and headed to the Majik Market. The clerk said, "Hey, what's up, Jay, come for your lunch?" when he walked in the door.

"Fuck you, man," Josh said, laughing. Jones, the clerk, laughed with him, knowing Josh was here to pick up his afternoon quart.

"A little early today, huh?" Jones asked.

"Yeah," Josh replied. "We off for the holidays."

They chatted for a minute after Josh pulled a quart of malt liquor out of the cooler. He paid Jones and took the brown bag with the malt liquor inside out to his ride. As soon as he got in, he screwed off the cap and took a long chug on the brew. Then he fired the car up and headed toward Regina's. He eased up to the light at the corner of Campbellton and Centra Villa. It was red. He ended up taking two more big swigs out of the quart bottle while waiting for the light to change. Damn, he needed to be more careful.

Bad enough he was driving on a suspended license. No telling how far under the jail they'd toss him if the cops caught him drinking, which—oh, by the way—was the reason they had taken his license in the first place. He looked both ways as the light changed. He raced across Campbellton past the bank on the corner and headed up Centra Villa, quick timing it to beat Genna to Regina's. He swallowed the last of the malt liquor, rolled down the window, and tossed the empty into somebody's front yard.

He lit another cigarette and smoked until he reached the stop sign at Cascade. Out of respect for Regina, he mashed out the butt in his ashtray. She hated his smoking. He had bought a bag of peanuts at the store, hoping to kill the smell of liquor on his breath.

Good, he'd beaten Genna there. He parked and waited down the street from Regina's for Precious, Regina's nickname for her youngest child. He grabbed the box of mints and popped a couple more in his mouth. Faith had told him once, "Boy, you know you love to put stuff in your mouth." He laughed at the thought, remembering the nasty way she had said it.

Leaning against his car door, gazing around the neighborhood, he considered which style of home he would prefer if he ever came back to stay. Would it be just one of the basic models, or would he prefer something more ornate? He liked Gina's place, a tastefully done little spot with pink roses in the yard that accentuated the well-manicured grass surrounding her home. Yeah, this was a really nice place to be, peaceful as you would expect, well kept like you would hope, even inspirational, something he never would have imagined until Gina had moved in and he had started visiting on a regular basis. It was one of the neighborhoods you noticed every so often as you rode down Cascade, but never really gave its proper due until you had a reason to pass through.

Nineteen eighty-five, he thought. In a few hours, the new year would be upon them. Yeah, here it was, another New Year's Eve. Tomorrow would bring the new beginning a new year represented. Not that anything would necessarily happen for the better. It was just the thought, especially standing here in this neighborhood. Yeah, nineteen eighty-five just seemed to have a nice ring to it. He thought about Genna and how she kept insisting he had to meet this Morehouse professor with all these great ideas. Kept telling him they would benefit the school.

Her name was Adrienne Johnson. Regina knew her Aunt Leah. Regina and her Aunt Leah had taught together for ten years at Slater Elementary School when Gina was younger. As a Morehouse man himself, her pedigree and position at Morehouse carried some weight with him. He figured he would at least listen to what she had to say. It was the polite thing to do. He wasn't expecting much, though. Of course, he didn't tell Genna this was how he felt.

There were grumblings amongst some of the parents about the black supremacist positions they were taking in the classroom. Denise Burke went home and informed her father that Mr. Josh told her class they're "going north." That was okay with her dad. It was when he asked her what Mr. Josh meant and she said Mr. Josh had told her class modern Negroes were happy little darkies because they had traded in the sweltering cotton fields of South Georgia for the seemingly swank cubicles of corporate America, that because they had a desk and a phone line they thought they were free. "But you don't pick Massa Tom's cotton," he cautioned. "He will tie you to the modern whipping post known as the unemployment line."

"Besides, Daddy," Denise quoted him word for word, "black people have been taught to go to white elementary and high schools, so we can go to white colleges and universities, so we can go to work for white corporations, so we can move into white neighborhoods. All I want to know is where the celebration of our blackness is in all of this, and if you won't celebrate yourself, don't demand someone else do it for you."

Denise's father showed up with what their Uncle James liked to call the "scared Negro look" on his face. He wanted to know what they were teaching the children and what did Josh's exhortations have to do with getting them ready to go to Harvard? Josh looked at him and replied, "I'm getting 'em ready for Howard." Her father threw a fit, saying he thought they were preparing the kids for the best schools, not some second-rate HBCU. If it hadn't been for Denise, Josh would have gone ballistic.

Instead, he asked, "How do you know Harvard is a good school?"

The dad mumbled some answer about, "Well, everybody knows Harvard is a good school and all the papers say so—" and Josh cut him off right there.

He innocently asked, "Is there any racism left in America?"

Old dad said, "Well, of course there is."

Josh said, "Well, the white man says there isn't any more racism in America, but you don't believe him. But let him tell you Harvard is better than Howard, you swallow that hook, line, and sinker. That doesn't make sense to me. Why you believe one and not the other?"

It took Genna two weeks of begging to get Denise's parents to bring her back.

He didn't like the guy and said good riddance. Genna told him, "It's not him I care about, Josh. I'm worried about Denise." So he called the dad up and apologized and promised to tone down the rhetoric.

But being the children of two avowed Mau Maus, Josh and Genna were determined to bring love and celebration of self into the school's agenda. One day, a parent had introduced Genna to Adrienne Johnson. Genna had been raving about her ever since. She swore Ms. Johnson was the answer to their question of how to celebrate themselves without putting down others and scaring off the clients. And it didn't hurt that Genna had gone to high school with one of Ms. Johnson's cousins.

He checked to see if he saw any signs of Genna. He didn't, so he lit a cigarette. But damn, here she came, just as he took a good, long drag.

Chapter 4

Genna

Genna turned on to the street and saw Josh standing by his car waiting for her. "Dang," she murmured to herself. She was late. Normally, she was the punctual Gibson sibling. Somehow he had beaten her here. She knew he would give her a hard time about it.

She frowned. "I caught you," she said to herself, seeing Josh trying to hide the cigarette he was holding. She shook her head and smiled, then pulled up beside him and rolled down her window. "Boy, put that cigarette out. What would Momma say?"

She watched him drop the cigarette and step on it. "What cigarette?" he asked.

"Josh, you are something else, you know that? Let me park."

She pulled her car in next to his and sat looking at him before she got out. She thought about all the times they'd shared together, both good and bad. *He is the sweetest man*, she thought. *And he is always trying to hide it.*

Josh was not quite four years older than her. He would be twenty-nine the thirty-first of January. She had turned twenty-six on November the eleventh.

When she was eight, she got hit by a car running across the street behind him in front of James Hall on the campus of Hampton Institute, where their father, Lawrence, was teaching. He heard her scream and ran back out in the street and fell to her side. She would never forget the look on his face when he looked down at her leg.

It had broken in two places. Her thigh bone had pierced the skin. Her shin had bent so bad, Josh told her later it looked like she had an extra elbow. She had been in the hospital for weeks. The doctors had told her parents that even if they saved her leg, she would probably never walk again.

Josh wouldn't hear it. Every night, he would come to the hospital with Regina and sleep in a chair in her room. A lot of nights after Regina went to sleep, he would crawl on the bed and stroke her head, telling her everything was going to be okay.

She had whimpered, eyes watering, "Josh, I'm scared. I don't want them to cut my leg off."

And he always said, "Hush girl, ain't nobody gonna cut your leg off. And you gonna walk again."

Daddy had taken a job at his alma mater, completing a journey back home to Morehouse that had taken them from Tuskegee to Fisk to Hampton on his way to securing a tenured professorship in Atlanta while Momma had finished up her last year as a teacher at an elementary school in Newport News, the town right next door to Hampton. Daddy would ride to Virginia every Friday to be with Genna, taking off on Sunday in time to get back to school on Monday. So Josh had been the man in her life five days a week.

Sitting there, she had felt him encouraging her, missing so much school to be at her side he got left back in the sixth grade. He hadn't cared. "Genna comes first," he had told Momma every time she had worried out loud about his circumstance.

It had taken a year after she got out of the hospital, but she learned to walk again. She still walked with a slight limp. Her leg had healed, but it wound up two inches shorter than her good one. Even now, she had to wear special shoes.

A lump welled up in her throat as she sat considering the paths they'd traveled to get to this place. Daddy had died of lung cancer when she was thirteen. It was hard on all of them, but Josh had suffered the most. He and Lawrence had been really tight. Something tore in him when Daddy died.

When Daddy died, Momma insisted God had needed him and had called him home to heaven. Genna still remembered the tears welling up in Momma's eyes when she whispered those words to her grieving children. Josh had hated God for a long time, unable to understand why God needed his father so much more than they did, why He needed him so much He couldn't spare him a while longer, why God couldn't see the heartbreak He caused in their mother's eyes, and why He had to call Lawrence home July twenty-eighth, Gina's birthday.

Josh started smoking about six months after Lawrence died. Regina would jump all over Josh, berating him about how smoking had killed his daddy. Did he want to go the same way? Josh would mumble, "Gotta go some way, some time." And Regina would shake her head in exasperation.

He brought her back to the present by beating on her car door. "Come on, Hopalong, what you waiting on? Scared Regina's gonna get you about being late?"

"What did I tell you about calling me that?" she snapped playfully.

"Oh, I'm sorry. Hoppy, would you please get your ass out the car so I can go see my mother?"

"Now see, just because you talked to Sarah, don't get smart with me. You did call her, right?"

"Yeah, I talked to the esteemed Miss Smith," Josh said as he opened the door for her.

"My, aren't we formal today; the esteemed Miss Smith? You still like her, huh?"

"Nah."

"Josh Gibson, you lie!"

Josh stared at her. "Why you say that? Just 'cause I called her? You told me it would be a good idea, Regina Jr. You know how you and Gina are always right about everything."

She walked over and wrapped her arm around his. "Why don't you just say Momma instead of Regina?" He started to speak, but Genna cut him off. "'Cause you crazy like that. That's why, and as long as you can't call her Sarah, as long as you have to call her 'the esteemed Miss Smith,' or 'the black girl with the white name,' or, what's your favorite, that bi—but I'm not going to be like you and call her names."

"All right, Hoppy, you got that one. Tell you what, you want to race me up the hill?"

She smiled at him. This was a little game they played. She knew he was going to let her win.

She also knew he was easing away from talking about Sarah. *You think you're slick, Josh Gibson.*

"How much you had to drink today?" she cracked.

"Uh, two sodas and some fruit punch."

"Hush, Josh. Come on, let's go see Momma."

"What?" he said. "You think I'm drunk?"

"I didn't say you were drunk, Josh. I just asked what you had to drink, but a hit dog will holler. And you sure smell like alcohol. And it is past noon." She smiled to take the bite out of what she said.

"Damn, you mean the peanuts didn't work?"

"No, Josh, the peanuts didn't work. You okay? I mean, I know what time of year it is, and you know how I worry about you."

He paused before he spoke. He looked her in the eye. "Yeah, I guess I'm all right."

He swore she acted like she was the big sister. She couldn't help herself. He needed watching over.

He was a sensitive soul who took most everything to heart. The Gibsons were from Tuskegee, so it worked out really well that Lawrence's first teaching job was at the institute. They had a bunch of aunts and uncles and cousins who lived in and around Tuskegee, and everybody called Lawrence and Regina by their first names. Josh joined the chorus of "Regina this" and "Lawrence that" instead of calling them Momma and Daddy.

It was fine until Regina's sister Vivian had come for a visit. She had been confounded by the idea anyone's child would address them by their first name and had ordered Josh to stop. It was the last time Josh called Regina and Lawrence anything to their faces. Regina had ripped into Vivian for scolding him about such a minor thing, but Josh had already shrunk into himself, forever unable to call his parents anything but "hey."

Well, except that one day in Hampton. Josh had wanted to see some movie really bad. So he had crept up to Regina as she was on her way out to the store and said, "Can I go to the movies, Mom?" Genna had listened to him straining to get the last word out. You could barely hear it. Genna and Regina had both been stunned.

Regina had turned and said, "What did you say, baby?" in the most encouraging voice she could muster.

And he had said it again, "Can I go to the movies, Mom?" This time it had come out even lower.

Regina had asked him again, excitement mixed with disbelief in her voice, "What did you say, Josh?" He had tried, but he hadn't been able to get it out again. He had said, "Can I go to the movies?" Regina had snapped no and marched out the door.

Even now Genna couldn't bring it up. Genna, being a mom herself now, hurt even more for her mother and her brother. Lord, kids could get on your nerves, hollering "Momma this" and saying "Mom that." Sometimes you wanted to say, "Quit calling me." Then came, "Mommy, I love you."

By now they were almost to Gina's. They were careful not to step into someone else's yard because she knew Josh would have a fit. Finally, they arrived. Josh stared for a long time. *Are you okay?* Genna thought. She was lucky. She had Daniel and the twins. Josh was pretty much alone.

She looked down at her mother's tombstone. It read Regina Washington Gibson, Born July 28, 1930, Died December 6, 1982. It felt like it had been longer; it felt like it had just happened yesterday.

If Lawrence's death had torn something in her big brother, their mother's death had just about finished him.

She understood. If Daniel, her husband of five years, had not been there, she would have crumbled. And of course, her twins Brittany and Lawrence gave her two good reasons to get up out of her sorrow and go on. And her faith sustained her—a faith she could not mention to Josh without him getting upset. He was so angry with God about Regina, she just knew if he could, he would fight Him about his mother. He told her once he thought about being an atheist, but hell, that was letting that bastard off too easy for taking Regina.

Josh talked about Regina like she was still alive. She could barely drag him to her grave once a year. Even then, he talked about coming to Regina's house to visit. She sure wished he could find peace. She knew Momma would not want him suffering about her the way he did.

Part of it was guilt. Josh was her prodigal son. That's what Momma had called him. Somewhere along the way, he started drinking and getting high. For a while it was redbud and mescaline. And those hoodlums he loved to run with.

One of them—Dad, Longeno, Hakeem, she wasn't sure who—had turned him on to cocaine. At first, he liked to toot a little. He'd actually done well for himself. He graduated with honors and hooked up a nice gig in marketing at Coca-Cola. Met Sarah, seemed to be living the American dream. It had all been a prelude to his descent into a smoke-filled nightmare.

Genna couldn't even trust him with his paycheck anymore. She had to cash it for him and dole it out a few dollars at a time so he could keep a roof over his head. Somehow he made it to work every day. Thank God for their school. It was Josh's idea. He felt guilty about his days in the moving business, as he liked to call it. Told her and Sarah he wanted to make up for all the harm he'd done to his people.

Of course, all he did was talk about opening up EDCO Academy until Regina had died and left them enough insurance money to give it a shot. She and Sarah went behind Josh's back to Uncle James—or the Ancient Mariner, as Josh called him, because he had been everywhere and seen everything—for some extra financing as well as some help in persuading Josh to quit his job and "go north" to the freedom of entrepreneurship like runaway slaves fleeing the South. The Mariner was Momma's baby brother, and he loved him some Josh. And Josh loved him some Mariner.

Their parents had stopped asking what EDCO stood for. Genna refused to let Josh tell them it was short for "educating colored folks," sure it wouldn't go over well with the new breed of Negro trusting them to teach their children. The humor Josh found in the school's moniker was a little too eccentric.

The school had to work. Cocaine was a thief. If it weren't for EDCO, Genna was sure it would steal him from her.

Business was good, yet unsatisfactory to both of them. They sensed a little too much of a white supremacist attitude amongst their kids. Josh was frustrated over how to turn them into race people when they encountered white supremacy everywhere, especially at home. The school needed a new narrative—a narrative calculated to celebrate black without denigrating white.

It was hard to get Josh to see this was the problem with his Howard versus Harvard tirade. It was like the Mariner told them, "Y'all need to understand, no matter how much you hear black people complain about white people, they secretly want to be just like 'em. They don't complain about white folks 'cause they hate 'em; they complain about them 'cause white folks don't want to be bothered with black folks. It's a big difference. They don't want some young Malcolmnette and Stokely teaching their kids to believe they're equal to white folks; they want them to be taught to grow up to be white folks."

So when a parent sympathetic to their plight had introduced her to a young sociology instructor at Morehouse named Adrienne Johnson, Genna sensed a solution. Listening to her share her unified theory of blackness, as Josh cracked when she mentioned it to him, Genna realized here was a chance to solve two problems at once—her school problem and her brother problem. Now the trick was to get Josh and Adrienne together. Standing here, she saw her chance. Josh was weak with guilt and grief and would talk about anything right now to avoid the Sarah conversation. So she sprang the trap.

"Josh, you know how Momma would love the school, right?"

He stared at her grave. "Yeah, you know, Hopalong, her and our father. They're a big reason why I want to do this. Them and a few other things I don't want to talk about right now."

"You remember how Momma used to tell us 'if you're going to do something, be sure to do it right'?"

"Yeah," he said, looking off into the western sky.

"Well then, don't you think it's time you hear what Adrienne has to say?"

"Who?"

"Sarah."

He looked at her. "Okay, how about Thursday? Can you set it up? It will be the first day back, and we might as well start the year off right."

She smiled at him. "How about ten o'clock?"

He sighed. "That'll work."

Relieved to have it settled, she changed the subject to memories of Momma. Josh filled her heart with memories of Daddy.

Finally, it was time to go. She asked him for about the umpteenth time this week if he was coming over tonight.

He rolled his eyes, pressed his hand against his heart, and reminded her, "I'm a professional drunk. My ethics won't allow me to participate in amateur night. I'm gonna run by Adams Park and smoke a cigarette. Then I'm on my way."

Chapter 5

The Prodigal Son

Josh woke up coughing, lungs full of smoke. His first thought was he was developing a smoker's hack. *The apartment is on fire* was his next thought as his eyes began to burn from the smoke rapidly filling his bedroom. The glow from the television screen illuminated things enough for him to see the thick, black smoke clouding up the apartment.

"Damn!" He'd forgotten to close the door to his room. He could see the red stuff blazing out of the living room and into the hall leading toward him. It was just a matter of seconds before it crept through the door. This was one time living on the second floor didn't work.

His room was beginning to feel like a heated oven. He rolled away from the side of the bed closest to the door, scrambling away from the flames that had invited themselves into his room in a blink of an eye, ready to climb into the bed with him. *So this is how it is to be cooked*, he thought.

Sarah had always insisted on sleeping with the door closed just so something like this wouldn't happen. He wondered if she would cry. "Damn, Gibson!" he muttered to himself. "Get out of here, that's what you need to have on your mind."

He threw the covers off, rolling over to the side of the bed near the window. He slid off the bed onto the floor.

The air was clearer down here. He could actually breathe again. He crawled the five or six feet to the wall where his escape stood about chest high.

He looked at the fire helplessly, trying to ignore its advance across the carpet toward him. He wondered if the television would explode from the heat. He then wondered how he would look standing outside naked. He always slept in the buff. Going to the closet to grab something to wear didn't appear to be a very good option at the moment. This corner wasn't burning yet, but it couldn't be long before he was barbecuing. He had a feeling it wasn't going to be a slow cook, either.

The last thing in the world he wanted to do was stand up and sip on some more of that smoke. He was going have to go out that window, though. It was his only hope. Sarah had always told him he ought to wear some clothes to bed, too! He'd be a sight, tumbling out that window naked. Of course, it would be a much worse sight if he couldn't fit through it.

Luckily, he liked to sleep with the window ajar. He wouldn't have to waste time sliding it open. His mind raced, thinking through the motions he'd need to follow to get out of the window once he stood up. He'd always heard smoke was the real killer in fires. He didn't figure to breathe it indefinitely when he stood up, no matter how used to it his lungs were from his "all day, every day" cigarette habit.

He was sweating now. He took a deep breath before he stood up into a thick, hot smoke cloud. He forced the screen out the window. He reached out into the chilly January night, pulling himself through the opening.

Josh hit the ground with a *thud*. "Shit, that hurt," he muttered under his breath. Luckily, he had landed on the ground and not the concrete. He stood up, realizing he wasn't totally naked. He had on his drawers. In his panic to get out, he hadn't noticed. Well, things were looking up a little bit already. Now when he knocked on his downstairs neighbor's door, she would only be greeted by a half-naked man.

"Oh shit, the kids!" He remembered now why his door had been open and why he had been wearing underwear. It was because the kids had been in the living room in sleeping bags. He'd left the door open so they could come right in if they needed him, and he'd worn drawers so they wouldn't be scandalized if he got up and met one of them roaming through the apartment.

He dashed back up the steps. He had to get them out or die trying. He reached the door, grabbing the knob. It was hot. Realizing the fire had to be raging right on the other side of the door for the knob to feel the way it did, tears began rolling down his face, and he knew it was too late to do anything for either one of them—

Josh sat straight up in the bed with a start. Damn, he was having another nightmare about those kids doing their best lit-candle imitations. Mmmmmph. He reached over to the nightstand, grabbing a cigarette. His hand was shaking.

Three days into the new year and he was ready to give up his resolution not to drink his breakfast. Every time he slowed down on the drinking, he had that dream. *Oh well, when Faith pays me, I'll go get a bump,* he thought. *Yeah, it would be just what the doctor ordered.*

He lit the cigarette, letting the smoke rush down into his lungs, filling every corner. He wasn't so shaky anymore. He wanted a beer, but thought better of it. He glanced at the clock on his nightstand. It said six a.m. Josh reached for the telephone and dialed Sarah's number.

She picked up on the fourth ring, voice thick with sleep. "Hello?"

"Hey, Sarah Smith," he whispered into the phone.

"Oh! Hey, how are you doing?"

He heard sheets rustling.

"You got company?" he asked.

"Hold on," she whispered into the phone. "Felton, it's six o'clock. It's time to get up, okay?" A male voice said something unintelligible. "It's my boss. I better take this in the kitchen," she replied. "Just a minute," she said into the phone.

Josh's chest tightened while he waited for her to come back on the phone. He took a long pull on his cigarette.

"Hey, Josh, what's the matter? Is Genna all right?"

"She's fine," he answered, hesitant, bothered by Felton being over at her crib. "I had that dream again. It fucked me up, Sarah," he said, not caring about how she hated to hear him curse.

"No, Josh," she whispered into the phone. "It's going to be okay. It was just a dream."

"Look," he snapped, "you're busy. I didn't mean to disturb you."

"Josh, don't be that way. You have no right," she snapped back into the phone.

"I'm sorry. Sarah, I'm just scared. I'm trying to do better, but I'm not sure what I'm gonna do if every time I go a couple of days without a drink this is going to happen."

A pause, then she spoke again. "Look, call me back this evening. We'll talk. I don't like for you to be like this. Josh, you know that."

"Okay, Sarah, I'll call you back."

"Josh, call me," she pleaded. "I'll call you. And answer the phone, Josh. Okay?"

He hung up without answering. *I shouldn't have called*, he thought, swelling with jealousy. He dragged himself out of the bed. The phone rang. He started to answer, but didn't. It went to voice mail. He heard a loud dial tone when the message started.

The thought of getting a brew crossed his mind. He quashed it. Today was the day for his meeting with Genna and the professor. He wanted a clear head for this conversation because it meant a lot to Genna.

His throat was dry. He grabbed a box of mints and popped three of them into his mouth. Daydreaming about Gina, Josh lit a cigarette. Remembering Gina brought a smile to his face. Genna was right, Gina Gibson would have appreciated her son and daughter running a school.

Gina used to call him every night at eleven thirty sharp, figuring if Josh was home, her child was safe for one more night. They had talked the night before she died, fussing about her wanting to buy him a coat. "Josh, it's cold and I know you won't buy one," she told him, knowing his drug habit wouldn't leave him be long enough for him to do something like purchase a coat. Josh argued with her just to give Gina a hard time. She was buying him that coat.

An eighteen wheeler flipped over the next afternoon, dodging a stalled car on 75 South near the University Avenue exit ramp, falling on Gina's ride, crushing it, and killing her instantly. She'd been on her way to pick him up. Sarah bought him a coat once she heard it had been Gina's dying wish. Sarah had loved Gina and Gina had loved her back—she had just known Sarah was not right for her baby.

Pulling his charcoal gray suit out of the closet, Josh got down to the business of getting ready. He planned to get there a little after ten so Genna and the professor could sit on pins and needles awaiting his grand arrival. The Mariner told him all the time, "Let somebody trying to sell you something wait on you. Nothing wrong with letting them sweat a little."

This was January third. The year was young, life was good, and today was a chance to begin to solve a problem, a shot at easing his little sister's vexation. He slipped into his clothes as he mulled over the coming day. He loved January. A new year always made him feel optimistic about the future.

He walked into the kitchen, sat down, and fired up another cigarette. He shook one more mint out of the box to go along with the cancer stick he was so thoroughly enjoying. A brew would sure go good right now, but he was committed to not drinking until nightfall today. Then he could drink himself stupid right here in the confines of his apartment, where nobody would know or care if he slumped over and fell asleep at his table.

Time to go, Jay, he thought.

He walked out of the apartment and down the stairs to his car, glancing up at his bedroom and thinking about how he had tumbled out the window in his dream.

He got in his car, cranked it, and lit up a smoke. He sat there for a minute or two, allowing the car to warm up while he puffed on the cigarette. He shifted into gear and pulled out of the parking space, thinking to himself, *On to Decatur*. He drove over to 166 headed toward work. He thought about the school as he drove toward I-20.

Genna was an excellent administrator. She made sure everything worked, from opening the doors on time to keeping the books balanced. Theirs was a good partnership. They both knew the business couldn't function without her. He personally believed it would do just fine without him, but she refused to concede the point whenever he brought it up. She reminded him there wouldn't be any business to run if it hadn't been for his inspiration.

He was already getting off on Candler Road. It was surprising how quickly he had gotten to Decatur this morning. He glanced over at South DeKalb Mall as he approached the top of the exit. Naturally, the red light caught him. Once it changed, he darted out into the traffic, cruising across the lanes, and turned left onto Rainbow and headed to the office. He pulled into their complex and found a parking space in the back of the school.

They were renting a two-story building in the complex. This was the employee entrance. The front of the building sat on a hill, where the parents dropped off their kids upstairs. The back of the building sat at the bottom of the hill. Staff and teachers parked there.

Aaron, one of their older students, was coming out the door. He stood about five-feet-eleven, weighed maybe one hundred and sixty pounds, and wore his hair high and tight with a part on the side. Medium brown with a bright smile, the girls loved him. Aaron's father had abandoned him and his mother and younger brother and sister three years ago. He was a good student until then, but had started getting into things the last couple of years. The final straw had been when his cousin Al moved to Atlanta from Los Angeles. Al was bad news, and Aaron's mom had turned to their school to get him back on the straight and narrow. It was tough with Aaron sometimes, but they were beginning to see progress

"What up, Mr. Josh?" Aaron said as Josh got out the car.

"What's up, Aaron?" Josh replied. "Where you headed?"

"Up to Kroger. Miss Genna asked me to pick up some coffee. Y'all having a meeting this morning and she forgot to pick it up on the way in."

"Hey man, pick me up a quart while you up there."

Aaron laughed and shook his head. "You crazy, Mr. Josh. You know Miss Genna will kick my ass if I get you something to drink."

"Aaron, you know I'm just messing with you."

"Yeah, I know."

"And one more thing."

"What?"

"Quit that damn cussing!"

Aaron nodded. He popped into Genna's car and headed up the street. Barely sixteen, he was the only person on earth Genna would let drive her beamer without much experience behind the wheel. He had it like that. He was everybody's favorite.

Josh watched him pull off. He stood in the walkway at the bottom of the stairs leading into their offices. He liked to smoke out here where he could talk to himself without worrying about being disturbed. Genna would come out to see him sometimes, catching him deep into an animated conversation. She'd say, "Talking to your friends again, huh?" and go right into whatever conversation she needed to have with him.

Here she came now out the door to greet him, undoubtedly wanting to check his breath. He wished he had some kind of spray he could put on his breath that smelled like beer, just so she could panic about him being drunk before noon again. He laughed out loud at the thought.

"What's so funny?" she said as she walked up to him with her head cocked slightly to the left and her arms crossed.

"I was just thinking, here comes Genna with the breath-alyzer."

Genna smiled, recognizing he was sober. She knew he would have been defensive if he had been drinking. She walked right up to him, looking him up and down. He could tell she was nervous about how he might behave this morning.

He reached over and put his arms on her shoulders and said in a really gentle voice, "I wouldn't do you like that."

"Josh, I know you wouldn't mean to, but you know you would."

He feigned hurt, putting his right hand over his heart. "You really think I would show up here with brew on my breath? That was last year's Josh. Told you I turned over a new leaf."

She laughed and shook her head. "You must think you're still talking to yourself."

"That was cold."

"Come on. Let's go inside, she's already here," Genna told him.

"Already here?"

"Yes, she is. She's been here thirty minutes. She really wants to get involved with the school. I think she wants to make a good impression."

"Okay, sis. Well, let's go meet her, then." He held the door open for Genna and followed her up the steps.

Chapter 6

First Take

Adrienne sat waiting. She was impressed with EDCO. Genna had told her about the setup, but it was much more than she expected. Genna had showed her around when she arrived. There were seventy-seven students at this facility. Fifty of them were in the lower school, which they called the kindergarten. They were in two large rooms downstairs, having a ball learning their times tables. It blew her mind.

"Girl, I could barely do my ABCs at that age, and you have them multiplying. Wow!" Adrienne said.

Genna told her, "You know how black people are. You have to make an impression. Besides, it's memorization. Just like learning your ABCs. My Uncle James suggested it. And it made sense. My father used to tell us, 'Your mind is like a muscle. You have to work it to make it stronger.' But don't be too impressed, soror. They can barely add and subtract. And you better believe we have to explain that to their parents."

"What do you mean?" Adrienne asked.

"Well, Adrienne, it was a couple of parents who were like, 'You mean my baby can tell me ten times ten is a hundred, but doesn't know what ten plus ten is?'"

"Your people are a trip," Adrienne replied.

Genna waved her off. "It's okay. We'll have them adding and subtracting like pros before the year is up. We're going to raise a whole tribe of black engineers."

"You sound like my cousin. He swears black people need to learn how to make things so they can build businesses."

"Yeah, CW is right. As a matter of fact, he's where we got the idea about the engineers from. I went to high school with him. We were pretty good friends."

"Why do you call him CW?"

"It's short for Chicken Wing. I'll let Josh explain to you why we call him CW. He gave him that nickname."

Genna had taken her upstairs as they continued their conversation. There were twenty-seven more kids scattered among four classrooms. Genna explained they grouped several grades together because they didn't really have enough students to warrant a single class for each one. There were seven students in the high school class. They were all in either the ninth or the tenth grade.

Genna had brought her to this suite of offices after they completed the tour. She led her into a big office that opened out into the hall they had just come down. Genna invited her to sit at a round table with three chairs around it. There was a huge desk with a credenza behind it facing the hall.

Adrienne said, "This is nice."

"Thank you, this one is mine. That's Josh's right across the hall. He insisted I take the bigger office."

Adrienne glanced at the office diagonally across from Genna's. "You two must really like each other," she commented.

Genna tittered. "I have to keep my eye on Josh. And yes, we do get along. You make yourself comfortable while I go look for him."

Adrienne saw a picture of a handsome black couple on the wall above Genna's credenza. She noted Genna bore a strong resemblance to the woman and surmised the couple must be her parents. On her desk sat a picture of a man and two children—a girl and a boy grinning mischievously out of the photo. *Must be Genna's husband and kids*, Adrienne thought.

Her stomach fluttered.

She thought about Reggie yelling at her this morning before she slammed the phone down. *Come on, Adrienne, isn't your plate full enough already? Now you're trying to get involved with a school—a black private school. Wow, that's a fine use of your time. Those people aren't interested in your little theory.*

A little voice in her head argued, *Reggie's right*. She stood up and paced the floor next to the table. Suddenly, she heard people talking. She recognized Genna's voice. And a man was with her. It must have been Josh. She sat back down, smoothing her dress as she did. The last thing she wanted was them to realize she had been pacing the floor.

She had changed her mind about four or five times this morning trying to pick just the right outfit. She finally settled on a blue dress with a pattern of concentric squares and a pair of brown boots. It had seemed like a good choice when she left home, but now she wasn't so sure. *Father help me*, she thought as they came through the door.

"Adrienne Johnson," Genna said. "I would like to introduce you to my brother Josh, Josh Gibson. Josh, this is Adrienne Johnson. She's here to share some ideas with us I feel can benefit the school."

"Josh Gibson, huh," Adrienne cracked as she rose to greet him. "Can you live up to that name?"

He looked surprised for a moment before his face burst into a big smile. "What do you know about the black Babe Ruth?"

"Don't you mean Babe Ruth was the white Josh Gibson?" she corrected him. "My father's from Pittsburgh. He saw him play when he was a little boy. I'm the youngest of nine and the only girl. My father loves baseball. He raised all of us on it, even me—especially me. He'd take me to the barbershop with him when I was little, and they used to talk about Josh Gibson a lot. They said he was the greatest baseball player who ever lived." She smiled, lost in some long-ago memory.

"You from Pittsburgh?"

"No, I'm from a place called Lima. It's in Ohio."

"Lima, Ohio, huh. You like Atlanta?"

"Yes, I do. I love all the trees."

"Here, let me get that for you," he said as he pulled out the chair for her. Genna was smiling at him. "I gotta be nice to a guest who knows about Josh Gibson."

"You a baseball fan?"

"I'm a Braves fan. I don't know if that really qualifies me as a baseball fan. I like you. You're a trash talker," he said. "I love your outfit. Blue is my favorite color. And those boots really look nice on you."

"Thank you," she replied. She thought, *You are fine.*

"So Chicken Wing is your cousin? I went to Morehouse with him."

"Yeah, Genna told me. We both teach over there. Why do you call him Chicken Wing?"

"You not grown enough to hear a story like that," he shot back.

"Josh, behave," Genna interjected.

"Yes ma'am," he said with a smirk. "So, Ms. Johnson, how you enjoying my alma mater?"

"It's great! I just started this fall, but I'm having a ball so far, Mr. Gibson."

They chatted for a few more minutes. She sensed him checking her out once or twice. Once, she caught him and really turned on the high-beam smile. He froze in mid-sentence. She got a kick out of the way he stumbled back into the conversation.

He seemed really nice. Her nervousness dissipated as they talked about Josh Gibson and baseball and what it was like to have eight older brothers.

Finally, the conversation slowed. She reached into her valise and handed Josh and Genna an outline containing key points from her presentation. She informed Josh that what she was about to share with him was taken from her doctoral dissertation.

"What field?" he asked.

"Sociology, "she replied.

He took a few moments to study the paper she had provided. He frowned once or twice. She felt a touch of nervousness return. *He doesn't want to hear this.* She could hear Reggie attacking her again. Josh shook his head. She tried not to sit on the edge of her seat. She didn't want him to know how anxious she was for him to agree with her. She really liked what she saw here. She felt proud. It touched her to see two young black people pull this off.

Genna had told her a couple of weeks ago about their satellite campus in College Park: forty-three more young voices singing their times tables, celebrating themselves, being raised to revel in the sweetness and strength of their darkness; young, black, and gifted with the knowledge of their first-class status in the eyes of every adult around them all day long.

She heard him grunt. Josh shook his head again. Adrienne bit her lip, wondering what he thought so far.

She reflected on her brother Norman for a second, wishing he could have lived to see this place. Adrienne looked at Genna for some hint of what Josh was thinking. No luck. Genna was busy studying Josh.

He looked up and stared her straight in the eye. She shifted in her seat. Genna had emphasized to her that Josh loved these kids. He wouldn't let anyone near them if he smelled a hint of white supremacy on his or her breath. He only wanted people around them who truly believed in the goodness and greatness of blackness.

Adrienne understood his point. They were exposed, well, overexposed to white supremacy every day of their lives. The only way to fight against it was to emphasize the specialness of who they were. *How can I convince him we're on the same page?*

Josh started speaking. "Chicken Wing and I heard Muhammad Ali give a speech at Morehouse a few years ago. He was speaking on how black people are constantly bombarded with these negative images—a bad day is a black day. The bad guys are the guys in the black hats. A black cat is bad luck. Black is scary, black is evil. He went on and on about that thing. But then, he turned it around. He told us to understand the truth about black, you have to look to nature. He said if you look to nature, you can see for yourself black is a good thing. He told us the blacker the berry, the sweeter the juice. He said a strong cup of coffee is a black cup of coffee; good dirt is black dirt. I'll never forget him saying those things. Something all the young brothers needed to hear. Adrienne, we don't tell our kids enough how special they are. We don't teach them being black means you have to be strong—you learn to take the bitter and turn it sweet. That black people are good people. That's what I'm about. What are you about? 'cause if this isn't it, you're wasting my time."

Adrienne, hold it together. She could feel her legs shaking, glad they were crossed under her dress. Glad it fell to midcalf so he wouldn't see how his comment affected her. Another bigger part of her grew angry, really angry. *How dare you question my love of my people!* "I love black people," she replied, speaking more tersely than she wanted to.

He kept staring at her, not saying a word.

"Give her a chance, Josh," Genna said plaintively.

Seeing Genna pleading her case helped her decide how to approach him.

"Well, I certainly don't want to waste any more of your time, so why don't you hear what I have to say and then get back to whatever it is you were doing that was so important."

"Well, all righty then. Genna, you want to take this down the hall? Ms. Johnson, we have a board set up for you in our meeting room. You ready to do your thing?"

Asshole ran through her mind as he came around and pulled her chair back. "Hey, Genna," he cracked. "I bet this is going to be even better than you said."

Chapter 7

The Great Crossing

Josh took the rear so he could watch Adrienne walk down the hall. He was trying to see if he could figure out how his comment about wasting his time had affected her. If her purposeful stride was any indication, she was pissed. *Bowlegged! Boy, you look just like a cowgirl marching down my hall in those boots—a really pretty cowgirl.*

He figured he had to do something. She was so nervous she was tapping her feet. She even appeared to be biting her lip. He glanced at the pictures—Malcolm; Martin; Miss Harriett, the honorable; and all the other inspirations on their wall of fame. He swore Malcolm winked and gave him the thumbs-up as she flashed by. He smiled, thinking to himself, *This is why I drink so early in the morning—to avoid hallucinations.*

Fresh-brewed coffee awaited them in the meeting room. Genna asked Adrienne if she needed her bag. "No, I'll be all right." Adrienne glared at him for a second as she prepared to set up before cutting her eyes away.

"Explain the unexplainable. Your people," Josh said as he took a seat next to Genna.

Adrienne smiled. "I'll try," she said. She sketched a graph on the board. The vertical line she marked as Level of Discrimination. The horizontal one she named Years.

Josh watched her intently, wondering where she was coming from. She wrote the terms "effective" and "efficient" off to the side. She placed definitions by each word. Effective—choosing the right approach. Efficient—choosing the fastest, least costly approach.

She turned to face him. Her expression had changed. It was intense, almost intimidating. She pursed her lips.

"Are you familiar with the works of Thomas Sowell?" she asked.

"You talking about that idiot who claims the civil rights movement was unnecessary?"

"I see you've heard of him," she said with a look of bemusement that made him suddenly wary. "Anyway, the theory I'm about to share with you is based in part on some of his writings from the early sixties. He does excellent research, but his analysis is ahistorical."

"Big word, Ms. Johnson, but why do you call him ahistorical?"

"He either can't or won't acknowledge a key point about our heritage. Have you read any of his works?"

"I saw a column he wrote on the editorial page of the *Wall Street Journal* a couple of years ago. He was claiming black people really hadn't made much progress during our time in America, when you compare our circumstances to other ethnic groups he claimed suffered discrimination in America. It was during my black Republican phase. He was one of the people who turned me away from that line of thinking. I thought his comparison was flawed."

She smiled at him. "Yeah, I read that column, too. I was troubled by what he had to say. It does seem like we could have done more in four hundred years than we have, but I couldn't accept his premise we were lacking in achievement when compared to other ethnic groups.

Actually, I got the ahistorical comment from Dr. Sims in the economics department over at Morehouse. I was asking him about Dr. Sowell's comments, and he pointed out Sowell chooses to ignore the disparities in the histories of blacks and the groups he compares us to in his analysis. He talked about the assault on the black community in Tulsa, things like that."

"So you know Dr. Sims?" Josh asked. "He was one of my favorite teachers."

"We talk sometimes,'" she replied. "I was troubled by our seeming lack of progress the past twenty years. I think all of us expected more than what we've seen, so I didn't just reject his commentary out of hand. I studied his research, particularly a book called *Ethnic America* he wrote in 1963, and concluded what he missed was the real nature of discrimination in America. The Irish, Italian, Jewish, and other immigrant groups he compared to blacks faced a different type of prejudice in America than what we confronted, but that doesn't mean they weren't discriminated against in their time. It means we were more discriminated against in ours."

Genna stole a glance his way to gauge his reaction to what Ms. Johnson had said so far. He looked back at Genna, nodding his head to signal his interest in her comments.

"I realized there are two types of discrimination in America—one that includes and another that excludes. Discrimination that includes is what immigrants from other countries have had to traditionally deal with in this country. It's generic in nature and over time it dissipates, or, I should say, it's the type immigrant males have always faced. Women, gays and lesbians, and the disabled have always faced an intracultural exclusive discrimination."

She took a breath and continued.

"They are part of America, but not allowed to assume certain roles. For instance, can you imagine a gay man being elected president? Or a woman? Franklin Roosevelt had to hide the fact he was in a wheelchair from Americans in his day. Then you have blacks and Native Americans. We have suffered from intercultural exclusive discrimination. It is the most difficult form of discrimination to deal with because it specifically excludes the aggrieved party from the nation-building process.

"I always think about the bicentennial celebration and how so much was said about the immigrants who were adopted by America, how they chose to come here and gradually made the transformation from Giuseppe Immigrant to Joe America. I remember how all the black people around me felt a lot less enthusiastic about this celebration. Instead of tall ships riding down the Hudson, we were forced once more to consider slave ships riding the Atlantic. Instead of celebrating our deliverance to the land of opportunity, we were forced to consider how few opportunities for a better life were presented to us through the nightmare of slavery and the cruel illusion of separate but equal under Jim Crow.

"I think about the American Indian and how his fate was in many ways even crueler than ours. We were taken from our home; his home was systematically taken because God chose to impose a manifest destiny on the new world. I think about the two sides of the story of the western movement in America, how it started on the beaches of Virginia and at Plymouth Rock in Massachusetts and how it ended on the shining shores of the Pacific. How Custer's Last Stand was a great Indian victory, while for America it represented the most stinging of all defeats."

Preach it, girl, Josh thought.

She continued. "Think football. Blacks and Native Americans are the blocking backs that sprang other immigrant groups free for a dizzying dash to the end zone marked Equality to score the touchdown of ideal status in America. We served as the parameters of American society, the low people on the hierarchy of prejudices that defines this and any other complex society. We were the dregs whom others stepped on to begin their ascension. If the white, heterosexual, able-bodied male of Christian descent is our society's ideal, then we two groups were his polar opposite. Everyone seeks out the ideal; everyone spurns the dregs, including the dregs themselves."

She shifted her weight, leaning back on her right heel and showing off those boots. She stared at him for a second before turning her gaze to Genna. He smiled at her to indicate he was open to what she was saying. Questions were forming in his mind, challenges to her thinking were popping up, but he sensed she should be allowed to finish. He had never heard anything like this before, and he knew his mind was instinctively bucking against so different a proposition. She continued.

"America could not totally disregard the immigrant, because they were at least superior to the niggers and savages who disgraced the country by their mere presence. The immigrant was therefore granted a role in the grand ball of American development. Immigrant males faced inclusive discrimination, but it was temporary in nature. Irishmen were confronted with employment discrimination in the form of signs that said No Irish Need Apply just as Jews suffered the same fate during their assimilation era when they were told Christians Only. Italians were considered genetically mentally inferior by the top social scientists of their assimilation era because they were such poor students. Dr. Shockley would have been proud."

Josh had to stop her now. "Can you back up all this?" He was surprised to hear her use such strong language.

She said, "I'll let you read my copy of *Ethnic America*. It's all there. I don't agree with his politics, but Sowell is a brilliant researcher."

"Okay," he replied.

"And if you're wondering why I put such faith in what he says, it's because of all the footnotes he provides that back up his assertions about the assimilation of ethnic groups into American society. He doesn't comment in the book; he reports. You can make your own judgments based on the facts he presents."

He shot back at her, "You read my mind, because I was sure gonna ask why you accept his words as gospel truth."

A twinkle briefly ran across her eyes. "Josh, the point I'm trying to make to you is that the two types of discrimination have to be acknowledged, because then and only then can we discern the proper approach to dealing with them. Exclusive discrimination requires an effective approach to its elimination. It is a subtraction problem. Inclusive discrimination requires more of an efficient approach to what would be its minimization. It is more properly described by differential calculus."

"Subtraction and calculus, huh? I know you're getting ready to explain—"

"Then let her finish!" Genna interjected.

She looked at Genna and said, "It's all right, he's just curious," as if to say, *I got this.* She turned back to the board, drawing a line across it right above the top of the graph. She wrote Area of Exclusion above the line. Below the line, she wrote Area of Inclusion.

She began again. "In a multiethnic society, there are often groups who don't fit, who aren't really a part of the society. Some examples are Jewish people in Germany before the Holocaust, Chinese immigrants in New Zealand, and blacks and Native Americans in our country. These people can play a role, often a substantial role within a given society, but they are in that society and not of it. They live in what I call the area of exclusion, because they are excluded from citizenship in the country where they live. Sure, they live on the same soil as the citizens, but they lack the same rights.

"A nation is much more than a physical territory—it represents the sum total of a shared history and culture, a collective mindset nurtured and refined over generations into an identity to which nationals can easily affix themselves. It is the derivative of a set of traditions, values, and myths bound together into common ideals. Ideals nationals draw upon for strength and direction.

"This common history and culture is the glue binding a nation's members together into a single whole. Resulting from generations of shared positive experiences, it develops in nationals a common ground of understanding—a shared view, guidelines for living, and cultural instincts. These instincts serve as a cultural navigational system, guiding individual choices, setting boundaries for appropriate behavior, defining concepts such as right and wrong.

"In this sense, the United States is a nation. There is an *American* way of life, an *American* state of mind, an *American* set of cultural instincts guiding this nation's citizens in their day-to-day decision making. Americans draw comfort, strength, and direction from this country's history and culture. Americans take great pride in their national ideals and hold up the creators of those ideals to be national heroes. Washington, Jefferson, and Lincoln are names Americans recognize and admire. They symbolize for modern Americans the magnificence contained in the nation's regal past.

"Three nations formed in the middle of the North American continent: black America, native America, and the United States of America. The only glue binding blacks and Native Americans to the United States of America was the severe mistreatment they bore as their lot in American history. Native Americans and Americans looked at two sides of the same coin; the Oklahoma Land Rush was a great moment in American history, but a dark moment for a people already subjected to numerous variations of the Trail of Tears. Custer's Last Stand was a great Native American victory, but a bitter American defeat.

"Black people know in the course of human events, for far too long and way too often, life, liberty, and the pursuit of happiness were inalienable rights America denied her black stepchildren, holding it to be self-evident no black man or woman could aspire to such lofty ideals. We see celebrations like the bicentennial, commemorating the nurturing nature of a land that drew people from the world over in search of a better life in a better world. And we feel bitterness about how we have been forgotten by opportunity and feel anger about our involuntary separation from Mother Africa, sadness about how America has denied us access to this nation's glory.

"The only proper American response to the conquest of the American Indian and the enslavement of the African was to dehumanize them, and this is precisely what happened. Dehumanization allowed America to reconcile her behavior toward these people and the evolving myth proclaiming America the land of opportunity for the world's downtrodden. Blacks were written into the constitution as less than human, and the case of a Ponca Indian named

Standing Bear, discussed in Dee Brown's *Bury My Heart at Wounded Knee,* showed a United States attorney arguing Indians were not persons within the meaning of the law. Standing Bear won his case and became one of the few Native Americans or blacks of that era to be considered a full-fledged human being."

"Our people and this continent's aboriginal settlers were specifically excluded from the nation-building process to the point they could not be considered Americans. They were denizens of two shadow nations who defined the dark side of Americana. Blacks and Native Americans are pieces left over from the construction of the United States. Left on the floor inside this grand edifice, they remain an unsightly pile in the corner for which the builders have yet to find a proper place.

"The natives, forced from the land they cherished, still inhabit a separate world. Black people, brought here in chains, found ourselves confounded by choices available to us that Native Americans did not have or want. We could migrate back to Africa. We could demand a land within a land or we could emigrate to the United States of America. These were the choices available to us as we lived a life in the exile of exclusion, strangers in our own home."

She went on. "Marcus Garvey exhorted us to go back to Africa, the Honorable Elijah Muhammad clamored for a land of our own. Their ideas didn't really resonate. They ignored a point Martin King embraced—black people love America, and what we want above all else is to be a part of this great country, not to be apart from it.

"Civil rights leaders understood they were dealing with exclusionary discrimination and knew how to deal with it, even though they called it Jim Crow racism. You had to humanize the Negro, as we called ourselves, so mainstream America could begin to see blacks as junior partners in our society; unequal partners, but partners just the same. This was a necessary first step. King understood you must create solutions both sides embrace. Back to Africa and Africa out West were dissatisfying propositions to Americans black and white.

"The movement's emphasis on nonviolent revolution was a brilliantly effective strategy. The peaceful assertions for full-fledged citizenship made by demonstrators in the South contrasted well against a backdrop of bullhorns, fire hoses, and biting police dogs. Coupled with imaginative legal attacks on Jim Crow by the NAACP legal defense fund, the movement gradually extracted enough discrimination from the American mainstream for it to be plausible for us to seek equality as we ended our stay in exile.

"The civil rights movement was the black journey across the ocean to America. We looked out across an ocean of racial oppression, imagining a land of opportunity, an ideal; a nation setting the standard for freedom and tolerance in the world. An America where by the sweat of his or her brow, one could create a better life for themselves, a better world for their children, an America where one could speak out with impunity, whistle at a woman without being hung. This was the America we believed in, but did not live in.

"We glanced out longingly into a stormy sea filled with racial hatred and drew solace from our captain's remonstration: We're not going to be discouraged, we're not going to be dissuaded; we're going to reach that land of freedom. Black America gathered its meager belongings, boarded a ship called Hope, and set sail for a new world. Black America offered so little, this other America so much, we decided like so many before us that no matter how dangerous the trip, no matter how high the price, we had to live in this land."

"Our journey traversed a seascape fraught with fear. Instead of disembarking at Ellis Island, we slipped off the boat beneath the Lincoln Memorial knowing in our hearts we, like our ethnic brethren before us, had a dream. What a great day in the morning it was when we landed on these majestic shores, lifted our heads skyward, and shouted with joy: 'America, we are here! Love us; take us in your arms as you have so many before us.' This was our fantasy at that historic moment. Only seldom does fantasy echo reality."

She looked him in the eye, turned, erased the board with long, graceful strokes, and strode away from the board, sitting down next to Genna. Josh found himself standing, shouting, "Bravo!" and giving her a standing ovation. She couldn't hide her smile before she turned her head toward Genna.

Chapter 8

The Girl from Lima

Josh sat back down quickly. *Jay, get a hold of yourself,* he thought. Adrienne stared at him triumphantly. She flashed a high-beam smile. *Wow. A definite number-one pick,* he thought.

He and Shaun and some of the other fellas had always thought assigning a woman a number like a nine was lame. What was a nine anyway, and how did that describe how well this particular player might fit with your franchise? Assigning draft numbers allowed for more nuanced comparisons. It allowed you to assess things besides looks, which faded in importance after a few weeks anyway. Was she well groomed? Did she have all her teeth? Could she talk in complete sentences? A number-one pick implied a great all-around talent, not just a piece of eye candy. What position did she play, was she a guard, a center, or a forward? Did she suit the direction you're trying to take your franchise?

They'd started this assessment when they first started getting high, picking joints out of dime bags. After copping, they'd roll up all the dope and pick which joints looked like they'd get you the highest. You started with the real talent and worked your way down, hoping to develop a strong bench to back up those future stars you tried to select in the earlier rounds. Some drafts were thin in real talent. Maybe you copped from some lesser dope hole and didn't get a chance to go to one of the stronger programs for your talent. Maybe you went to a strong program that was having an off year.

A pick that might go mid-first round in a good year might make it to the top of the draft board in a down year. What he saw sitting next to Genna was one of those once-in-a-generation picks that would immediately go to the top of any draft board in any given year. She reminded him of Jabbar coming out of UCLA, a no-brainer. Except she had a frame and game more along the lines of a Walter Davis—sleek, standing about five eight or nine, lean, athletic looking, smooth, and seemingly able to get off her shot from anywhere on the court.

And she was astonishingly attractive. Her face was defined by a pair of geometrically perfect cheekbones, rising high above her jawline to rest right below a pair of mesmerizing brown eyes. Her hair was so wavy it made him seasick. It was parted right in the middle with three waves on each side that looked like the crinkle-cut French fries they used to eat at Hampton games as kids. Her hair fell away from those crinkles, rolling down the sides of that face to rest on her slender shoulders—shoulders covered by that dress. A dress that he took in again, made up of concentric squares of different hues of blue, dark then light inside the dark, light then dark inside the light, all the way down to those boots that seemed to be whispering to him, *You need to check out these legs, you wouldn't believe. . .* And then he followed the squares back up to that face and hoped she hadn't caught him checking her out. She must have because she smiled at him again, only she turned up the wattage. He felt his heart simply get up to leave him and jump her way.

He caught it right before it leapt for her smile, nestling it tightly in his hand, muttering "traitor" as it squirmed, attempting to get closer to Ms. Johnson.

"Josh." Genna spoke, bringing him out of his thoughts and back into the room. "What do you think?"

Damn, I shouldn't have stood and cheered. He paused like the Mariner had taught him to do, grimacing, attempting to give off the appearance of being deep in thought, as though he were considering whether or not what he heard was anything worthwhile. The point was to throw her off balance. After all, good defense was the key to winning.

Ms. Johnson looked at him, smiled, and the words gushed out of his mouth. "I'm impressed. I hope Morehouse knows what they got and hold onto you." *So much for playing great defense;* there went the smile on high beam again.

He tried to fend her off, scrambling for some question to ask so she wouldn't see the devastating impact her smile was having on him. *Be cool, Josh,* he thought. It was hard.

"So, what happens next? I mean, is that it? We made the great crossing? I can see that, but what difference does it make?"

She smiled again. "If you want to know that, you have to sign on the dotted line and pull out your checkbook."

Damn, he thought to himself, hooked beyond all comprehension.

He laughed. "Okay, you got that one," he told her. "Let me talk to Genna. But I think we can definitely work something out."

He refused to look at Hopalong, not wanting to give her the satisfaction just yet of being right about Ms. Johnson.

Genna broke the spell by standing up. "Well, Adrienne, how about I walk you out? I've got a couple of errands to run. I'm sure Josh will want to read over the materials you left him."

"Yeah, I sure will," he told her. "I enjoyed meeting you, Miss Johnson. It is miss, right?"

"It sure is! Nice to meet you, too, Mr. Gibson. I hope to hear from you soon."

She held her hand out. He slowly reached for it as if were a piece of fine porcelain. "See ya, Josh!" she said, striding off behind Genna. Genna waved to him as she led Adrienne down the hall to get her bag. He watched her walk off with Genna, wondering if there was any chance the two of them could hook up. He wondered if she had a boyfriend. She probably did, but so what?

He waited until he was sure Genna had walked her out to go back to his office. It would normally be time for a cigarette, but at the moment a smoke didn't interest him. He walked down the hall into his office, slid behind his desk, and took a seat. Genna had placed a thick, bound document from Adrienne on his desk. He opened it, ready to get started.

He thumbed through it every so often, reading small snatches that caught his eye. It was fascinating reading. He reached a passage where she argued the current black condition paralleled that of the Irish in America a hundred years ago. He would have thought the closest comparison would have been Italians. This section seemed like a good place to start reading in depth.

There was a gentle knock on his door. He looked up. There she stood, Miss Johnson in the flesh. Her standing in the doorway sent a shock wave through him.

"Hey, I came back to apologize. I kinda snapped at you right before I left, when I made the crack about the checkbook. I wanted to make sure you didn't take offense."

"Nah," was all he could say. He thought, *You don't know how glad I am you came back.* "Oh, why don't you have a seat?"

he asked. She glided over to the chair right in front of his desk and floated down into it, crossing those long legs and folding her hands over her knees all in one motion. Once again, she smiled.

"So you've really thought this out pretty good, huh?" He asked, fishing for something to say.

"Yeah, I recently spent the summer in New Haven. I worked for a professor at Yale while I was there, running errands, typing letters, that sort of thing. He made me read *Ethnic America* as a part of my job. He wanted me to get a different perspective on America. Reading it opened my eyes. I guess I got curious, especially since the movement didn't really gain us equality. He was different in his thinking. He seemed to totally agree with Sowell. I don't buy Sowell's belief the civil rights movement was unnecessary, but this professor brought up the fact that urban blacks seemed to be mimicking some of the behavior patterns of the Irish migrants who came to this country after the potato famine. It struck a chord. So it's strange to be in the presence of a black Republican," she cracked.

It was his turn to smile. "Yeah, I tried that coat on for size for a minute. I had to take it off though. Didn't really fit me."

"What made you change your mind?"

"I came to the conclusion they don't really like black people. I'm not into self-hatred. What, you got Republican leanings?"

She frowned. A look ran across her face like she'd bitten into something bitter. She leaned back a little, settling into a more defensive posture.

"No, I don't think so. I'm like you. I don't think they really like black people, and I'm definitely not into self-hatred."

"So how'd you wind up here?"

"Somebody offered me a job."

"I haven't cut the check yet."

She laughed and leaned forward ever so slightly. "You act like a Republican." They both laughed.

"My mother died when I was ten. I used to come visit my aunt and uncle every summer after that. My Aunt Leah and my mother were close so she wanted to look after me. I love her for that. I always liked Georgia, so when Chicken Wing told me there was a position available at Morehouse, I applied and here I am. Plus, I lived here once before," she said. "I graduated from Fisk when I was nineteen. I got a job as a stewardess with Delta after I finished college. I did my training here."

"Why a stew?"

"I don't know; I guess I wanted to travel. See the country. It seemed like a good way to do it."

"Did you enjoy it?"

"It was interesting. It's funny—I was telling some of my students about being trained by Delta last semester. I had a white roommate. We got along pretty good. One night I pulled out my hair dryer, getting ready to wash my hair. She looked at it and she was like, 'What are you going to do with that?' So I had to explain to her how black women have to sit under the dryer after their hair has been washed. She had a hard time accepting that I only had to wash my hair once a week 'cause she washed hers every night and dried it with a blow dryer. She couldn't believe how long I had to sit there waiting on my hair to dry."

"She still in Atlanta?"

"Nah, she flies out of Dallas. We call each other every few weeks. So, Genna told me your dad taught at Fisk for a year?"

"Yeah, we were gypsies for a while there when we were kids. We lived in Alabama, Tennessee, and Virginia before we moved here. My mom and dad met over at the AU center and they always loved Atlanta. Yeah, Fisk was nice. So was Hampton. My dad worked there for a minute. This is home now, though. Think you gonna stay here?"

"I might. Atlanta's a nice city."

"You should let me show you around sometime. I could give you the native's tour."

"We'll see."

"I guess I got to break out my checkbook first, huh?" They both laughed again. There was an easy rapport building between them. It felt good. He always found it hard to connect with strangers. Breaking the ice had always been a difficult one step forward, three-steps-back-into-his-shell proposition.

She glanced at her watch. "I'd better be going. Enjoyed chatting with you though. I'm gonna have to call my dad and tell him I actually talked to Josh Gibson. He'll get a kick out of hearing that." She rose from the chair.

"You gotta leave?" slipped out of his mouth before he could catch it.

"Yeah, I got a class I have to get ready for at one o'clock. Besides, you got some homework you need to finish." She looked down at the folder on his desk. She opened her pocketbook, reaching in to pull out a business card. She handed it to him. It read Adrienne Johnson: *Have Book, Will Travel.*

"I like your card. I'm glad I found out how to spell your name. I thought it was A-D-R-I-A-N."

"No, that's how guys spell Adrienne. You mean I look like a guy to you?" she said.

He smiled at the thought. "No, actually, when I was a kid, I had a good friend named Adrian. She spelled her name A-D-R-I-A-N. 'Have book, will travel,' huh? I guess I'm going to have to call you Paladin."

"You caught that, huh? Maybe you *can* live up to your name. Call me," she said, "when you get ready to open that checkbook. My number's on my card. That's my work number though. Here, let me see it for a minute." He handed her the card. She took it, flipped it over, scribbled something on the back, and handed it back to him. He looked down. In beautiful cursive she had written: Home—233-8989. "Just in case you need to get in touch."

"You live in Buckhead?"

"Yeah, for the moment. I've got an apartment off Peachtree near Lenox Square. I'm supposed to be moving soon. My aunt has a house she's going to let me rent. Better yet, if I don't hear from you in a few days, I'll call you and see what you think. I know you're busy, so I'll check with you. That okay?"

"Sure, I'll look forward to it. I'm going to try and get a good start on this today, though. I don't really have to see the kids until the afternoon. I try to stay out of the teachers' ways until then. How about I walk you out?"

"Okay."

He got up and walked around the desk, motioning for her to walk out in front of him. He chuckled to himself.

"Something funny?" she asked.

"Oh nothing, I was just thinking how Genna kept telling me about you, how I needed to hear what you had to say and how I kept putting her off. Big mistake."

They were standing next to the glass double doors leading out of the building. He held the door open and she walked out. She turned and smiled and waved as she opened the door to her car and got in.

Aaron came up behind him. "Miss Genna wants you, Mr. Josh. Hey, that your meeting?"

"Yeah."

"Damn. Mr. Josh, she got you in a daze, doesn't she? I don't blame you, though. She's pretty. Kind of reminds me of Miss Sarah."

"She does, Aaron. You sure are right."

As they went back inside, he could hear Sinatra singing "The Girl from Ipanema," except he sang to himself, "the girl from Lima."

Chapter 9

Norman

Thirty minutes after she pulled out of the school's parking lot, Adrienne was walking up the stairs to her office. She paused at the door to the second floor with her hand on the handle. Smiling to herself, she opened it and started marching down the hall. She peeked in a couple of doors, speaking to colleagues before reaching her destination. She rapped gently on the door.

"Hey Adrienne, how you doing?" inquired the thin man with a medium afro who rose to greet her.

"Hey Chicken Wing, how's tricks?"

Her cousin stared at her. "Chicken Wing! I know who you've been talking to."

She came around his desk and gave him a hug. She stepped back, pressing her hands gently against his arms. "You never told me."

"Told you what?"

"That you were such a big lover of chicken wings."

"You aren't funny," he replied

"Well, then, how'd you get the nickname?"

Sighing, he replied. "How's Genna? And her crazy brother."

Adrienne sat down in the chair facing his desk.

"Hey, nobody invited you to stay."

She rolled her eyes at Chicken Wing. "Stop tripping and sit down and talk to your favorite cousin."

He grinned at her. "You didn't answer my question," he responded as he sat back down.

"She's fine. She told me to tell you hey. And her brother is crazy."

"So you did meet the nefarious Josh Gibson. What did you think of the school?"

"It's nice, really nice."

"Yeah, if Genna's involved, I know it's hooked up. She always liked her stuff just so. Momma said she acts just like her mom. She also told me you're supposed to stop by this afternoon."

She shuffled some of the papers on his desk. "Yeah, I told her I'd be by. You coming over?"

"I got something up. Besides, you know how the two of you are. I wouldn't get a word in edgewise anyway. But tell me how it went. I know how excited you were."

Why is everybody excited about this but Reggie? That wasn't fair. This was family, and old Chicken Wing was more like her brother than her cousin. She had been born four days before him, so she always called him her baby cousin. When Norman died, she had almost lost her mind. Norman had been two and a half years older than her and her favorite brother, and this cousin had sat in her room with her during the terrible night before Norman's funeral, watching her cry herself sick. Chicken Wing had always been there for her and had always been excited about anything his big cousin did. Maybe she was being too hard on Reggie.

"Well, Genna was nice as always. She took me on a tour of the school. I really like it. She told me they want to raise a whole tribe of engineers. She said she got that from you."

"Yeah, her and Jewel were tight. That's how we got to know each other. We talk every now and then."

"Adrienne shook her head. "That brother of hers, though. He's something else. Oooh, he made me mad."

"What'd he do?"

"He went into some long spiel about a speech you and he heard Muhammad Ali give at Morehouse about the virtues of being black. Then he told me that's what he was about and that I wasn't to waste his time. And why are you laughing? That's not funny."

"Made you mad, did he? Come on, Adrienne. You know how emotional you are. He was probably trying to get you out of yourself so you could give it your best shot. I bet you were tapping your foot, right?"

She wanted to hit him for knowing her like that. She balled up a piece of paper off of his desk and threw it at her cousin.

"Did it work?"

She lowered her eyes. "I guess so. He gave me a standing ovation when I finished."

"Adrienne, Josh Gibson's the kind of man who will help a little old lady across the street and snatch her purse when they get to the other side. I mean, Josh is cool, but he can come out a bag on you sometimes."

"Are you friends?" she asked.

"We're okay. The reason he calls me Chicken Wing . . . Nah, I better not tell you that."

"Why not? I mean what is it about you being called Chicken Wing that's so bad? He told me I wasn't grown enough to hear the story."

"I know how you are. If I tell you, you have to promise you won't get upset."

"Upset about what?" she asked.

"Norman."

"What does Norman have to do with it?" She felt herself getting loud, her voice growing shrill. *Calm down, Adrienne.* For a moment she was back in Chicago, in her Aunt Adel and Uncle Syl's kitchen. She and her aunt were laughing about something, she couldn't remember what, when she heard a *pop pop pop* like firecrackers going off. Tires squealed, and her cousin Slave came running in the apartment, cursing. He looked at her and she knew. She knew even as she ran out the front door.

Norman was lying on the ground. Her cousin Vince and a couple of the other Stones in his clique stood over him, cursing and crying. She ran to Norman. Vince tried to grab her arm and pull her away, but she snatched it from him, falling to her knees besides her big brother. His eyes were wide open—but not as wide as the hole in the center of his forehead. What looked like oatmeal appeared to leach from the wound. There was screaming. Aunt Adel cradled her in her arms, and Adrienne realized it was her own screams she heard. Knees scraping the concrete, Adrienne caressed her brother's breathless body as her heart cracked under the weight of her sorrow.

For a moment she was back in Chicago, wrapped in Aunt Adel's arms, tears running silently down her cheeks, until she realized she was in an office in Atlanta, her cousin's arms wrapped around her, whispering it was all right. She rocked back and forth, her hand on his arm, scared to breathe.

Chapter 10

Leah

"Hey, Momma."

"Hi baby, how you doing?" Leah asked in her raspy, smoke-tinged voice.

"I'm fine. Is Adrienne there?"

"She sure is. She just walked in the door a couple of minutes ago."

"Is she okay?"

Leah glanced at her niece. "She's fine, baby. Why, did something happen?"

"Well, she was real upset before she went to class. I just wanted to make sure she's okay. We were talking and I mentioned Norman and she fell apart. I haven't seen her that upset in a long time. I was worried about her."

Leah took a drag on her cigarette. "I'll talk to her. I'll call you back later." She hung up the phone. Her sister Carol bore the pains of birthing this girl sitting at her table, but she loved Adrienne like she was her very own daughter. Lord, she had been through so much. Adrienne and Carol were so close she could hardly tell where one left off and the other began. Carol's death devastated her whole brood, but it had hit her only daughter hardest of all.

Alonso had asked Leah if she would help him with her and Norman. They were his two youngest. She had said of course, and her Howard had immediately insisted they come to visit every summer. They would arrive every July, filling the house with noise and love. She'd shuffle the two of them and her three boys back and forth between here and her Aunt Addie Mae and Uncle Enoch's house down in the country. Adrienne had loved to help out in their store.

And she had loved her brother Norman. He had been so nice. He'd wanted to be a school teacher just like Carol and his Aunt Leah. Adrienne had wanted to own a store. Norman's death, however, changed that.

Leah had been sitting in this kitchen talking to her two youngest sons the day Alonso had called her with the news about Norman. Adrienne had been fourteen. In her mind, Leah could hear her wailing "Auntie Leah, Auntie Leah," when Alonso had put her on the phone. Adrienne had been so distraught she couldn't get anything else out. Leah sighed before easing back over to the table to sit next to her child.

"How you doing, baby?"

"I'm fine, Aunt Leah. Why?"

"Your cousin told me you were upset today. You know how he is about you. He wanted me to make sure you're okay." She watched Adrienne tap her heel on the linoleum. "Baby, you know you can talk to Aunt Leah. What's the matter?"

"Aunt Leah, I'm okay. I guess so much went on today. I didn't mean to cry. It's just when I thought about Norman, I don't know, it . . ." Leah watched her fight back tears. She reached over and took Adrienne in her arms. "Baby, you can tell auntie. I know it's more than Norman. What's bothering you?"

"I don't know. It's Reggie, I guess. He's so mean here lately. You know Genna Campbell, right?"

"Yeah, Regina Gibson's daughter."

Adrienne nodded really fast like she was ten again. Leah stroked her hair. She would always be her baby.

Adrienne caught her breath. "Well, I met with her and her brother today about doing some work for their school. I was a little nervous about it so I called Reggie this morning to talk with him about what I was going to say. He got real mad. He told me my plate was already full enough. And then he told me this wouldn't bring Norman back. No matter how much I tried to figure out a way to make black people love each other. I couldn't believe he said that to me."

Leah sat back. "Adrienne, now you know I can't stand Reggie, but I try not to dip in your business. But what kind of man calling himself your man would say something like that? And you know he said it to upset you. If he cared about you at all, he wouldn't talk to you like that. And he knew Norman and how close the two of you were. Now I'm going to tell you. You need to cut his sorry butt loose. I got a good mind to call Alonso. He'll straighten him out."

Leah could feel Adrienne's hand on her arm. "Aunt Leah, please don't call Daddy."

Leah turned her head. "Look, Adrienne, I can't tell you when to be tired of that trifling, no-good Negro. But do you really still care about him?"

Leah could see her relax a little. She seemed to need somebody to say it was okay not to like Reggie anymore. He'd been her boyfriend off and on since the tenth grade. Alonso couldn't stand him. Of course, he'd kept that from Adrienne, so she didn't want Leah painting a bad picture of him to her dad, afraid it would bother Alonso he had been so wrong about Reggie and his arrogant ass all these years. And her baby—when she loved somebody, she loved them hard.

Part of what was bothering her baby girl was she was coming to the realization she couldn't love Reggie anymore. He wouldn't let her. Old, arrogant ass couldn't deal with her beginning to blossom. He was in his third year at Yale Law School. He assumed she would marry him and populate the world with a bunch of arrogant little Reggies. This professional, PhD-seeking woman was alien to him. He was trying his best to change her back into the stewardess whose job he'd sniffed at.

Leah decided to change the subject. "So you think it went well today?"

"Yes ma'am! They seemed to be really excited about what I had to say. I mean, Genna was always big on my ideas, but she wanted to make sure her brother Josh was on board. He made me mad at first. But he acted like he was impressed."

"How, baby?"

"He gave me a standing ovation when I finished."

"Well, why you say he made you mad?

Adrienne laughed and told her how Josh said he didn't have time for any white supremacists hanging around his kids. Mentioned the crack about how she wasn't grown enough to hear the chicken wing story. "But you should have seen him when I was standing at the board. It's like he was hanging on every word."

Leah took a long drag on her Salem and put it in the ashtray. Adrienne reached over, picked it up, and crushed it out. Leah stared at her. "We sure are grown today."

"Aunt Leah, you know how I hate you smoking. And you can get mad all you want, too. I don't want to lose you."

Leah chuckled. "Girl, you something else. You sound like Howard."

"Well Uncle Howard loves you too," she responded. "How's he doing?"

"He's fine, baby. You know how he is. As long as there's a kid for him to take care of, he'll be okay."

"Yeah, Josh loves kids too. You should have seen the look on his face when he talked about them."

Leah smiled and thought, *My baby likes old Josh.* "Did he tell you his father was in school with your uncle?"

"Genna had told me."

"Yeah, it's a shame about their parents, Lawrence and Regina."

"What do you mean?"

"Oh baby, they're both dead. Lawrence died of lung cancer when they were young. And Regina was killed in a car accident a couple of years ago. It was awful watching those children bury their mother. I thought about you and your brothers."

"Wow. It never came up. I told him about Momma." Adrienne's voice trailed off as she spoke. She looked down at the table then back at Leah.

"Yeah, it messed Josh up real bad. Regina was awful worried about him when she died. The last time I talked to her, she was asking if Howard knew anything about drug addiction. She told me Josh was having some real struggles with cocaine. I guess he must be doing better from what you're saying."

"Do you think he got on drugs because of his father dying?"

"Baby, your daddy used to drink. Your momma almost left him several times. He was drinking when they met. And your Uncle Short Boy is an alcoholic. He hasn't had a drink in years, but he was something else in his drinking days. Nah, according to your daddy and Short Boy, it's something you're born with. I wouldn't believe it if I hadn't seen the two of them. The first time I met Josh, he was tipsy, and he couldn't been more than seventeen, eighteen then."

"I never would have guessed it. He looked like he had it so together. You should see how nice he looks in a suit. His fit so well, it looked like somebody drew it on him."

"Adrienne, you can't judge a book by its cover. You be careful with him."

"Aunt Leah, I'm not getting ready to marry him. I'm going to do some work for him and his sister. Or at least I hope so."

"Yeah, well like I said, you be careful." Leah chuckled. "You remember what I used to tell you when you were washing dishes?"

Adrienne laughed. "Yes ma'am." She sat up rod straight in the chair and pulled her shoulders back. "Girl, quit spilling that water on you. You keep spilling that water, you gonna grow up and marry a drunk." They both laughed.

"Like I said, you be careful about that man."

"Aunt Leah," she protested. "I got a boyfriend."

Leah asked, "You going to the Hawks game Saturday?"

Adrienne looked at Leah, surprise in her eyes. "Yeah, I was thinking about going with Michelle." *Lord, this girl doesn't think I know about that basketball player she's fooling around with. Want something kept, keep it from a man.* "Yeah, your cousin said you might be going. You want to hang around and eat? You can let your Uncle Howard see you."

"Okay."

Chapter 11

The Girl and the Darkness

Josh sighed. "I Say a Little Prayer" by Aretha Franklin was finishing up on his radio as he pulled into his space. He remembered how Regina used to love that song. Every time it played, he sang along and thought about her. He tapped a cigarette out of the pack in his shirt pocket. He lit it with the butt burning in his ashtray. A couple of drags later, he was climbing out from his car to make the long trek up the stairs to his apartment, a brown bag gripped tight in his hand.

He hesitated at the doorway. Briefly he considered leaving to go for a ride, uncertain his nightmare was merely a dream, fearing he might sight a pair of charred innocents jitterbugging amongst the flames, consuming his guilt-ridden mind if he stepped into the apartment. He could hear Dad yelling, "Hey, fireball!" He shuddered.

Quit tripping, Josh. He walked in and sat the brown bag on the kitchen table. Josh pulled the fifth of 151 rum out of the bag along with the two cans of soda and the clear plastic, four-ounce cup he had brought along to keep him company. A field trip on the way home to Stanley's Florist down on the other end of Campbellton had led him by his favorite liquor store. He stopped in to socialize and wound up bringing these new friends home. He knew they wouldn't stay long, but right now he required their company.

He poured a small amount of the sweet brown liquor into the cup, downing it straight. The burn of the liquor tumbling down his throat temporarily took his mind off the conflagration dancing around the backside of his mind. He thought about Sarah. He knew she would be salty. Funny how hanging up in her face seemed to always put her in a foul mood. He considered not calling her.

He popped two breath mints in his mouth and poured enough rum in the cup to fill it halfway. This time he opened the soda and filled the cup to the top with it. He swallowed half the cup's contents. Once he felt a slight buzz, he walked over to the phone hanging on the wall and picked it up. Sarah answered on the second ring. "Hello," she said.

"Hi, Sarah Smith, how you doing?" Josh asked. Silence for a long moment.

"You know what, you have a lot of nerve," she snapped. "You call my house disturbing me first thing in the morning. I try to help you even though I should know better, and what do you do? Hang up on me! What do you want?"

"You," Josh confided softly into the phone.

"What! You're crazy."

"Sarah, I'm scared. I am, I really am. I'm sorry. But you gotta understand."

"Stop it, Josh! I don't want to go there with you."

"I need you, Sarah."

"Well, now, you have a funny way of showing it. Hanging up on me."

"I need you, Sarah Smith." Silence again. "Sarah, I am so sorry. I didn't mean it."

"Josh," she sighed. "You never do, but that doesn't make it hurt any less. You okay?"

"No," Josh said, his voice cracking. "Sarah, Sarah, please, I need you. I can't help it."

"It's all right, sweetie. I know. I know."

"Sarah." His words caught in his throat. He missed her.

They talked for almost two hours, or about the time it took him to smoke six cigarettes. At some point, she mentioned she needed to get off. He didn't ask why, pretty sure he knew the answer. Instead he got her to agree to lunch on Monday, wanting to make sure those flowers showed up at her job before they ate together. After that, he finished the bottle. Unable to sleep, he walked down to the store and bought a quart of the Bull.

He enjoyed the stars on the walk back. It was a nippy January night. Good thing he had consumed plenty of antifreeze, because he forgot his jacket. Josh came back through the front courtyard to his apartment. His front door opened into his living room. He plopped down on his couch without turning the light on, figuring he would clutch the darkness a while longer. He lit a cigarette and sat and swigged the Bull and drew on the smoke.

He stared out his front window at the Georgia night, his mood the color of his unlit surroundings. The Bull finished the job the rum had started. He dozed off on the sofa, waking up in time to get ready for work the next morning.

Chapter 12

Race Woman

Adrienne bounced up her stairs, humming "I Say a Little Prayer." She and her mom used to sing it together when she was little. She fumbled for her keys in her pocketbook for a minute, finally digging them off the bottom of her purse. She opened the door. "Chelle," she called, checking to see if her roommate was home. No answer meant she was alone.

She deposited her valise on the kitchen table and started singing out loud. "Forever and ever," she yodeled, chortling after a moment. Reggie insisted she couldn't carry a tune in a bucket. They disagreed about a lot here lately, but she had to give him his props on this critique.

She plopped down in one of the four chairs sitting around the table and unzipped her boots. She kicked out of them. *What a girl goes through to be cute.* She rubbed her right foot.

Then she got up and went to the bathroom she and Michelle shared. She surveyed herself in the mirror. There was no denying that she was beautiful, no matter how hard she tried sometimes. She was conflicted about her looks. Sometimes they could really get in the way. If they weren't intimidating some guy she really wanted to work up the nerve to say something to her, they were allowing somebody to presume she was an airhead. Of course, some days her looks worked to great advantage. She thought about how one Mr. Josh Gibson couldn't take his eyes off her, and she smiled. She had needed the attention. Reggie had hurt her bad with the comment about Norman. He could be such a jerk lately.

Oh well, the NBA's coming to town, she thought to herself. Dinner at the Ritz late Saturday, followed by her for dessert. She felt her body anticipating being in the ballplayer's arms. The phone rang.

She answered it in her room. It was Michelle's friend Derrick. She told him she wasn't home and wondered what her roomie was up to. After she hung up, she decided to call her father. Alonso Johnson picked up and said, "Hello."

"Hey, Daddy," she said.

"Hey, little girl! How's my favorite daughter doing tonight?"

"I'm your only daughter," Adrienne responded with a tone of mock exasperation. She loved to hear him say that. "Guess who I met today."

"I don't know. Who'd you meet, somebody I know?"

"You wish. Josh Gibson in the flesh."

"Josh Gibson! Now see, you're pulling my leg."

"No, I'm not."

"Adrienne, don't tease me like that. You know he's been dead for years."

"I did, Daddy," she said. "He's the brother of the soror who has the school I was telling you about. They own it together. I did a presentation for them today. Cross your fingers because they're considering hiring me to be a curriculum consultant."

"Well, now, if they have any sense and he has eyes, you won't have any trouble getting hired."

"Daddy," she protested.

"You know I'm right. How did it go?"

"I think it went good, Daddy. Genna, that's the sister's name, has been talking to me about this for several weeks. They're trying to teach their kids to be race men and women."

Alonso cut her off. "Well, then I know they must love what you had to say. I mean, nobody is more of a race woman than you."

"Yeah, do you know Josh asked me was I a white supremacist? He made me so mad. But he turned out to be really nice. He gave me a standing ovation when I finished. And then we talked for a little while afterwards. I like it there, Daddy."

"Well I'm glad to hear you sound so good. Leah called me."

"What'd she say?"

"She told me you were upset, almost in tears. Is that right?"

"Yes sir."

"Adrienne, what did Reggie say?"

It all came pouring out like Leah had known it would. It was why Adrienne didn't want Leah to call Alonso but, like always, her aunt knew best. Reggie didn't believe in her theory. Wouldn't even listen to what she had to say. At first, he ignored her when she talked about it. Here lately he was belligerent. This morning, he had hit her with the worst thing anybody could say to her.

Alonso let her get it all out. "Adrienne, I never have liked that boy. Not for you, anyway. I should have told you that a long time ago."

She sat listening, surprised to hear him say he didn't want her with Reggie.

"You know you're my daughter, and I love you to death, but you're not an easy cup to swallow. You know, ever since Norman died, you've been obsessed with the idea it's something wrong with black people. Baby girl, everybody doesn't want to hear that, especially not Reggie. What's that you call him—a race-neutral Negro. Now, if he's race neutral, how in the hell do you expect him to want to hear you going on and on about how black people need to do this, and black people need to do that? He doesn't care about that stuff, baby. He figures he's making it and that's good enough for him—and it ought to be good enough for you."

"But Daddy."

"'But Daddy' what? It's like your aunt told you. You don't need a man who can't believe in you—and Adrienne, he doesn't. The sooner you acknowledge that, the sooner you can move on to somebody who's right for you."

"I guess so," she said, perturbed that everybody appeared to have agreed behind her back that Reggie wasn't the man for her.

"Adrienne, what's that you told me? Race-neutral Negroes are bad for the community and bad for America. That America is always made better by her immigrant children's demands that she stretch herself to a point where they not only accept her on her terms, she accepts them on theirs. What is it that you said—if Germans hadn't brought the kindergarten here with them and if America had been unwilling to accept their ideas about education, the nation would have been poorer? Don't you always tell me America needs black people to do the same thing—demand she stretch herself to accept what is good about black culture and accept it as a part of her culture?"

"Daddy, have you been taping me?" She was only half teasing.

"Nah, just listening. And if he is race neutral, you don't want him. Quit blocking your blessing. You know that's what a pastor would tell you. You found a church yet?

"I'm still looking."

"You need to be looking to let Reggie go, too."

"Daddy," she snapped this time.

"Okay, you're right. All I'm getting ready to do is push you toward him if I keep running my mouth."

"Anyway, Daddy, I do like the school. And Josh knew all about baseball. He agreed with you about Brad Komminsk. Said the Braves made a big mistake by picking him. Even if he was from Lima."

"Well, he sounds like he got sense. And he asked you if you were a white supremacist. I bet he did make you mad." Alonso laughed, picturing steam rising off her ears.

"You think that's funny, huh? He even knew I got the idea for my card from *Have Gun—Will Travel*."

Alonso remembered how she loved that old Western. It and *The Rifleman*. She was practically bubbling talking about Josh Gibson and the school. It was good to hear her like this. When Leah called, he feared she would be all broken up when he talked to her. He had started to call her, but Leah had said to wait and see if she would call him tonight.

"I heard 'I Say a Little Prayer' on the way home."

"Adrienne, girl, come get these shoes out the floor. What I'm gonna do with you! You just nasty," a voiced bellowed in the background.

"Gotta go Daddy, Chelle's home." She giggled into the phone.

Alonso laughed. "Tell Chelle I said hello. Call me Sunday."

Chapter 13

The Tin Man

Faith brushed her teeth, mapping out the day ahead. She stood eying herself in the mirror. *You need a haircut, Faith.* She ran her hand through her brick-red afro, wondering if she would have time to run by the barbershop later on this evening. *Nah, you better wait,* she thought, remembering Mr. Tillman would be here tomorrow. She planned to hit him up for some ends.

"Oh well," she said to the mirror. "It's time to clear my house out." She knew her daughter Mona Lisa would be home soon. And she was supposed to be hanging some sheetrock with Josh later this morning. Faith marched back into the bedroom. She looked down at her bed. She sure hated to put such a fine piece of ass out so early on a Saturday morning, but she had shit to do.

What was her name? Oh yeah, Ramona. She leaned over and shook her. "Ramona, come on, get up." The girl moaned, but didn't move.

Girlfriend was going to have learn when Faith said move, she'd better move—no matter how good that ass was. "Hey, get up," Faith barked, shaking her hard. "Come on, now, it's time to rise and shine."

The girl rolled over, an annoyed expression on her face. "What's wrong, Faith?"

"Nothing other than you got to go."

"I'm sleepy, Faith."

"What I say," Faith replied in a really no-nonsense voice. "I got things to do and I need you to get gone."

"Okay, Faith," she said, pouting as she rolled out of bed. Ramona stood stretching, not a stitch on. Faith ogled that body in her mind, but outwardly she stood impassively, like she wasn't fazed. She knew the girl was trying to work her. She sure wanted just one more little taste, though.

Bam, bam, bam, bam, bam, bam!

Faith and Ramona jumped, startled by the banging on her front door. *What the hell? That's that damn Josh.* Faith put her fingers to her lips, shushing Ramona. She eased her bedroom door closed behind her as she went to answer the door.

"Boy, what is wrong with you? Hitting my door with that police knock this early in the morning," Faith said as she opened the door. "You like to scared me to death."

"What's up, Faith?" Josh replied. "Just trying to make sure you up. Look at your ass. Standing here in your robe. Ain't it time to go to work?"

"My, my, we in a good mood this morning. What you get up to last night?"

"Damn, can't I be in a good mood? Where's Mona Lisa?"

"Josh Gibson, I know you. Don't change the subject. You been with that damn Sarah, haven't you?"

"Nah, Faith, fuck you talking about?"

"Uh-huh."

Faith looked him up and down. "Lean over, I bet I can smell her grand ass on you."

"Damn, Faith. Okay, we hung out together last night. Why you always so down on her? She's cool."

"Faith," Ramona called from the bedroom door. Josh looked down the hall.

"Hold up. Let me go check her. You have a seat and I'll be ready in a few minutes." Faith turned to go down the hall.

"Hey Faith."

She looked back at him and snarled, "What, Josh?'

"I know what you were up to last night," Josh cracked. She rolled her eyes.

Josh sat on the couch in her front room. A carton of cigarettes sat on the table. Faith was always looking out for him.

A few minutes later, Faith escorted Ramona out the front door without the slightest introduction. Ramona was young, looked to be nineteen or twenty, about Mona Lisa's age. Cute, too. Small, maybe five-two, but packing those jeans she had on. She was ebony, like Faith liked 'em. Mr. Tillman was about the same complexion.

Faith came back in about ten minutes later. Josh shook his head. "Damn, Faith, where you get her from? She's fine as hell."

Faith gestured for him to follow her down the hall. "I picked her up at the club last night. She needed prayer, so I brought her home and laid hands on her."

"Faith, you ain't shit," Josh cackled.

He followed her into her room. She sat on the foot of her bed and patted the spot next to her. "Come sit with me for a minute, Josh." He sat down next to her.

"Thanks for the cigarettes, Faith."

"Boy, you know I'd do anything for you. Don't even worry about it. Genna told me you had that dream again."

Faith watched him closely. She couldn't let him know, but she was really worried about him. She could sense him hesitating, trying to find some lie to tell to make her feel okay about him.

Josh shook his head. "You mind if I smoke?"

She responded, "Go ahead, Josh."

He reached in his shirt pocket and pulled out a cigarette and his lighter. He looked straight ahead, avoiding her eyes. "Yeah, Faith, it fucked me up." There was a slight tremble in his voice. "I'm tired. Every time I feel like I'm getting it together . . ." His voice trailed off and he pulled on his cigarette.

Faith patted his hand. "Damn, Tin Man, you ain't even gonna tell me a lie to make me think you doing all right? You must be shootin' bad for real. Josh, what's done is done."

"Yeah, I know. You ready to go lay some sheetrock?"

"You want me to drive?" Josh asked when they got outside.

"Sounds like a plan. So what did you and your girl get up to last night?

"Nothing. We hung for a while. That's all."

"So y'all an item again."

That's none of your damn business. "Look, Faith, why don't we talk about something else, 'cause we both know you don't like Sarah and all we gonna do is talk shit to each other about her. I ain't feeling that this morning."

They walked out her front door and Josh heard Faith sigh. "Let's take my car, Josh." She handed him the keys to her Hog and Josh came around and opened the passenger side door for her. He walked around the car, got in, started it up, and whipped it out of the driveway onto Mt. Gilead heading toward Lakewood Freeway. In no time, I-285 beckoned.

He saw Faith looking him over out of the corner of his eye. He swung around Lakewood, scooting onto 285 headed toward Riverside Drive. She muttered, "You ain't got to cop an attitude. I just asked a question. We sure are sensitive this morning."

"Yeah, I guess I am."

They rode in silence for a few minutes. He didn't want her upset, but what good what would it do for him to explain about he felt about Sarah Smith?

"So you remember the new girl I told you about?"

"Nah, who, Josh?"

"You know, Faith, the one I told you Genna kept going on and on about. Her name's Adrienne. She's a sociology instructor over at Morehouse."

"Oh, the one y'all were thinking about hiring? Yeah, what about her?"

"Well, I've been reading her dissertation draft and it's off the chain."

"What you mean, Josh?" Faith was perking up. She always liked it when he treated her like an intellectual.

"Well, she's got this idea black people are, in a sense, immigrants to this country. She goes on and on about how you have to draw a line of demarcation between pre- and post-civil rights movement black America. She claims if you do and you see black people as recent arrivals in the United States of America, you can get a better understanding of what's up with our community."

Faith turned her head toward him, interested in what he was saying. "Boy, you gonna have to tell me more than just that."

"Faith, she says we're eerily similar to the Irish immigrants of a hundred years ago. She says when the Irish lived in Ireland, it was illegal for the Irish to teach their children to read, that a British planter could demand an Irishman's wife come to his bed and there was nothing the guy could do about it. An Irishman could not testify against the British in court. Basically that, by law, you were designated to second-class status in Ireland if you were Irish."

"Go on, Josh, I'm listening," Faith said as he hesitated for a moment.

"You know, Faith, my dad made me read *Dred Scott* before he died, the entire decision."

"What is *Dred Scott*?"

"It's a famous decision involving the legality of slavery. Dred was a slave who sued for his freedom."

"That was stupid."

"Yeah, you right. It was, 'cause the Supreme Court said since black people weren't citizens, we could not hold standing to sue in federal court. Said it was written right there in the Constitution—we weren't citizens. The court said the Negro had no rights a white man had to respect. That Native Americans could be viewed as members of a sovereign state, so they had greater standing in court than us. And then there was *Plessy v. Ferguson*."

"I know that one. The separate-but-equal decision, the one where they said the white guy was black because he was one-eighth a nigger."

"Yeah, that one. Faith, my dad always complained about *Plessy*. It bothered him more than *Dred*. Part of it is because of what you're saying. Plessy was for all intents and purposes a white man. A judge named Harlan wrote a famous dissent upon which *Brown v. Board of Education* stands. Harlan said that white supremacy was and always would be the way of this country. White people didn't need separate but equal to make this so."

"Yeah, Tin Man, it's the attitude America was built on."

"Yeah, exactly, Faith. And she says the civil rights movement had to happen because before we could be equal, we had to end Jim Crow."

"But Josh, what's different about what she's saying than a whole bunch of other black folks with their mouth to the mic and their eyes on the camera?"

"I'll tell you what. She says that there are two types of discrimination—one that includes and one that excludes. She says that the pre-movement discrimination excluded us and the post-movement discrimination includes us in the same way it does every other immigrant group—slowly and painfully. She insists the problem for us is not discrimination, it is our approach to how we deal with it."

"Well, Josh, what is wrong with what we're doing? How 'bout white people is just evil? What are we supposed to do about that?"

"Tell you what. We're supposed to have lunch on Wednesday. I'll ask her then. Fair enough?"

"Damn, boy, you having what? What she look like?"

"She all right."

Faith glanced at him. "Well, Josh, she sounds like a real smart girl. And she must be pretty since you hollering she 'all right.'"

"Yeah, Faith, as soon as Genna introduced us, she cracks me, 'Josh Gibson, can you live up to that name?'"

"I like her already."

"She's cool."

"Well, you make sure you don't bat those big pretty brown eyes at her while y'all eat. I don't want Sarah to have to kick your ass, Tin Man."

"It ain't like that. This is strictly business."

"Uh-huh. I bet she ain't thinking it's just business."

"Faith, you think every woman wants me. It ain't like that.

She shook her head and said, "After while, after while."

They rode on up to Riverside Drive. They were fixing a house with severe lightning damage. It was a direct hit on the roof. The front section of the house was almost totally destroyed, but after some work, it was starting to look like someone's home again.

Josh loved helping Faith out on jobs like his. He enjoyed rebuilding damaged goods. This house was the same way Aaron was a project for him at school. Damaged, sure, but with a little tender, loving care, they both would be fine.

Faith paid him half of the three hundred dollars she owed him. He cussed and ranted, but he knew he was wasting his time. She figured she was protecting him. Nothing he said was going to get his money.

"Come by Tuesday and you'll thank me 'cause you'll have some money to take that girl to lunch."

Chapter 14

Slave

The water slowly rose to a boil in the pot sitting atop an eye on the stove. Longeno pressed a spoon on the cooker's cap, making sure it remained standing as the water around it roiled from the effects of the heat. Longeno, being an old-school cocaine cook from the genteel days when there were certain rules surrounding the pipe, prided himself on his ability to bring a package back. Hakeem may have turned Josh on to the pipe, but it was Longeno who taught him the aesthetics of freebasing.

Cook always got first hit, house always got a free one; those were the rules defining proper cocaine-smoking etiquette when it remained a pastime exclusive to the upper and middle classes. Those were the days when a good cocaine chef was worth their weight in hits because no self-respecting master of the stove top would ever teach anyone how to cook, knowing they might get cut out of the next package.

Bringing back a package on the stove top was a skill hard-earned by fucking up a sack or two on the path to knowing how to mix soda, water, and product well enough to make all the dope fall. A bad cook left dope in the water by going too light on the soda, or even worse, applying bad soda, which ruined even the best dope, or by diluting the solution with too much water to start.

Cooking was a simple process now. You grabbed a test tube, a little baking soda, some grain alcohol, a torch; struck a match and you were in business. A test tube was much more forgiving than a cooker. The smaller diameter of the cooking surface and the tiny space where dope, baking soda, and water combined minimized mistakes. It was easier to adjust soda and water in the tube. There was no dope turning over in the boiling water with a tube, a nightmare without equal when you were down to your last half G and it flopped over into the water. Even an old pro like Longeno generally cooked in a tube these days. Only on special occasions would he resort to the old ways.

No, as everyone called him, picked the cooker up, unscrewing the cap. "Damn, Gibson, smell that medicine," he said in a flat, unexpressive voice, trying to hide his pride in the product he had brought back from across the street. He held the cooker up to Josh's nose. No was right, this was the real deal. Good cocaine gave off a powerful, medicinal scent when it first began to free itself from the cut in a cooker. Josh nodded. Longeno poured a little water into the cooker, covering the dope rapidly melting on the bottom of the glass container. He placed it back in the pot to resume its chemical conversion.

He motioned for Josh to come over to where he was standing. "Check that out, man."

Josh could see from where he sat the dope coming back right. No placed a pinch of soda in the water, and cocaine began to fall to the bottom of the cooker. He poured in more water, and the dope began to congeal into a knot on the cooker's floor.

No grabbed the piece of coat hanger he had broken off to coax the dope out of the cooker, stuck it into the ball of dope, and began to make tight circles, causing the cocaine to harden around the metal. He expertly pulled it out of the water, putting it down on the small plate lying on the kitchen counter. Taking a single-edge razor off the plate, he scraped the cocaine off the torch stem onto its smooth surface. Dope seemed to fall off the stem for days.

Josh felt his stomach flip, adrenaline surging through him in anticipation of the rush sure to come in the next few minutes. Longeno was putting a small piece of rock up on to the bowl of the pipe stem. He dipped the torch into the bottle of grain alcohol. Josh lit it with the lighter Longeno had sitting on the counter. No held the pipe to his mouth in his right hand while he bounced the torch up and down on the bowl with his right. Slowly, a white cloud formed in the stem, draining down into the bigger bowl of the pipe, filling it on its way out the other stem into Longeno's mouth.

Longeno got a good flow going. The white cloud filled the pipe, running out the backside through Longeno's lips, getting ready to hop aboard the express through his bloodstream to the upper reaches of his mind.

No's eyes were bugging. He trembled from the force of the hit. The dope made him say uncle, forcing him to put the pipe down on the counter to regroup even though it was full of smoke. He looked at Josh, unable to speak. But he caught himself, picked the pipe back up, and repeated the process of dipping the torch in the grain alcohol. Josh lit it again. No bounced it more gingerly against the bowl this time. He turned the pipe in his mouth so it was tilted sideways, holding the flame on the stem so the cocaine that had drained into it would turn to smoke.

He slowed his pull down, creating an enormous cloud in the pipe and pulling it out for what Josh knew had to be one hell of a hit. His hands quivered as he put the pipe down and blew out the torch. He put a penny on the bowl so it would get ready for Josh's turn faster. No leaned over the trash can and spat. Coke did him like that. He would probably have to go take a shit next.

Sure enough, No told him to hold up while he went to the bathroom. Josh always liked for No to hit first for this very reason. He could tolerate waiting before drugs entered his system. He'd be bouncing off the walls if he had to wait on No after he had pulled on the pipe. Neither one of them believed in putting a hit up on the pipe when the other left the room. It kept down confusion about whether anyone put up too big a bump while the other one was gone.

Josh fired up a cigarette. He took a couple of quick drags, then crushed it out. He wanted to have his head clear for when No came back. Josh stared at his fingernails for what felt like hours until Longeno returned to the kitchen. He looked at Josh and asked if he was ready.

Josh nodded. He prepared to step up to the plate. He took the razor and cut a chunk of cocaine off the rock lying on the plate. He dropped the razor, picked the penny up off the pipe, and placed the dope into the bowl. He took a deep breath before dipping the torch in the alcohol. Josh picked up the pipe. No lit the torch with the lighter. Josh took another deep breath, hunching his shoulders as he readied himself to start pulling on the pipe. He held it to his lips, slowly inhaling as he gently sat the torch on the cocaine. It began to liquefy.

He bounced the torch up and down about a half an inch below the bowl to prevent the dope from overheating and burning up. It began to drain through the screens, turning from liquid to smoke. Josh tilted the pipe to a forty-five-degree angle, holding the flame underneath the sizzling bowl. Smoke swirled through the stem. He inhaled slightly harder, thinking *up* so he would not suck the smoke into his lungs where it would blow the high. He ran the torch under the stem, watching smoke billow into the bowl and out the other stem. Smoke filled his mouth, numbing his tongue.

He pulled on the bowl steadily, watching it turn pearl white with smoke gusting through the stem he held in his mouth. His mind detonated from the powerful convulsions the cocaine sent coursing through his brain, causing his eyes to pop and knees to rock; forcing his hands to shake. He almost dropped the pipe, hanging on for dear life, inhaling as long as he could before putting it down on the counter. The bowl mocked him, still full of smoke, looking as if it dared him to pick it up again.

Adrenaline raced through his body, causing his heart to pound uncontrollably in his chest, his body trembling from the concussive force of the cocaine pummeling his mind. Longeno looked at him knowingly, nodding his head in recognition that Josh had gotten a good one. Josh sat down for a moment trying to get his bearings. *Damn, KG always had the good dope!* Sweat was already popping off his forehead.

Josh thought, *Time to go back for round two.* Longeno dropped a couple of crumbs on the bowl, filling it with even more smoke. Josh picked the pipe up and tilted it sideways so the liquid would not run all the way down the stem into the bowl. Longeno lit the torch. This time, Josh held it far enough from the stem so that the flame barely touched it. Josh could feel the adrenaline-fed tremors throughout his body almost immediately.

An elevator rose through his mind, forcing the high up, up, up until it hit the top of his skull where the dope exploded again. Josh could feel his teeth grinding. His knees buckled. He signaled for Longeno to finish off this one. It had gotten the better of him, as much as he hated to admit it to himself. This was the bomb! He had been smoking cocaine for six long, hard years. It didn't normally affect him like this anymore.

Josh sat down, unsure his legs would hold him. His hands were still shaking as he pressed them against his knees in an effort to get a grip. Almost as quickly as the coke had taken him up to the sky, it began its rapid descent back to a slight buzz. He picked up a butt out of the ashtray and relit it. A long pull on the cigarette sent him beaming up again, though with nowhere near the force the cocaine had exerted on his mind and body.

His mind bent into a cocaine-induced craving for the next hit. Already the room was beginning to close in on him. Now his world consisted of the plate, the pipe, and the ashtray. One hit and it felt like they were almost out of dope.

Longeno was letting the pipe cool getting ready for his turn. He cut two more small rocks off the knot of dope sitting on the plate. Then he crushed the rest with a spoon, the dope making a crunching sound as he mashed it against the plate. He scraped it off the plate with the razor, and then used the sharp edge of the blade to chop it up into fine particles so the dope would stretch farther.

The bowl was already starting to turn cloudy with dew. Either this was super strong shit or they were wasting dope. He decided to smoke powder this go-round. He scooped up a hit of it off the plate with the razor blade, pouring it carefully into the bowl. He sat the pipe down on the counter to take a deep breath. This was his ritual. You could always tell the league vets because they all had one.

No's was the hunt. And after a couple of more hits, he was going be running his hands over everything. Counter, refrigerator, furniture, his clothes, trying to search for the hit he dropped. It didn't make any difference that he had never found one; he always looked. Big Dad liked to fiddle with the plate and play with the screens, trying to get 'em just right. Hakeem liked to direct you on exactly how to do everything just so.

He dipped the torch, trying not to rush. Rushing would make him mess the hit up, but it was hard not to when his mind was demanding he get on with it. He picked the pipe up, motioning for No to light the torch. Longeno lit it and stepped back. Josh hunched his shoulders, inhaling as much as air as he could before blowing it all out of his lungs. Now he was ready.

He began to inhale after placing the stem between his lips, thinking about the old pipes that used to come with the words *base hit* written on the side underneath a drawing of two baseball bats crossed like swords. Those were the days when the pipe's bowl was round. Now most of them were shaped like a cylinder.

The cocaine cloud formed rapidly in the bowl this time. He was pulling it just right. The dope started the steep ascent to the top of his skull. *Damn,* he thought. This one was about to rip his mind apart, it was so strong.

They were going to be here a long time. Dope like this made you respect it. Every now and then, you had to stop to take a breath. KG had outdone himself with this package. Josh could feel his ears ringing.

They took turns for a long while until they were finished with the first gram. The pipe was no longer clear. It was foggy from the residue build up on the sides of the bowl. Longeno asked him if he wanted him to clean the pipe before he cooked the next batch. Josh nodded. The cloudier the bowl got, the more dope it would trap on its side—dulling the high they pulled out of the stem.

Longeno eased the top stem out of the pipe. He took a torch and poked the screens out of the bowl onto the plate. He scraped the thick brown resin off the stem's walls and dropped it on the plate. He then removed the second stem from the pipe and laid it on the counter. Next, he extracted the rubber coverings that held the stems in place from the holes in the bowl.

He poured a little grain alcohol through each stem into the bowl and swished it around until the bowl was clear. Josh grabbed a small plate and put it on the counter. Longeno poured the alcohol out on the plate and set it on fire. It burned brightly for a few moments before the flame petered out. No took a spoon and made circles in the slushy mixture lying on the plate until it turned hard. It was a least two or three hits worth of dew on the plate. Much weaker than the base they had been smoking, it would serve as filler for their first couple of hits off the next package.

Longeno then poured a tiny amount of alcohol on the screens and burned them, too. He turned on the faucet and ran water through each stem into the bowl. He blew the remaining water out of the stems before draining the bowl again. He shook the bowl while motioning to Josh to blow out the stems. He wanted to be sure the pipe was dry before they started hitting it again.

No carefully packed the screens back into the bowl at the head of the stem. About halfway through, he decided he didn't like the way they were seated in the stem and poked the screens out and started over again. He wanted to be sure the screens were packed tight in the bowl, or the dope would run through them down the stem once it liquefied. This dope was way too good to waste. He got them right the second time and pushed the last one down with his finger to be sure it was in good.

Now, No stuck the rubber caps back into the pipe, screwing the stems back in. He picked up the plastic dope bag and poured about half the remaining dope on the plate. Paranoia setting in, No tasted the baking soda to be sure it was fresh. Cook with stale soda and the package would just dissolve in the water and leave him cursing the fact he was too lazy to go to the grocery store. He had already cooked with this same soda, but basing got him edgy and jittery, making him check out things he wouldn't have paid attention to before that first good bump.

He put on the plate about a quarter of the amount of soda as he had cocaine and mixed them together. He scooped up the mixture on the razor blade and poured it into the cooker. He had already turned the stove back on, and the water was coming to a boil. He cooked up the second package. He asked Josh if he wanted to start this second go-round with a back to back. Josh agreed and suggested they save the dew. He didn't want to fuck up a good back to back with some damn residue.

The first hit was just crazy. His mind reeled from the strength of the cocaine washing through his mind, surging across whatever barriers of sanity and self-restraint he had managed to hang onto from the first package. Powerful winds roared inside his head, rocking his brain and popping his eyes and ears with the sheer force of the high.

No put a supersized one up for the second hit. The second hit sent him straight to the stratosphere. His knees were quaking. He had to lean against the wall to finish this one.

Maybe he should have cut the second one with a little dew. He sat down. Not quite able to fire up a cigarette, he stuck his thumbnail under his fingernails, one after the other. This calmed his nerves enough to light up a smoke and watch his boy suffer the same fate he had just endured.

They split the remaining dope into two piles to cook, prolonging the inevitable heartbreak of the dope running out. No matter what they did to stretch it, the last hit was gone by about four thirty in the morning. Josh had fifty dollars left, but it was what he planned to use to buy groceries for the week. *Fuck it*, he thought, *Faith owes me some change.*

After a night of action like this, he couldn't let it end with that weak-assed dew hit he finished up with. He asked No in a really shaky voice if he knew anybody who might hook them up with a last package for the night.

No beeped Alton. He lived about twenty minutes away and would make deliveries to him. Josh smoked two cigarettes in the time it took Alton to call. *Hurry, motherfucker* ran through his mind several times. He said he'd do them a gram for that price.

Josh could remember when he could smoke half an eight ball and take the rest home to toot for a couple of days. Now, it was just a good start on a major-league fuckup. He long ago realized the futility of smoking cocaine. One hit or one thousand, it was never enough, no matter how much dope you were holding. You still wound up jittery, craving just one more. He'd hit once with Hakeem's girl Duck and the shit got so good she wouldn't buy sanitary napkins, even though her period was wide open. She had pleaded with him to let her sit on some newspaper so she wouldn't stain his car's front seat. She'd wanted to put her last twenty up on the pipe. The cat they were copping from didn't believe in credit or coming up short. So he handed her some newspaper he had on his backseat, and then off they drove to the dope house. When dope started talking to you, you'd do all kinds of dumb shit.

They heard a knock on the door. It was Alton. "What's up, Gibson? Damn, y'all niggers already been fucking up, ain't you?"

"What's up, Alton, man?" was all Josh could get out. He wanted Alton to hurry and transact business so they could cook this last package. Josh had slipped No the money knowing Alton would hook him up. Sure enough, he sacked up about a gram and a quarter of some butter.

Longeno asked him if he wanted to hang, but Alton knew better. This was a ploy to get him smoking so they could hit him up for some more dope later on when this ran out.

It seemed like five minutes after Alton left when the dope disappeared, gone up in smoke. Day was breaking as Josh headed home.

Chapter 15

Dying Embers

Sarah lay soaking in her tub, daydreaming about Friday night. Felton was out of town on business for two weeks, and she had let Josh creep back into her life. She was contemplating whether this was a good idea. Like always, the past few days with Josh had been part exasperation, part exhilaration.

She stuck her big toe in the faucet. Lord, when he'd called that morning two weeks ago upset about being visited in the night by those two apparitions, she could feel her heart reaching past her better sense to cradle her poor, broken Josh. That man, he could be so sweet; that man, he could be so cruel. She would have slapped him if he had been in reach when he hung up on her. Had the nerve to act like he was jealous because Felton was there. She smiled to herself.

She was surprised when he'd called her later on. It wasn't him. Normally he'd brood for several days, wrestling with his conscience about how he had treated her. This time he was on the phone, every other word letting on how sorry he was. He told her he needed her. She fought hard against his begging, but her heart won out over her common sense.

This man—she thought about her trip down the soup aisle in Kroger that day. Men could be so slow sometimes, especially this one. She had seen him checking her out all the while trying to be subtle so she wouldn't catch him. So of course she had. She had bent over, letting him catch a good long look at her assets. He hadn't said a word. Stood there gawking, even smiled at her with those big pretty brown eyes.

She had given it a minute and moved on, and all of a sudden, there he stood in line. She had popped in behind him. His rap had been so lame she wanted to school him on how a woman wanted a man to be confident, a hunter, who was going to give strong chase. So she got his number. She had surprised herself and called him a couple of days later. She thought he might be married since he'd given her his work number. She almost hadn't called him. Lord, she was glad she did. Turned out he had a bad habit of not answering his phone. It took her a good six months to break him of it. He was so slow, she had told him later after they hooked up, she thought she was going to have to send him a note in the mail inviting him to make a move.

She had still been dating Anthony off and on. Never seemed to faze him; Josh kept coming around. She even got mean a couple of times, making a point of letting him know she and Anthony were getting it on. He'd purse his lips, frown, but wouldn't make a move to push Anthony out of his way. And that's all it took, a little push. Ooh, he used to make her so frustrated. But she could always count on him.

She found how much when she got laid off. He had been the first person she called. It bothered her. He wasn't her man, she should have called her parents, but no, it was Josh whose voice she needed to hear. And every word he said had been perfect. He told her how heartbroken he was about what she was going through. He said he couldn't stand how people pretended it was all right when your world felt like it was crumbling around you. He promised her he wouldn't play that game, because he knew she was hurting. And then he said, "They made a mistake, but we're going to make their mistake your opportunity."

Somewhere in her hurting, she let on how she was worried about her rent. He told her he'd be right over. He brought her a thousand dollars and told her if she needed anything else to let him know. Wouldn't let her pay it back, either. And his Uncle James pulled some strings and had gotten her the job at the bank where she now worked.

When she got a promotion after six months there, Josh sent her a plant with the note "Some Blooms for the Desk of a Budding Star." If he hadn't of been out of town, she might have gotten a rape charge for what she wanted to do to him for all the things he'd done for her—and asked for absolutely nothing in return. When it finally happened, she swore it felt like they were levitating over the bed.

She was so mad at him for making her wait so long, but she couldn't give him the satisfaction of knowing how much and how long she had wanted him. She came to realize he didn't much love himself. And that was all it was to Josh. All he cared about in this life were the people he cared about. And he wasn't one of those people. He'd do anything for you but had a hard time letting you do anything for him.

He reminded her of her daddy. The way every day was a parade when he was around and how needy he could leave you feeling when he got into his cups. She used to cry for her daddy, and Lord, she had cried so many tears for Josh. Many times, she'd wished it was another woman so she could compete. But it was cocaine, and it finally took so much of him there was almost no Josh left for her.

She lay in the tub, conflicted about what to do. Lord, she loved Josh Gibson. And she knew he loved her. But she wondered if love was enough. They'd made love Tuesday night on the couch in his front room. It was okay, nothing to write home about; both of them had been holding back as if it was a stranger in their arms. Friday night, on the other hand, was heaven.

Now, she found herself lying here again in a Josh-inspired hell on Saturday night, waiting for him, knowing he was somewhere with his one true love. Oh, he didn't mean it. Her daddy didn't, either.

The phone rang. She started not to answer. But she mustered the strength to get out of the tub.

"Hey, Felton, how you doing? When you coming home?"

Chapter 16

A Spot on Crescent Avenue

Josh watched her striding down Crescent Avenue twenty minutes late, past the chairs sitting outside the window. Adrienne Johnson walked hard, on the balls of her feet. He could almost hear her shoes clacking on the pavement. She turned left, came up the walk, and opened the door to Vickery's. He got up from his seat at the bar to greet her as she entered the restaurant. She smiled upon seeing him walking toward her. He held out his hand and she shook it.

"How ya doin', Mr. Gibson?" she said. She looked incredible. He'd have to ask her if she had a thing about checkerboards because today she was wearing a flowing, black-and-gray checkerboard dress. It hit about midcalf on her. She wore a black sweater and heels with the dress. She was mighty impressive.

Vickery's was his favorite midtown eatery. It was a good place to do business and a good place to relax. He wanted her to be able to open up about her work. He was blown away by much of what she had to say, but he wasn't sure he completely followed her thinking. Here would be a good place to get a better grasp of her theory.

The waitress led them onto the porch. "How was class?" he asked. He walked behind her chair and pulled it out for her. She sat down, and he pushed her chair under the table. "It was great," she replied. "We kind of got off the subject, but it worked."

She said she wasn't sure at first how she would handle teaching at the college level, especially since she would be doing so at an all-male school. However, after the first lecture, she felt like it was what she was born to do. Her students loved her so far, always hanging around her office for a chance to talk.

She asked about what made him leave a well-paying job, because, after all, wasn't it lovely up there in corporate America? Next thing he knew, he was telling the saga of Lawrence and Regina Gibson, those two black nationalists who had raised him and Genna. And he admitted it took a big push from Genna and a friend for him to make the leap.

She told him about her dad, how he had slaved away the hours at a Ford engine plant in Lima, coming home too tired to move, as the old folks used to say, but never too tired for his little princess—that's what he'd called her—sitting in his chair with her in his lap and reading to her and telling her stories about his days in the navy.

It was those stories that made her lust for the larger world outside of Ohio. Those stories led her to Fisk and to Delta and right here to good old Atlanta, Georgia. Josh told her he loved it here. They had moved so much when he was a kid. He liked being settled in one spot.

She looked off for a long moment. Then, she smiled at him. "Yeah, I like it here too. It's my home away from home. My Aunt Leah and my Uncle Howard have always been good to me, Josh. In fact, my aunt is like my second mother. She calls me her baby girl. It doesn't bring back my mom, but it helps to know she cares about me so much. And when my brother died, I don't know if I would have made it without her and Chicken Wing." Her voice caught.

Josh instinctively reached over and patted her hand. "I'm sorry. What happened? Wait, you don't have to talk about it if you don't want to."

"No, it's okay, seems like he keeps coming up here lately. Maybe I need to talk about him. He was two and a half years older than me and had always been my favorite brother. I suppose you shouldn't have favorites, but he sure was mine. We were in Chicago visiting my aunt and uncle. We hadn't been there in a while. My dad didn't like the neighborhood. Thought there were too many bad kids hanging around. It's a place called Woodlawn. It's the home of the Black P Stone Rangers. My cousins Vince and Arthur were Stones, and some of their enemies rode through and shot at them. They knew to get out the way when they saw the car swinging past. Norman didn't, so he got shot in the head with a .45. I hate the sight of oatmeal to this day. That's what his brains looked like draining out of his head down his face."

Josh squeezed her hand. They sat there in silence. Josh looked down at the table and then back at her. She was looking right into his face, as if to ask him how he would take this story.

"I guess you and I have a lot in common. When my dad died, it tore me apart." He could feel his eyes watering. "He was so sick. I hated to see him like that. You know, it was a relief, in a way, when he passed, because he didn't have to suffer anymore." He shook his head.

"I hated God for taking my dad. I still don't understand. But I got all right with it. Then my mom got killed in a car wreck. It broke my heart. I mean, it hurt so bad it made me almost scared to love anybody. And I blamed myself. I took her through so much." *Why I am telling you this?*

She squeezed his hand. "I felt the same way when my mom died. I hated God, too. That's okay. That's what my pastor told me. He said God understands, and if you let the Lord, He'll see you through this. I was getting better. Then Norman got killed." Her voice cracked again and tears snuck down her face, stealthily snaking through the tiny crevices leading down to her chin, a few of the more adventurous ones diving off her face onto her skirt below.

She caught herself. "I used to ask everybody, 'Why don't black people love one another?' after Norman got killed. I couldn't understand why kids were shooting people who looked like them in a fight over street corners they didn't own. I hated going to church for a long time. Daddy and Aunt Leah made me. I'm glad they did. But I don't mean to be Weepy Wendy. It's just, I know you know how I feel. You've been hurt the same way." Then she started smiling again, the gleam in her eyes enhanced by the glistening of her tears.

Josh liked the way she bounced back. He wished he could do the same. "Yeah, well, nobody could make me go to church after my mom died. I still don't go, and I'm still not okay with God. Maybe one day, but not right now." She patted his hand and smiled at him again.

"When I was on my way home from my aunt's the day we met at your office, I heard 'I Say a Little Prayer' on the radio. You should have heard me singing. It was one my mom's favorite songs. We used to sing it together when I was little."

"The Aretha Franklin version?" Josh asked.

"Is there another one?" she said, her voice full of indignation and a teasing note.

"I heard it, too! Me and my mom and Genna used to sing it together when we were kids. I knew I liked you."

The waitress came back and brought their lunch. He had a burger and she had the amberjack. The conversation quieted while they ate. They took up business after they finished eating, agreeing on a contract for $2 thousand for what Genna called *curriculum enhancement*. They also agreed she would answer to Genna directly. It sounded like a good idea.

He felt a tug he didn't want work to interfere with. The past weekend had been a fiasco as far as he and Sarah went. He still couldn't believe how he'd stood her up to go get high. First, he was telling himself *I'm not gonna get high*, then he lost one word, *not*, and it was off to the races. By the time he called her Sunday, she was back on the defensive again. He was afraid he'd blown it for sure this time. Maybe this newfound friend could help him through this struggle.

Even as they were chattering, he could feel Gina saying, "Josh, you can't enjoy the rainbows in life without suffering through some rain." This girl sitting across from him sure looked like a rainbow. So of course it began to rain.

She asked, "Why do you call my cousin Chicken Wing? And don't tell me I'm not grown enough to know. He won't tell me. Said because of Norman. What's up?"

"See, you gonna get mad."

"Don't try to play me off like that. Be man enough to tell me and see."

"Okay. When we were teenagers, me and three of my fellas were riding around looking for a street. We pulled in this high school parking lot and we saw this kid sitting on a bike. Somebody asked him how to get to the street. He said he didn't know. I was sitting in the back on the driver's side, facing him. I rolled down the window, pulled a .38 out my coat pocket, pointed it dead in his face, and said, 'You sure, motherfucker?' He started flapping his arm up and down in front of his face like a chicken wing and said, "Nah, man, I don't know,' in a whiny little voice. We laughed and pulled off. Turned out he was Genna best friend's boyfriend. We met a couple of weeks later and I said, 'Hey, ain't you that dude who was sitting in front of Therrell High School flapping your arm like a chicken wing?'"

She sat glowering for a minute. "I hate guns. How dare you treat my cousin like that."

"Look, Sister Kate, you asked why I call him that. I told you. Don't sit here judging me by some shit I did a hundred years ago. The gun wasn't even loaded. I was just trying to scare him."

"Wait a minute. You need to check yourself. I don't know who you think you talking to, but it damn sure isn't me. You got that?" She leaned over right in his face when she said it, too.

Even though he was mad, Josh ate that shit up. *Miss Snappy*, he thought to himself. "Look, Adrienne, I'm sorry, okay? And I hate what happened to your brother, but this ain't Woodlawn. I had no intention of shooting your cousin. Why don't you ask him how he feels about it? We laughed that off a long time ago. Can't you tell we cool? Don't you think if he didn't like me, he would have told you not to fool with me and Genna? And I know you talked to him about it because Hopalong mentioned it to me before you and I met. She said he told you to go for it with us. He wouldn't have said that if we weren't okay with each other."

She looked like she was wrestling with what he'd said. "Okay, well, I have to go. I will call Hopalong and talk over the contract with her."

"Let me walk you out."

"I guess," she snapped. "You won't shoot me if I refuse, will you?"

Damn girl, I like you.

"Adrienne, stop it."

He heard her say under her breath. "You know, I would do this for free—I think so much of what you're doing. Two thousand dollars is really too much!"

"So you're saying you're not worth it?"

"Am I?" She got up to go. He rose with her, scrambling to figure something to say in response—not so much to the comment, but the look that ran across her face when she made it.

"Where you park?"

"Down the block around the corner there." She gestured toward the direction from which she'd come. They walked off the porch back into the restaurant. He opened the door for her, and they sauntered out of Vickery's down the walkway to the street. "I'm parked that way, too. Mind if I walk with you?" he asked her.

"Two thousand dollars? Yeah, I guess you can walk me down the street. Cost you extra to talk, though!"

They burst into laughter. He reached over, pushing her on her shoulder. They strolled down to the corner in silence. He spotted her Camaro as they approached the corner. He didn't want to leave her. Being around her was intoxicating.

He walked her to her door, opened it, gesturing for her to get in. She slid into the driver's seat, looking straight ahead as if he weren't there. "Mind if I holler at you a minute before you go?" he asked.

She glanced at him and said, "Sure."

"Look, talk to your cousin. You and I click, and I don't want that messed up by something stupid I did a long time ago. Okay? He'll tell you how much I regret what I did. And if he doesn't—well, you just work with Genna so we can do right by those kids."

She looked at him. "Okay."

"Okay, Adrienne, you have a good evening and I'll talk to you soon."

Chapter 17

Once Upon a Time

Once upon a time in America, there lived a people who cast their lot with this great nation, seeking a life better than the one they knew before. Unlike others who sought refuge in the land of opportunity, they came determined to stay. There was no turning back. Life in their old country was so bereft of hope, so lacking in the gifts America had to offer, they had to live in this land of hope, this land of oppression forgotten; they knew they had to live there no matter what the cost.

So they loaded their belongings, boarded a ship to freedom, and made off for the Promised Land. It was a long, difficult journey that quite a few of the brave many did not live to complete. The ride was that long, that hard. It was worth it, though. Even at so great a cost. They were in America.

They left behind a land where oppression was their lot. A land where laws were once passed making it illegal to educate their young, where the oppressor's rule was so all-encompassing he could snap his fingers and demand a man's wife or daughter. Where separate but equal was accepted as a matter of course, the way things ought to be between a superior and inferior people.

Politically excluded, legally impotent, they nevertheless struggled for equality and sought justice. They mastered political organizing to better fight the laws that segregated them from the finer *things in life in their own home. They mastered and grew to love florid oratory, rhetoric a prized weapon in their hands, inspiring the masses to continue the daunting struggle against oppression.*

Like so many other victims of exclusion and oppression, they drew religion and its visions of pie in the sky and a better world in another world to their breasts. They turned to the church for guidance and comfort. Their religious leaders in turn became the community pillars, speaking out against oppression, providing shelter to the haunted, succor to those beaten down by the oppressor's whip.

Forced to work the master's fields from can't-see-sunup to can't-see-sundown, they were a rural people at home in the pastoral settings where they lived and worked. They lived in beautiful country, yet the veil of oppression denied them the chance to enjoy this beauty to the fullest. They worked hard, played hard, and died young.

It had to be a great day in the morning for those who survived the journey when they arrived in America—freedom from the desperate times and desolate outlook they left behind in the colony of repression they fled. They so looked forward to a life of equality, of separation from the want that had ruled their old lives, of opportunity in America. This must have been their fantasy at that moment. Only seldom did fantasy echo reality.

They became an urban people in America. They tried to be good Americans, but were met with frustration at every turn. They moved into a neighborhood, the neighbors moved out. They searched for jobs only to be rebuffed by employers who made it plain they didn't want their kind working there. Mainstream Americans considered them inassimilable and unworthy of the title Americans.

Still they persevered, scratching and clawing their way up the ladder of opportunity. Having acquired political acumen, oratorical flourish, and excellent social-organizing skills in their struggles against exclusive discrimination, they were well equipped to struggle against the inclusive discrimination they confronted in their new home. They won political office after political office in urban areas using block voting and almost innate political abilities to put their own in office. Political patronage led to middle-class status for many, and many in the community began to prosper.

People began to make at least some distinction between the two emerging classes within the group. This was the mainstream's attempt to acknowledge the gains these people had made in America. They took to law enforcement and public safety, taking over the top management jobs in many big-city police and fire departments. They turned the office of mayor into their own personal possession in many cities. Slowly but surely, the community formed a large middle class.

They provided the nation with great entertainment, dominating the major team sports. The heavyweight boxing crown was presumed to belong to them, they held the title so many times. They also became legendary as entertainers in the various media. Mainstream America loved to watch them perform even if it didn't want its daughters to marry one of them. Their only Achilles heel in these areas seemed to be swimming, which they were unable to master.

There was a dark side to their various successes, however, because even as the middle class grew, the problems associated with the underclass began to strain relations with the mainstream. It became fashionable politically to criticize their overrepresentation in the nation's jails and on the public dole. The fatherless household became endemic in many neighborhoods as males of the group became notorious for child abandonment.

Mainstream Americans tended to judge all by the terrible but attention-grabbing example set by the underclass. The middle class grew frustrated, wanting to be accepted as full-fledged Americans. Community intellectuals challenged conventional history, asserting they had played a much greater role in the development of Western civilization than had been acknowledged by American historians. The community imposed its own national day on the nation, holding parades and celebrating their triumph over a dark and bloodstained past.

Religious leaders, who still played a prominent role in the community even in America, and others sought to better the lower class. The rampant substance abuse in the lower-class community was of particular concern. However, the high dropout rate and the disdain for education held by many in the community made it difficult to accelerate the group's advance into the middle class.

The most disheartening element of the group's assimilation equation was that the longer it stayed in America, the worse the problems seemed to become. Fatherless households grew as a problem even as the middle class community grew and seemed to take. Decades after assimilation began, crime and violence still ravaged the community. Life expectancy, incomes, educational levels, and intermarriage rates were all slow to advance to the national average.

Jack Kennedy and Ronald Reagan's Irish ancestors must have been a vexation to America during assimilation. They became legendary for their political acumen—and the political scandals that always seemed to follow. The Irishmen who built the Illinois Central Railroad were notorious for having committed a murder for every mile of track they laid. They forced St. Patrick's Day into the national consciousness even though mainstreamers could not relate to Ireland's patron saint. Shanty Irish neighborhoods acquired nicknames like Hell's Kitchen and San Juan Hill.

Josh crushed out his cigarette, mulling over this section. It was his third time reading it. He still wasn't fully convinced she knew what she was talking about. Gradually as he deconstructed her argument, like his sociologist father taught him to, he could see the validity in her claims.

He lit another smoke, standing up to stretch. He had been here at his kitchen table for hours, studying her dissertation draft. It was too breezy in places to be accepted by a doctoral committee, but so what? More and more, he agreed with Genna. Adrienne was definitely on to something.

A big problem would be the two groups she discussed and their reactions to her claims. Blacks would refute her declaration that the Irish suffered equally terrible injustice. And this was true—if you only looked at America. His people were proud of their struggle and would accept only reluctantly the idea some other people somewhere had possibly suffered just as much. Black people would argue slavery was just as bad as the Holocaust, that Jews were fortunate in America because black people were the excluded party here.

And the Irish, notorious nigger haters that they were, would certainly take offense at the suggestion they had something in common with black people. Hell, one of their own had started a presidential campaign in Philadelphia, Mississippi, advocating states' rights.

But he was beginning to understand. She wasn't trying to group them together for any other reason than for black people to learn how an inefficient approach could have painful consequences over the long haul of history. And she pointed out how apartheid, Jim Crow, and the British domination of Ireland carried a common theme—legal suppression of a people by a British-created government. He knew there were laws like the Vagrancy Act of 1809 passed in South Africa that effectively turned

Africans into slaves by decreeing any African who did not work for a white person was breaking the law. And she also pointed out that in South Africa, political organizing and church-supported social activism were being used to break the back of apartheid.

Lawrence would have really appreciated what she said here. He wished he could share it with him. Josh put up the draft and went to bed.

Chapter 18

A Couple of Little Squares

"Brittany! Larry! How y'all doing in there?"

"We're almost ready, Mommy," they shouted in unison.

Genna smiled to herself. They'd be excited when they found out Uncle Josh was riding in with them this morning. She sat down on the bed so she could put her shoes on. Thank God for heel lifts and knee-highs. She wished she could wear nice shoes like other women. *Girl, be grateful you can walk. Quit worrying about some shoes.*

She slipped on her flats. Her back was killing her. She'd been walking around without her shoes on quite a bit the last few days, and she was paying the price for it this morning. If Daniel hadn't gone in early for a meeting, she would have got him to massage it. Genna sighed.

She heard the twins rumbling down the hall. "Mommy, Mommy," they shouted. Lord, did they ever *not* shout? "We're ready."

"Okay, come on. We'll get something to eat when we get to school."

"Burger King, Mommy, Burger King," they shouted.

"Oatmeal," Genna retorted.

"Ew, Mommy," Brittany said.

"Calm down, baby. You can't eat that for breakfast. It's bad for you." She saw another comment forming in Brittany's mouth and shot her the look. The same I-ain't-playing-and-you-better-not-go-there look Regina used to give her.

The comment died, resurrected as "You okay, Mommy?"

Genna reached down and hugged her. "I'm okay, baby. My back hurts a little. I'll be all right, though. Larry, sweetie, you okay?"

"Yes, ma'am."

She smiled at him and thought of Josh. "Tell you what. Uncle Josh is going to ride with us this morning. If he wants Burger King, we'll get Burger King. I guess it's all right every once in a while."

"Yay, Uncle Josh! Yay!" they yelled, waving their arms above their head. Genna felt the same way. Her spirits were low this morning. She knew her big brother would cheer her up. She picked up the telephone off the nightstand and called to let Josh know they were on the way. He sang the *Hopalong Cassidy* theme song to her before she could get him off the phone. She laughed to herself as she hung up.

"Come on, Larry, Brit, let's go." It took about ten minutes to ride from the lower end of Cascade Road to Josh's apartment. She sent Brittany up to get him. Josh brought her back in his arms. He put Brit down and knocked on Genna's window.

"I hear your back hurts. Want me to drive?"

Genna nodded and slid out of the car's front seat. She shuffled around to the passenger side. Josh came around and opened the door for her. "Thank you, big brother," she murmured.

"For you, anything, Hoppy." She smiled and shook her head.

They were on the road in no time. "Hey, back seat. Let's show Mommy our new trick. Larry, let's go. Two times two is . . ."

"Four," Larry snapped.

"Two times five is?"

"Ten," he answered. Josh and Larry proceeded to call off several more times table problems and answers.

"That's good, Larry," Genna said, proud of her four-year-old.

"Let me, Uncle Josh, let me," Brittany yelled.

"Okay, here we go. Four square is?"

"Sixteen."

"Five square is?"

"Twenty-five."

Genna looked at Josh and turned to stare at Brittany. "Brittany, when did you learn how to do squares?"

"Uncle Josh has been teaching us. We've been saving it for when you didn't feel so good. Uncle Josh said it would make you feel better."

"I can do them too, Mommy!" Larry was bouncing up and down, straining against his seat belt, seeking Mommy's attention.

"Okay, Larry, let's see." They did twelve squared, three squared, and eight squared.

"You better, Hoppy?"

Genna beamed. "Josh, what am I going to do with you?"

"What do you mean?"

"Nothing. How long have y'all been working on squares?"

"About a month. They're pretty good, huh?'

"They sure are. I'll have to let Dan hear them tonight. He'll be really proud."

"Nah, I think he's going to be tied up."

"What do you mean?"

"I called and told him I would keep the kids tonight. Y'all need some 'me' time, and I need some time with my niece and nephew."

"All this without telling me?"

"Yep, Dan thought it was a good idea. I'm broke, so no worries about me doing something stupid."

He'd read her mind. She loved Josh, but she wouldn't leave her kids with him if she even thought he could get near some alcohol or, even worse, cocaine. They rode in silence until they got off the expressway. Brittany mentioned Burger King. Josh told her it sounded like a plan, and they pulled in to order breakfast.

In no time they were walking into the building. The one perk the kids were allowed was eating breakfast with Mommy and their Uncle Josh when he was at school first thing in the morning. "Say It Loud—I'm black and I'm proud" pumped through the intercom, signaling it was time for morning prayer. To Genna's surprise, Josh got up to join them.

"Are you all right?" she asked.

"What, a brother can't come to join in prayer?"

"No, not when that brother's name is Josh Gibson."

"I told you, I'm turning over a new leaf."

They walked down the hall together and entered the room where the entire school gathered each morning. It crackled with the energy of young spirits. Aaron led them in the Twenty-Third Psalm. Mrs. Graham then stood and led them in prayer. They broke up after about fifteen minutes and went to their respective rooms.

Josh and Genna went back down the hall to her office. "You feeling better, sis?"

"I am, I really am. I can't believe you have them doing squares."

"It wasn't that hard. I mean, it ain't like picking cotton. It's learning something new. That's all."

"So Adrienne's bringing the contract by this afternoon."

"'Bout damn time. I talked with her about it over a week ago."

"Well, Josh, she's been busy. She told me last weekend she was going to sign it."

"Yeah, I was rereading her dissertation last night. The more I think about what she's saying, the more I agree with her."

Genna listened to Josh drone on for a few minutes. Josh liked Adrienne. Her plan was working. Sarah was her girl, but she could not deal with Josh. She was too nice. And she couldn't understand. Josh didn't know Genna knew about his latest stunt. Sarah had called her upset about Josh standing her up.

Poor child. Sarah deserved better. The bad part was Genna knew Josh loved Sarah. Or as much as he was going to allow himself to love anybody. That was part of why he always pushed her away. He was scared of how much he cared for her. Probably scared loving her would lead to some terrible end to her or their relationship.

Adrienne seemed different; sweet, yet full of vinegar. Genna liked the way she reacted when Josh made his "What are you about?" crack to her. Genna wasn't surprised to see her get angry. What she enjoyed was how it fueled her presentation. And when Josh gave her the standing ovation, she played it off, but Genna could see her filing it away for future reference. Besides, Adrienne understood the pain of loss the same way she and Josh did. Genna knew about her mother. Her heart had reached out to her sorority sister when Josh had told her about her brother. And unless Genna missed her guess, Adrienne was feeling Josh, too. *How do I get them together?*

One thing Sarah got—Josh didn't love Josh Gibson. Sarah didn't know why. Only Genna and Faith and Big Dad knew why. She was crazy about Sarah, but some secrets didn't need to see the light of day. The consequences could be too severe.

Chapter 19

Chicken Wing

"Oooh, may I have one of those pickles?" Adrienne pointed to the jar of big, fat dills sitting on the counter. The Korean girl standing behind the register screwed off the cap and reached into the jar, spearing a juicy-looking one with a fork and placing it in a piece of wrapping paper. She smiled and handed it to Adrienne.

"Minsook, this is my cousin Adrienne. We teach together. I told her about these pickles, and she had to have one. We used to get them at a store over off McDaniel Street in the summer when we were kids."

"Where have you been? I've missed your smiling face," the girl said to Chicken Wing.

"I was out of town at a conference," he stammered.

Adrienne glanced at the two of them and smiled to herself. *Wait 'til I tell Aunt Leah.* Yeah, the first place he had wanted to come when he got back to work was here. *And now I know why.* She paused to take a bite, a twinkle in her eye. "These pickles sure are good."

"Where's Hyung-Ju?" Chicken Wing asked, cutting his eyes at his cousin.

"He had to run some errands."

"I'll bring her back soon to meet him. You remember I told you my aunt and uncle used to own a store when I was a kid?" Minsook nodded. "Well, Adrienne worked there with me when she came to visit. She always wanted a store. I wanted her to see how well your parents are doing here."

Minsook smiled. "He always tells me he wishes more black people would do this."

Adrienne replied, "He's right. I'm jealous."

"Come on, cousin, time for us to go to work." Chicken Wing grabbed her arm and gently led her out the door. He waved at the Korean shop keep as they left, and she gave him a big grin.

"And here I thought you were so anxious to come to the store because you love the pickles," Adrienne cracked. "You know I'm going to tell Aunt Leah."

"Tell her what?" Chicken Wing grunted.

"About your friend."

"I barely know that girl."

"It ain't her fault. What'd she say? 'I miss your smiling face'?" Adrienne cracked, batting her eyes as she imitated Minsook. "I owe you anyway."

"Owe me for what?"

"Oh, let me see. I'm sitting at the table gabbing with Aunt Leah right before you went out of town, and she asks me, 'You going to the Hawks game?' Now, I know my aunt. Every question contains a question. So who could have told her about my friend the basketball player? Couldn't have been Chelle. They haven't talked in a long time. Who else knows? Oh, my big-mouth cousin. That's who. So I'm going to call her and say, 'Aunt Leah, you know you always said he had a thing for yellow girls.'" She dashed around the car, laughing.

"You better run. She just misses my business."

"Uh-huh, you tell that to Aunt Leah. Let me see, Jewel . . . what's that other girl's name? Oh yeah, Rhonda. I knew you liked 'em light skinned, but you took it to a whole 'nother level this time. Went all international on me."

Chicken Wing laughed and said, "I ain't studying you. That's two girls. You don't know what I was doing when you were in Ohio. Besides, Momma ain't gonna say nothing, but at least she ain't white."

"Does Hyung-Ju know?"

"Know what?"

"You been hitting on his daughter, 'cause she sure was grinning at you."

Chicken Wing laughed and shook his head. "What am I going to do with you?"

"Seriously, why did you tell her? I can't have my aunt knowing all my business."

"It's your fault."

"My fault?"

"Yeah, Momma always said if you want something kept, keep it from a man. The way I see it, it's your fault for not listening."

They got in the car and rode back to Morehouse. They chatted about how they wished more black people could see the need for black businesses. The place they got the pickles when they were kids was called the Jew Man's store. It was in the south Atlanta neighborhood of Pittsburgh. Leah had taught summer school at W. H. Crogman, an elementary school in Pittsburgh. Kids would line up to spend their nickels and dimes with Jew Man. And he would load that money up and take it back to his community.

Alonzo Herndon, the first black millionaire in Georgia, got his start running a string of barbershops that catered to a wealthy white clientele. Black people used to understand business was a good way to attain some semblance of freedom. Chicken Wing admired his big cousin. She had taught him why black people had turned away from the small-business ownership that had been a routine part of their lives growing up.

A people who were held down by the law had to deal with the law first. Making money didn't matter when people could take that money from you anytime they got ready and the law would sanction the theft. Black people displayed good sense by attacking the illegality of blackness in America through legal and social means. Their Irish counterparts in Ireland would have been proud.

She argued this was an appropriate approach when racism totally excluded black people from American society through the rule of law. The laws had changed, and now the approach had to change, too. The way to overcome the inconvenience of being black was to build organizations owned and run by black people that catered to a white clientele. Be like the Jew Man and Hyung-Ju. Go to someone else's community and provide them with a needed service. Then, take your profits and invest them in your own. She believed the real problem for black people was not racism, but the black approach to it.

Before they could resolve black America's problems, Chicken Wing pulled in the Morehouse parking lot. He parked and they got out and walked across the lot to Wheeler Hall. Adrienne said to him, "That Josh Gibson is a real asshole!"

Oh boy, where is this going? "Why don't you tell me how you really feel?" he replied.

"He told me why he gave you your nickname."

"And?"

"He pulled a gun on you. He—"

"Whoa, whoa, Adrienne, hold up! Quit going off half-cocked. Damn!"

"How can you stand here okay with him pulling a stunt like that?"

"Look, cousin, I know how you are about guns. And believe me, I understand, but you talking Atlanta in the seventies. Kids didn't shoot each other. Yeah, I was scared, but I didn't really think he would shoot me. And when we met a couple of weeks later, he was mortified about what he'd done. He couldn't stop apologizing. We got past that. Now if you can't, fine, but you some kind of Christian."

"What do you mean?"

"The Bible I read says turn the other cheek."

"It also says thou shalt not kill."

"And who did he kill? I'm standing here talking to you, so it couldn't have been me."

"Why do you take up for him?"

"Maybe you ought to get to know him and see for yourself. He's a good brother. Like I told you, he's got his ways. But he always looked out for me once we got to know each other. As a matter of fact, you remember you came here one time and we went to Adams Park and smoked on some good gold Colombian? Remember how high we were?"

"Yeah."

"He gave me that dope because I told him my cousin was coming to town and I wanted to show her a good time. A quarter ounce he gave me so you could get high. Didn't ask for a thing in return. How many people you know do stuff and don't want anything back? That's Josh Gibson, too."

Adrienne shook her head.

"Adrienne, he could have told you anything. He chose the truth. Let that count for something."

"You really like him, huh?"

"I really do. We haven't talked in a minute, but if I needed the shirt off somebody's back, he'd be one of the first people I'd call."

She said, "That reefer was the bomb. Thinking about it almost makes me want to get high."

"Look, professor, let's let the past stay in the past. And I promise you he's a good guy.

"I'm going to class—Chicken Wing."

Chapter 20

He Calls Me Hopalong

Adrienne saw someone wave at her out of the passenger side of a black Mercedes as she pulled into EDCO. It was Josh. Against her will, she smiled and waved back. She took a long look at the man driving. He was older, maybe in his fifties, but boy he was good looking. She got out and went in the building.

"You Miss Adrienne Johnson?" a teenager asked her as she walked in the door.

"I am," she replied.

"Hi, ma'am, my name's Aaron. Miss Genna wants meet to escort you to her office."

"Why hi, Aaron, you're the coffee maker, right?"

"Yes ma'am," he replied.

"It's good to meet you. You make good coffee," she said, extending her hand to him.

He beamed and shook her hand. "Thanks, Miss Adrienne. I had a great teacher. Miss Genna taught me how to make it."

He led her down the hall. Once again, she had a good feeling about this place. She was impressed by Aaron's manners. She glanced at the pictures on the wall. She especially liked the one of Harriet Tubman.

"Hey, soror, I'd get up but my back is killing me," Genna said.

"Girl, don't worry. You stay where you are."

Genna gestured for her to have a seat. "I see you met Aaron." Adrienne nodded. "You just missed Josh and my Uncle James. They're on their way to go over some documents with our CPAs."

"Yeah, I saw them leaving. I was wondering who that good-looking man was with Josh. Aaron, you kind of remind me of my brother Norman."

"He must be cute," Aaron said.

"Aaron," Genna shrieked and they all laughed.

"Almost as cute as you, sweetie," Adrienne said. "I think you got him by a hair, though. That'll be our secret, okay?"

"Yes, ma'am."

"Aaron, don't you have an assignment you need to finish for me?" Genna asked him.

"I'm on my way. You gonna work here, Miss Adrienne?"

"I am."

"I'll see you around, then." Aaron turned to leave.

"Close my door, Aaron." He pulled it shut behind him as Genna thanked him.

"He's sweet," Adrienne told Genna.

"He is," Genna paused. "He's come a long ways." Genna explained how angry Aaron had been when he first came to EDCO. He couldn't understand why his father had deserted him. He couldn't get over feeling like his dad didn't want him. It had been rough. They hadn't been sure he'd make it. The first week, he'd beaten a kid up named Ronald. Ronald's only crime had been having a father.

Adrienne said, "He beat him up because he had a father."

"He sure did. I was ready to show him the door, but Josh begged me to let him work with Aaron for a while.

Even now, every afternoon when Josh is here, they sit down and have man time at three o'clock."

"Man time," Adrienne ventured.

"Yeah, Josh calls it that because they're both working on being better men. It makes Aaron feel proud, Josh treating him like he's grown for an hour each day. It helps both of them."

"Josh is really hurt about your dad being dead, huh?"

"Adrienne, you just don't know. It ain't just that, though. Josh has been through a lot. My mom—Lord, it 'bout killed him when she died. It was so sudden. And it was so close after his friend Slim dying." Genna stared at her, not saying a word.

Finally, Adrienne asked, "What happened to Slim?"

"Somebody shot him four times with a rifle. He had moved to New York. Faith, Slim's aunt, told Josh. I can still hear him crying. And it's some other stuff, but that's not important. All that changed Josh. I miss my brother."

"What do you mean?"

"Did you ever find out where Chicken Wing came from?"

"No, why do y'all call him that?"

Genna repeated the story exactly like Josh had, except her voice was tinged with sadness. Josh had relayed an angry version of the same tale. She felt her foot start to tap. Genna glanced at it and looked back in Adrienne's face.

"When I was a little girl, I got hit by a car. The doctors weren't sure they could save my leg, forget about me walking. Josh used to lie in the bed with me every night in the hospital and tell me it was going to be all right. He made me believe I was going to keep my leg. And he made me believe I could walk again. He missed so much time out of school they kept him back. Nobody could make him leave me, Adrienne. That's my big brother. Sometimes I still have that brother. Sometimes I don't know what happened to him. All I know is I can walk, and I owe that to him." She looked down at her desk.

Adrienne sat speechless.

Genna looked back up, smiling. "He calls me Hopalong. People who weren't there don't understand. I'd say, 'I can't, Josh. It hurts too much.' And he'd say, 'If you can't walk, just hop along and I'll help you. Come on, Genna. Hop along for me.' Every time he calls me Hopalong, I can hear my big brother, the one I had when I was a child, and I know he's saying he loves me."

"He sounds like a special brother," Adrienne said.

"He is."

They chatted for another hour. Genna gave her a check for $5 hundred when Adrienne gave her the contract. Told her Josh had insisted. Genna called Aaron to walk her out, apologizing for not wanting to get up.

As they walked out, Adrienne said to Aaron, "Mr. Josh sounds like a good man."

"He's the best."

She nodded and got in her car and went home.

Chapter 21

Just a Couple of Children of the Seventies

Josh paced the floor in his office. He stopped to snuff out the cigarette he had been smoking. He looked at the clock on the wall. It read one fifty. He opened his door and walked down the hall to the front entrance. Maybe a little air would calm his nerves.

Adrienne swung into the parking lot as he walked out the door. He looked at his wrist and tapped it. She smiled and shook her head as she pulled into a parking space. Getting out, Adrienne said, "I'm not late. Why are you fronting me? Besides, the effect would be better if you were actually wearing a watch."

"You might have a point." Josh laughed. "You ready for the native's tour of Atlanta?"

"I am. Hey, Aaron, how you doing?" she said, seeing him coming out the front door. "I'm fine Miss Adrienne. Getting ready to grab a bite to eat. You wanna come?"

"Maybe some other time. Mr. Josh is about to take me on a fabulous tour he's been promising me."

Aaron looked at Josh funny. "Okay, well y'all better out of here before Miss Genna sees ya."

"Why, Aaron?" Adrienne asked.

"Oh, no reason. Anyway, I'm out of here. You driving, Mr. Josh?"

"Hey, man, ain't you gonna be late getting back if you don't get going?"

"I'll see y'all when you get back."

"Bye, Aaron," she told him.

"Come on, that's my car right over there. I brought it around since I knew you were coming." He opened the door for her. She looked up at him as she got in. *Where do I know you from?* he thought. It was the same feeling he had when she waved to him as she came in the parking lot with the contract three weeks ago. Oh well, he'd figure it out. Maybe he'd seen her with Chicken Wing or his brother James.

He started the car and rushed off. Aaron was right. He didn't want Genna to see them. Josh wasn't sure what Genna had told her. It must have been good. She'd called him a couple of days later asking for the tour he'd asked her about. He'd wanted to do it before now, but they'd both been busy. It had worked out, though. It was a beautiful day. The temperature was in the low sixties, and the sun was pretending it was spring. The Temptations song "Just My Imagination" came on as they headed up Rainbow to the expressway. *You sure are pretty today,* he thought. He said, "So how you been?"

"Good. I see you like oldies."

"Yeah, I do. This is one of my favorites."

She hummed along with the song. "Yeah, I like it too. Guess we're two children of the seventies."

"How old are you, Miss Johnson?"

"I'm twenty-six. I'll be twenty-seven in July."

"Damn, and you're working on your dissertation?"

"Sure am. I graduated from Fisk when I was nineteen."

"Wow, I was twenty-three when I marched."

"Genna told me you're kind of slow."

"She told you what?"

"I'm kidding. Actually, she told me about her leg and how you supported her. Did you really get left back taking care of her?"

"Yeah." He sighed. "She was messed up pretty bad. Our mother used to get so mad at me. Said it was the only time I ever sassed her. Genna's my heart. She needed me."

"That's sweet."

"Does it make up for Chicken Wing?"

"No, but it's a start. Does it matter?"

"A lot," slipped out of his mouth, eluding his grasp as he tried to catch the words.

She turned her head to look out the window. "Chicken Wing said I shouldn't hold it against you. He told me you're good people."

"You should listen to your cousin. You know how smart he is."

They rode down I-20 to Cascade Road. He pulled off the expressway and drove up to Cascade. "I'm going to show you middle-class, black Atlanta. The world I grew up in. White Atlanta, the ghetto, you have to find somebody else to show you them. I want you to see the city I love the way it ought to be seen."

She nodded. "Sounds good so far."

"When I was growing up, we used to say everybody who was anybody in black Atlanta rode down Cascade at least once a week."

"Boy, this really is going to be the native's tour."

"You know, Adrienne, my dad told me once black people suffer from Stockholm syndrome."

"What do you mean?'

"Well, it's this idea that hostages tend to bond with and take on the ways of their captors. He said black people had been held captive so long by white folks we'd taken on their ways. Even to the point of not loving ourselves because they don't."

"Wow, I should have met your dad. I've spent my life looking for the answer to that question. It took me years, but I figured that out. Stockholm syndrome, huh? I like that."

"He would have loved what you have to say."

"You think so?"

"Yup. Girlfriend, you are deep. You know you're going to have a hard time getting black people to listen to you, right?"

"Now you are right about that. My friend hates to even hear me bring up the subject. He says the same thing. Black people aren't going to listen to that."

Friend? "So what does he do?"

"He goes to Yale Law School. Remember I told you I spent a summer in New Haven? I was visiting him."

"Is it hard being separated like that?"

"Sometimes. What about you, Mr. Gibson, you got a girlfriend?"

"*Had* is a better way to put it. We broke up about six months ago. I tried to get back together with her, but I did something stupid and she won't talk to me."

"Men," she said.

"Anyway, that's The Beautiful Restaurant over there on the left. You ever want a home-cooked meal, it's not too far from Morehouse. This is Cascade Heights, the real beginning of Southwest Atlanta. I'm going to go down Mays Drive. It's named after the president of Morehouse when Dr. King was over there. They used to tell us that anybody can build buildings, but Dr. Mays built men. The street coming up is Peyton Road," Josh said, slowing down so she could get a good look.

"My aunt and uncle live off that street," she said, excitement in her voice.

"Veltre Circle is the street on the other side of Mays," Josh mentioned.

Peyton Road undulated across a ridge from Hightower Road through Peyton Forest until it reached the corner of Peyton and Mays, infamous among natives as the Atlanta compromise's line of demarcation. A gentlemen's agreement established between Mayor Ivan Allen and the leadership of black Atlanta decreed no black families would cross what was then known as Sewell Road. The sons and daughters of segregation proceeded down Peyton, paused, and crossed the proverbial Jordan, reneging on the agreement en route to establishing Cascade as the black neighborhood in the city. Like Sooners invading the Oklahoma Territory, they pursued a seraphic perception of a better life over yonder. Josh wove a tale of a neighborhood filled with real-life Cosby kids, the progeny of Atlanta's black elite, her cousins starring in the tale he told his tourist.

They circled around Lynhurst Drive, passing Camelot—his friend Shaun's nickname for Southwest High School—a place Josh told her where legend held that the girls were prettier and the boys more handsome. It was home to the community's Lancelot, the young leader of the Black Knights of Sewell, Anthony Flanagan. The West, as it was known, was the home of the only high school in the city of Atlanta to win the state championship in football during the integration era. A team so sublime in its athletic accomplishments it would be ranked the number-two high school football power in the country in 1974. Its quarterback Flan, as everyone called him, was so gifted athletically he would lead the basketball team to two state championships starring at point guard, magic in his play long before Johnson. He had been so famous in the area he had had his life story featured on the front page of the local paper when he was seventeen years old.

"James and Chicken Wing told me about him. They said he was featured in *Sports Illustrated* when he was a senior in high school. What happened to him? I always thought he would wind up in the pros."

"Best I can tell, he was ahead of his time. He went to the University of Georgia. UGA wasn't ready for a black quarterback. And he tried to play basketball, too. I don't think the football coach was too keen on that. He probably would have been better off playing wide receiver. It's a shame, though. He could throw a football fifty yards with his left hand and seventy with his right. Or that's what people say."

"Josh, he should have gone to a black college. They would have known how to develop him."

"A lot of people in the neighborhood feel that way. I mean, he could have gone to Grambling or, even better, Winston Salem State and played for Big House Gaines. Basketball was probably his ticket."

"Stockholm syndrome," she said.

He glanced over at her. "What do you mean?"

"Well, isn't that why we make white people's ideals our ideals, their dreams our dreams? He didn't have to go to UGA, except black people are like, 'Wow, our boys can play in the big time,' meaning for white teams. Look at all the football players Grambling sends to the NFL. And why aren't our institutions the big time for us? I mean, if you read what I said, you know I'm no fan of the

Brown decision, but Thurgood Marshall must have been a pretty good lawyer and he didn't go to Yale."

"Wait a minute. What do you have against *Brown*?"

"All deliberate speed."

"Okay, so tell me a better way, then."

"Why didn't they integrate the schools by sending their kids to our neighborhood schools? I mean, the real problem in schools was unequal access to money."

He cut her off. "You're right. I never thought about it like that. I went to elementary school at the Hampton Institute laboratory school in the early sixties when my dad was working there. It was integrated, but it must have been ninety-five percent black. White parents chose to send their kids to school there. But what does that have to do with all deliberate speed?"

"School busing, affirmative action—they are well-meaning but bad ideas. They foster an adversarial relationship between white people and black people. And both promote white supremacy. Their stuff is intrinsically better than ours."

"Intrinsically? Go 'head, Miss Social Scientist."

She laughed and shook her head. "You're silly."

"I am, but I didn't mean to cut you off. Go ahead with what you were saying."

"In *Plessy versus Ferguson*, there's a famous dissent by a justice named Harlan. He argues white supremacy will always be predominant in America, so there was no need for separate but equal. So far, our behavior makes him appear right. If white supremacy was a song, it would go to the top of the charts in our community. Two four six eight, we didn't need to integrate."

"My dad made me read Harlan's dissent when I was a teenager. I always tell the kids if you won't celebrate yourself, you can't ask someone else to do it for you. So you think busing is wrong?"

"I think the buses ran in the wrong direction. I mean, what's wrong with our stuff? Didn't Morehouse give you a good education? I know Fisk gave me a good one. Genna told me she went to Spelman. Do you think she would have been better off going to the Seven Sisters to be sanitized, or do you like her better having gone to Spelman, where I bet she found some soul? But see, mainstream America's ideal is Harvard. Works, but I think ours ought to be Howard or Hampton or Tuskegee or A and T or Clark. You feel me?"

I feel you. "So what's the matter with affirmative action?"

"It's bad for black people."

"Hold up, Kate. You gonna have to explain that one," Josh said with more bite in his voice then he intended.

"Well, specifically for black women. You read what I said about the hierarchy of prejudices, right?"

"I did."

"Well, then, you know how I feel. Our society has a hierarchy of prejudices. Straight, white men of a Judeo-Christian background with no disabilities sit at the top, going through white women, gay men, all the way down to black and Native American men. The further down the hierarchy, the tougher you have it here. Well, affirmative action supposedly relieves the bias related to the hierarchy. Only because women are higher on the hierarchy, it benefits them more. So you have twofers—black women. And white women are better positioned to take advantage of affirmative action. Black men are low men on this totem pole.

"So the progress of black men is slowed by the white supremacy inherent to affirmative action. This hurts black women too, because who are we supposed to marry when our men are being cast aside by mainstream America? It's just like the Irish community one hundred years ago. They had an inefficient approach to assimilation, so the men became highly dysfunctional. You can already see that in our community. Just like Irish kids grew up fatherless, so will more and more black kids because this adversarial approach we're taking slows our assimilation into mainstream America."

"I don't agree with that. So you're saying black men's prospects are actually receding? I mean, I'm not big on the whole 'chasing after white folks' mentality we have, but aren't we owed something?"

"What difference does it make?"

"Hey."

"Hey, if you have a daughter, you want her to have shot at a husband, right?"

"Well, according to you, she can just marry a white man."

"Okay, you can read. I did say interracial marriage will increase just like it did in the past for other ethnic groups. But I got a bunch of brothers and cousins and nephews, and I want them to prosper. We have to choose the better path. Chicken Wing likes this Korean girl in West End. Her father owns a store over there. We need to be more like them and pick a complementary path to assimilation. And isn't that what you are doing with your school? The only affirmative action there will be for white kids. Let them be the minority for a change."

"I'm going to have to study on that. Let's get back to the tour."

"I'm not letting you off that easy," she retorted.

"Well, at least let me tell you this neighborhood is called Ben Hill. This is home to the Chicken Wing incident."

"You need to watch yourself. Josh, people tell this lie, especially your folk the Republicans, that all we want is an equal opportunity for everyone. Of course, you know their line is you can't have equality of results. Well, that's the biggest lie since 'the check is in the mail.' What kind of fool wants the same chance for everyone? Is that what you want for your kids? Is that why you opened your school, so your kids could have the same chance as everyone? Or did you open it so you could provide them with an advantage in life? The parents of your kids aren't making sacrifices so their kids can have the same chance as any other black kid. They're trying to equip their kids—your kids—with every advantage they can give them in life. Believe me, it's the only reason they fool with your crazy butt.

"An earned advantage is truly what we all should and do seek. I'm trying to earn every leg up on you I can, because if we're equal, you might just beat me. In the parallel universe, I envision black lawyers would do work for black clients, but that means eschewing corporate America to start our own companies. Affirmative action encourages us to fight over a piece of the same pie with white people, and since they own the pie, they feel like we ought to be happy with any piece they give us and can't understand why we think we should have access to the best parts. I don't know about you, but I'd rather make my own pie instead of running behind somebody else, arguing with them about a piece of theirs.

"We make our pie, we make our own advantage. We don't have to argue with white people about their pie. I don't know about you, but I prefer sweet potato pie to pumpkin any day of the week! And see, we are automatically at a disadvantage in corporate America because we don't have the same cultural instincts as the people running it. It's just like women. Why argue about maternity leave at a male-dominated company? Why not start your own? Then you have the advantage of setting your own pace."

"Wait a minute. You telling me after four hundred years of this bullshit, you don't think we deserve a leg up?"

"Is it really a leg up? You think Charlene Hunter and Hamilton Holmes were really better off going to the University of Georgia than, say, Fort Valley or Albany State?"

"Yeah, I mean I wouldn't have wanted to and it's not what I want for my kids, but we ought to have access. That's only fair."

"Fair, huh. I'm going to tell you like I tell my students. Life isn't fair. So don't bring that fair argument to me in a conversation as a rationale for anything. Life is unfair and what you should do is make it unfair in your favor rather than crying about how unfairly you are being treated."

"Look, Adrienne, one of my favorite lines is we were taught by integration to go to white schools so we could go to white colleges so we could work for white corporations so we could live in white neighborhoods, and I don't see the celebration of ourselves anywhere in that approach, but isn't education the key to assimilation?"

"When you talk about affirmative action, you have to break it down into three components: employment, education, entrepreneurship. The first two are what I should have called mistakes. Our focus should have been on the last one. "

"Like the family in West End?"

"Exactly," she replied.

"But once again, what's wrong with affirmative action in employment and education?"

"They both have a negative impact on the assimilation rate. They encourage an adversarial relationship between blacks and the mainstream."

Josh sensed her getting on a roll. He started to cut her off to point out the Therrell High parking lot, where the nickname Chicken Wing was born, but decided against it.

"Remember, there are two areas of discrimination—one that excludes and one that includes. Effectiveness of approach is more important in the area of exclusion, efficiency in approach is more important in the area of inclusion. The most efficient approach is one based on economic self-reliance and educational self-development. Black people have chosen the most inefficient approach to assimilation, one based on social activism and the acquisition of political power. This approach is the most confrontational one. It is hard to meld into one from the many when every step of the way is fraught with confrontation. Every time you look up, there's an argument going on about some black kid getting in a school with a lower test score than someone white who was denied entrance, or some black person being hired for a job for which they are not qualified.

"Now understand at this point in time, according to my theory, black scores should be lower than mainstream ones. Test scores are a 'lagging indicator' of assimilation, to borrow a term from economics. So you could argue allowances should be made for the difference, since it is a byproduct of being less-than-fully assimilated into the mainstream culture. The focus should be on the decline in the difference between black and mainstream scores over a time frame rather than the difference at any given point in time. But here again, Josh, it's an argument that denies us our real goal—treatment as an individual rather than being stereotyped by our status as a member of a group. That's the only way to achieve true equality! Be an individual."

"But Adrienne, if there is no affirmative action, what do you do? I mean, black people need an education, right?"

"You argue for equal access to funds, not institutions. See, *Brown* said separate is inherently unequal and that we should move forward with all deliberate speed, which is exactly what black people are doing—moving ahead at all deliberate speed. The way to speed up the process is not to send black kids to the University of Georgia; it is to send the money needed to educate the black kids to Fort Valley and Albany State. Of course, Georgians wouldn't want that to happen, but it's a more honest fight, access to funds. Then white kids might someday actually choose to attend HBCUs if they were funded and administered properly."

"You're a dreamer. You know that, right?"

"So was my hero. Josh, listen to the mountaintop speech sometime. Right before he starts to prophesize on our reaching the Promised Land, King discusses the need for black people to shift our focus to economics. He talks about how we need to consider a bank in, an insurance in; we lost a lot when he was shot.

"Remember, Josh, what we are talking about is ideals. I know you're thinking there aren't enough black businesses to support all the black people who need jobs, but it should be our focus, not working for white people. The more we strive to open our own shops, the more we consider this to be our ideal, the more willing we will be to make the sacrifices required to make this approach work. And realize discrimination is not really our problem."

"Well, then, what is our problem? I'm going to have a hard time going along with you on that one."

"Our problem is our approach to discrimination. Look, everybody who is not a member of the societal ideal gets discriminated against. It's the American way. Even if I was white, I would have to deal with discrimination. I'm a woman. Think about if you were white and gay or white and disabled. Wouldn't you be discriminated against? Quit making this a black thing. It limits your thinking.

"Josh, I don't deny discrimination is an issue. But making it *the* problem leaves our destiny in the hands of others. After four hundred years of this, don't you want be in charge of how we overcome, rather than going hat in hand to mainstream America saying, 'Uh, Massa, the crops sho' was poor this year, could you give me a hand, uh, handout, suh?'"

"It's not a black thing, huh?"

"Approach is always paramount. Jews approached discrimination in Europe with an emphasis on economic self-reliance and educational self-development. Unfortunately, they dwelled in the area of exclusion, so they were relentlessly persecuted. Look at the Spanish Inquisition, the pogroms in Russia, and finally the rise of Hitler in Germany.

"Discrimination certainly affected them, but it was their inappropriate approach to the elimination of discrimination in the area of exclusion that left them vulnerable. It was only after they got it and came up with the proper approach—the migrations to America and the formation of Israel—that they were able to mitigate the effects of exclusive discrimination.

"It was our approach to exclusive discrimination which allowed us to eventually shake the bitter shackles of slavery and Jim Crow. We chose revolution, nonviolent revolution, which is the only way to go when you are outnumbered or outgunned—and we were both. The Jewish approach will never work against exclusive discrimination, because you have to conquer, revolt, or flee to eliminate exclusive discrimination. Theirs is too complimentary an approach. You have to be confrontational. And exclusive discrimination is so oppressive anyway—what do you have to lose by raising a ruckus?

"But the Jewish approach was highly successful in America. Jewish people were able to assimilate at an accelerated pace here because they seldom confronted the mainstream; they sought conciliation. If they couldn't get in a club, they built their own, hence no argument about what's unfair."

He cut in. "Maybe you have a point about exclusive discrimination, if the Irish were treated the way you claim in Ireland. And I guess they did eventually become included in America. Our problem is we saw no need for a transition. If I'm hearing you right, inclusive discrimination is a part of a pledging process—wonder where we got that from, Miss Skee Wee? —and is based in attitudes drawn from the hierarchy of prejudices. I can see that. It's no longer illegal to be black, but it's still an inconvenience, right?"

"Right, and you're right that pledging AKA at Fisk helped me to understand the difference between the two. We had to write our big sisters letters the summer before we pledged, we had to know their likes and dislikes, we had to learn the sorority's history, we had to—"

"Pass the paper-sack test."

"That is not true! Some of our founders were dark. People just like to say that."

"Yeah, I bet!" She rolled her eyes. "I'm just messing with you," he said.

She cut back in, "Anyway, before I was so rudely interrupted." He laughed.

"You think it's funny, huh?" She smiled at him as she spoke. "We are in many ways like immigrants. We are the new kids on the block and we have to prove we are worthy to be considered for membership, instead of pledging Alpha Kappa Alpha, we are pledging America Phi America. Fisk is a Pi chapter, so we really had to prove ourselves. Chelle, my roommate, pledged with me. She'll tell you how tough it was. Since Americans view America as special, each new group of pledges has to prove they are special.

"Americans are traditionally suspicious of newcomers, wondering if they can live up to being an American. They have to prove they are worthy, they have to earn this, and it takes time to be accepted. Some people are more readily accepted than others. It has to do with your approach. I made it a lot better for myself when I called one of my big sisters to wish her a happy birthday while I was visiting my aunt here the summer before I was pledged. She invited me to her birthday party and she looked out for me after that.

"She appreciated my call. Now imagine if I had antagonized her or, how would you say it, pissed her off." She dropped her voice a few octaves as she mocked him. "Then she would have required a great deal more convincing to allow me in. I bet she would have given me a few more whacks with that paddle. Affirmative action is like that. It antagonizes mainstream America because they perceive it as an advantage we have not earned.

"And see, that goes to approach. You can't control discrimination; you have to defeat it by forcing people to change their attitudes. If your approach is perceived, rightly or wrongly, to be one where you demand advantages to make up for your shortcomings, it won't be accepted by others. And it doesn't matter if that's fair or unfair; it's the way it is. We can only control our approach to racist attitudes.

"My friend Reggie's college roommate works for a consulting firm. He was in a meeting once, and his boss called him his top spear-chucker. He pulled the guy to the side afterwards to explain how insulting that was to him as a black man. The boss was apologetic, but it was uncomfortable for him for a while, and he hasn't gotten the promotions his white counterparts have. He can't say for sure it's 'cause he's black, but the question is always in his mind. When you come in your shop and ream an employee out or somebody doesn't get a promotion, they don't have to deal with that question. You ever thought about how nice that must be? Not to have to ask yourself that question—is it because I'm black?"

She paused before saying, "And I'm going to be honest, Josh, if I was in charge, I don't know if I would promote him, either."

"Wait a minute."

"Nah, you wait a minute. A firm like that has to promote people who can eventually generate new business. Who can do that better in America in nineteen eighty-five, a black man or a white man?"

"Well damn, Adrienne. Okay, you got me on that one. I mean, white people run America, so of course the white guy is going to have an advantage. You gonna tell me he earned it."

"His ancestors did. And we have to earn one for our kids by utilizing the proper approach. We have to hear what King was saying at the end of his life and what the Honorable Elijah Muhammad taught as a way of life—an approach based upon economic self-reliance. A strong base of black businesses is the best employment program for our community.

"Yeah, affirmative action will certainly bring forth the talented tenth, but what about the others? Sure, we can maintain the Irish course and have the same results, a couple of black presidents one day, but we'll also have the same schism in our community. A large group moving forward, which they called the 'lace curtain' Irish, and a large group left behind, which they referred to as the 'shanty' Irish. The middle-class/ghetto-black dichotomy we are experiencing even now is because of our approach to discrimination. I'd rather seek the Jewish path where we all come forward together. If I attain economic power, I can buy access. If I have political power, I have to fight to get it. I don't like to fight. I love to shop!

"There's no point in American history where the Jewish family broke down, yet I would argue they faced greater discrimination than the Irish because they were more distinct from the ideal. Yet the Irish family suffered in the last half of the nineteenth century. It was a truism that an orphan was Irish. Can't you see our community collapsing in the same way? The Jewish gangster rose and fell in a matter of forty years, the Irish and Italian gangster are still around."

"You telling me it's okay for a few black elites to enjoy the spoils of victory while so many of us continue to be ground up by the racial discount rate?"

She asked where they were. "This is outside the city, but I want to show you Niskey Lake. We're in South Fulton County, right outside the city limits."

She told him a story as they rode. "My Uncle Pete lived in Savannah. He worked for the city as a janitor back in the days before the movement began. He and my aunt had eight kids.

"He worked for the city back when they had colored and white bathrooms. One day, he had to go to the toilet. He was standing right outside the white-only bathroom and he didn't feel like going all the way down the hall to the colored one. He looked to see if anybody was coming and nobody was, so he went in and used the bathroom. Sure enough, a city department head came in and caught him. The white man asked him, 'What you doing in here, nigger, using a white man's bathroom?' Uncle Pete couldn't say anything. The white man had caught him dead to rights and took him down the hall to his office to fire him.

"About this time, Uncle Pete's supervisor caught wind of what was going on. He was white and he was crazy about my uncle. In fact, Uncle Pete used to call him his good white folks."

Josh thought about how Grandma Gibson used to sit on her front porch and talk with her friend Miss Johnnie about the good white folks. Back in the day, black people used to say if you had some white people who would watch out for you and really liked you, they were your good white folks. Miss Johnnie was a maid, and she had raised her white family's kids from the time they were babies. The three kids called her Mama Johnnie. The whole family loved her and they were a big deal in that Alabama town. Folks with sense, both white and black, knew better than to mess with Miss Johnnie or her kids because her good white folks would come down on you like a ton of bricks if you did.

"Anyway, the guy comes in and starts begging for Uncle Pete's job. The department head wasn't hearing it. Uncle Pete's supervisor kept saying, 'Boss give the nigger another chance.' The department head kept saying, 'Nah, that nigger messed up good. I ain't letting that go.' Finally, the supervisor says, 'Boss, let him go this time. It ain't his fault. The nigger can't read, Boss!' Boss thought about it and said, 'If the nigger can't read, I guess I'll let him go this time.' Only the nigger could read, and his good white folks knew it."

All Josh could do was laugh and shake his head. Her Uncle Pete told them there wasn't a thing he could do. They'd have fired him for sure if he'd told them how he really felt about what both of them were saying. And where else was he going to get a job like that in those days? "Back then, you had no recourse. Your boss might have called you a nigger at Coke, but you could have at least tried to do something about it. Back then, you just took it."

He thought about it. She had a point. "My Grandpa Gibson was murdered before we were born. He was the principal at the black school in a little camp in South Georgia. The good white town fathers decided to build a new black school. My granddad didn't like the blueprints, so he complained to the town fathers. They paid some black dude ten dollars, and he shot my granddad in the chest with a 12 gauge. Killed him dead as a doorknob.

"My gran cried her eyes out, got up from her bed, and broke to Tuskegee. Nobody ever even looked for who killed him. Yeah, my gran just had to take it."

She looked at him with pain in her eyes. "How do you know somebody black shot him?" He told her how the guy had made a deathbed confession sometime in the fifties. How sad it was. A black man had killed his grandfather.

"My grandmother always taught us to love, though. She said, 'You let a man make you hate him, you're allowing him to make you as small as he is, but if you can love a man even when he does you wrong, you're being bigger than him, and it's the Christian thing to do.' She'd always say, 'To whom much is given, much is asked.' And she figured God asked so much of black people in the South, He must have given us a lot."

"You think she was right?" She asked.

"Adrienne, I wouldn't have missed being born black in America for anything in the world. I love being black and I absolutely love black people. My Aunt Ella has a little rhyme that goes 'House, field, porch, or the yard; you black in America, life is just hard.'

"Hey, you see those apartments?" he asked. She nodded. "That's Windjammer. We used to party there back in school. One night your cousins got to jamming so hard the apartment we were in starting swaying back and forth."

"You lie," she said laughing.

"I'm not shitting you about that. It 'bout scared us to death. We got up out there. The Jammer used to be the spot. We'd party to the black national anthem."

She frowned. "You danced to 'Lift Every Voice and Sing.'"

"Nah, Adrienne, not the James Weldon Johnson version. The real one— 'One Nation Under the Groove' by The Parliament Funkadelics."

"You are insane. And I fell for it."

It was time to head back. Five hours they had been gone. He promised he would finish the tour of middle-class, black Atlanta soon. On his way home, Jermaine Jackson came on the radio singing, "I Found That Girl."

Chapter 22

About Riding with My Brother

Adrienne studied the exam lying on the bed in front of her. Surrounded by papers scattered on her bed, the floor, and her dresser, she was grading her first test of the semester. She struggled with scoring tests. It was the worst part of her job, grading the first exam of the term. No matter how well the class seemed to be doing, you could not be sure if they were getting the material until you gave that first exam. She learned her first semester that tests were a referendum on her ability to teach as much as they were on her student's capacity to learn. She took bad grades personally. She always came to grading edgy and unable to relax until she had a sense of how well the class was doing.

She heard the phone ringing. Michelle would get it. She knew not to disturb her unless it was an important call. "Adrienne, phone," Chelle said, sticking her head in her door a few seconds later.

Adrienne mouthed, "Do you know who it is?"

Michelle cupped her hand over the mouthpiece and whispered, "Genna."

Adrienne got up and took the phone. "Hey, Genna, how you doing?"

"Girl, I'm okay. Just trying not to let these kids run me crazy. Did you and Josh go somewhere yesterday?"

Adrienne frowned before answering. "Yeah, he took me out for a tour of black Atlanta. He ought to organize groups and do them for a living."

"He is pretty good. I don't mean to pry in your business."

"That's okay," Adrienne said a touch of wariness in her voice.

"I'm going to assume you drove, because Josh's driver's license is suspended."

"His driver's license is suspended?"

"It sure is. I didn't think he had told you. I saw your car yesterday and noticed his was gone."

"No, Genna, he didn't mention it. We rode around for hours."

"Girl, all that smoking didn't bother you?"

"Smoking? No, he never lit up once."

"Wait a minute. You sure you were with my brother? Josh smokes likes a chimney."

"I mean, I smelled cigarettes on him, but I thought maybe he smoked one or two a day. One of my brothers smokes a pack a day and he would never go that long without lighting up."

"Adrienne, Josh smokes three or four packs a day."

"Are you serious?"

"He sure does."

"And his license is suspended. How does he get back and forth?"

"Oh, he has permission to drive back and forth to work. But don't let Josh ride you around like that. He's hardheaded. I don't want you to get caught up in his mess. At least, not without knowing what's going on, okay?"

"Well thanks for telling me. I know he's your brother, but Josh is something else."

"He is."

"Well, anyway, I'm grading some tests, so let me get back. Oh, and Genna. Don't tell him you told me. I want to have that discussion with him myself."

"My lips are sealed. I'll see you Monday, then?"

"At ten o'clock."

Adrienne hung up and walked to the kitchen. "Michelle!"

Chapter 23

The Old Country

"Hey, doctor! How you doing?"

"Hey, Uncle James, I'm straight. What's up with you?"

"I wanted to touch bases with you about this young lady your sister's been raving about."

"What did Genna say about her?"

"Tell you what, doctor. Why don't we sit down for a meal, and you can fill me in on what's up?"

In other words, the Mariner wanted to be sure his money was being invested properly. The Mariner loved his sister's children dearly, but money was money. Josh and Genna were Regina's beneficiaries on her life insurance policy. Her death provided most of the capital needed to fund their idea of a school designed to bring the best out in young black children. The Mariner had stepped in and made a substantial investment so Genna could set aside some money for her young family. He had insisted Josh put up his entire share, except for $5,000 locked away in a certificate of deposit in Josh and Genna's name. This was the Mariner's way of keeping Josh from spending every dime to his name on drugs.

The Mariner was slick like that. A veteran of the movement, as he called the civil rights movement, James Washington had moved to France not long after the

Sixteenth Street Baptist Church bombing in Birmingham. Said to Josh, he had grown tired of the struggle. He'd wanted to seek a different path. Europe had been good to him in the fifteen years he lived there. He'd hit a couple of big licks and made enough money and connections to come back home and live well.

Always well dressed, one of his first acts after deciding to partner with them had been to introduce Josh to his tailor and have him fitted for a wardrobe of nice suits and shirts. He told Josh he had to look the part if he was going to play the role of someone dedicated to developing young minds. Black people were sight people. If someone didn't look like they had it going on, they wouldn't pay them much attention. They wanted their educators to look like the black people who taught them growing up, sober and upstanding like a deacon on Sundays in their spare time.

The Mariner had a black woman named Gloria who did his nails every two weeks. He hydrated his face every morning and instructed his barber to trim his moustache when he got his hair cut every Saturday. He took it a step further and had the guy skim his eyebrows, too. Stepping out of his Mercedes in his suits and those handmade English shoes he preferred, the Mariner always exuded cool.

The shoes were a European affectation. He had walked in a shoe store in London named Foster and Sons one day while living on the continent. A cobbler showed him a shoe last made for Duke Ellington, and the Mariner had been hooked. Sir Duke was his idol. If bespoke shoes were good enough for the Duke, they were what the Mariner had to have on his feet. He had eventually settled in with a shoemaker named G. J. Cleverly, who fashioned leather works of art for an establishment named New and Lingwood.

The old boy was kicking back in a pair of Cleverlys made from Russian reindeer hides painstakingly removed from a shipwrecked vessel lying on the bottom of the ocean when Josh sat down to break bread with him at Dailey's. The reddish-brown shoes were the foundation of an outfit consisting of a medium-gray suit, a light-pink shirt, gray socks, and a wine-grenadine tie straight out of a James Bond novel. Josh didn't think he would ever be smooth enough to pull off such a look, but the Mariner made it look good.

"Okay, nephew, what is it with this young lady? Genna says she is the answer to our scared Negro problem. You agree?"

Josh surveyed the menu while contemplating his answer. Too unreserved an endorsement of Adrienne's capabilities, and the Mariner would grow suspicious of his motivations. Too muffled a ratification of Genna's effusiveness, and the Mariner would question her judgment.

"I don't know, Uncle James. She talks a really good game. Good enough I've been willing to read her dissertation draft to see how strong I think her assertions about black people are. She seems to have some good ideas. I can't say I agree with everything she's saying, but she's got some good points."

"Such as?" the Mariner inquired.

Josh explained her theory of exclusive and inclusive discrimination. He mentioned her belief that the civil rights movement was the black journey across the ocean to America. The Mariner sat studying him, face inscrutable. Josh sensed he was okay with what he was hearing, but not overwhelmed.

"Uncle James, she goes into this thing about black America being the Old Country. She talks about how —"

"So she's a fan of James Baldwin," the Mariner cut in.

"Why do you say that?" "Josh asked.

"Baldwin wrote a famous essay called 'Notes of a Native Son.' In it, he refers to the South as the Old Country. Baldwin implies the blacks who lived in the Harlem he wrote about had fled their ancestral home for the promise of a better life. He speaks of their concern for the black soldiers deployed to the South for training during the Second World War. That's a great essay. But you were saying?"

"She makes the argument we are, in a figurative sense, immigrants to this country. And she goes on to say that what we are going through is the process of Americanization, transforming from cultural outsiders living on society's margins into mainstream Americans in good standing. She claims King pointed out our status as denizens of a psychological colony of oppression who lived in America, but were not of America at the beginning of 'Normalcy, Never Again.'"

"She doesn't call it 'I Have a Dream'?"

"Nah, she told me that out of respect for the people who wrote it, she preferred to call it by its given name."

"I like her. When are you going to get us together?"

"How about at the black history program? Genna asked her to come."

"Sounds good."

"One more thing, Uncle James. She says that all immigrants have to go through a phase she calls *values in transition*. It's where the young people in the group realize the Old Country ways won't work in their new home. That they have to toss out their parents' Old Country ways and adopt the cultural mores of America. Yet they can also see America refuses to accept them. She says these values in transition are what lead to street gangs and a rising crime rate in certain immigrant communities. For instance, she claims arson used to be called Jewish lightning."

"She's right. They used to have cartoons in the papers that had characters with names like Blazenheimer and Burnupski in them. So she knows about the Jewish mafia." Josh nodded. He'd learned a long time ago the Mariner knew a little about everything. "That's interesting, Josh."

"We're going to ask her to work with Aaron. Genna and I both think she can be a big help with him."

"That sounds like a good idea, doc. Now, let's eat."

Chapter 24

Aaron

"For the moon never beams, without bringing me dreams of the beautiful Annabel Lee; and the stars never rise, but I feel the bright eyes of the beautiful Annabel Lee."

"Yeah, Miss Adrienne, that's my favorite part," Aaron said to her as they rode to West End.

"I'm impressed, Mr. Jackson," she replied. "I would have never guessed you to be a romantic."

Aaron looked at her. He hadn't been sure about her being his teacher when Miss Genna first told him they would be working together. She was all right, though. Real down to earth, just like Miss Genna had said. Unlike most of the kids, math was his thing. He figured you could trust numbers. If you lined them up the right way, they would always give you a right answer.

People weren't like that. You line them up the right way, you could still get wronged by their response. Sometimes Aaron would look in the mirror and think about his dad. *I look like you spit me out. And you walked away. What did I do to make you hate me?* When he first got to EDCO, a kid named Ronald singsonged, "You ain't got no daddy" to him.

Aaron beat him good. Miss Genna had threatened to put him out. She couldn't get to how he could jump on

Ronald for teasing him. Yelled at him, "My daddy's gone, too." *Yours died. He didn't leave 'cause he wanted to, he left 'cause he was taken from you.* He had yelled back at her, "Fuck you!"

Mr. Josh had taken his side. Sometimes Aaron figured Miss Genna let him stay to spite him. *Like I ain't gonna let you off the hook that easy.* Now he and Miss Genna were tight. He loved it at EDCO. And he'd do anything to stay, even listen to another well-meaning adult trying to help him.

He'd liked Miss Adrienne from the beginning. She told him she reminded him of her brother. Mr. Josh told him later her brother was dead, murdered by Chicago gang members. That made him sad. Made him feel like maybe she hurt like he hurt, because he couldn't imagine somebody he loved dying on a tip like that.

And she acted like they were in some big conspiracy together. They were supposed to be talking about history. She told him they'd pretend to do history. She liked poetry and wanted to share some with him. Of course, he would have to know some history or they couldn't continue, or so she told him.

"Why do you like that part, Aaron?"

He snapped out of his daydream. "I want to feel that way about somebody one day, Miss Adrienne."

She smiled at his response. "Well, I hope you find that somebody, Aaron."

"What about you, Miss Adrienne? You feel that way about anybody?"

"I thought I did, sweetie."

"What happened?"

"You sure ask hard questions. Here we are. Let's go get a pickle."

166

After she parked, they got out and walked into a store named Kim's Grocery. He rushed to the door so he could hold it open for her. "Thank you, sir," she said to him as she strode through the door. "Hey, Minsook," she said to the tiny young woman standing behind the counter.

"Hey," the woman responded. "Bet you came for a pickle." Aaron watched the two of them laugh together as Adrienne nodded. The woman took a fork and fished a fat dill out of the jar filled with briny delights. She placed it in a piece of plastic wrapping paper and handed it to Adrienne.

Adrienne reached in her purse to pay her. The woman shook her head. "On me today. You a good customer."

"Thank you, Minsook," Adrienne told her. "Let me introduce you to Aaron. Minsook, this is Aaron. Aaron, this is Minsook.

Aaron reached his hand out. "Hi, ma'am," unsure if it was okay to call someone so close to his age by her name or if he should address her as Miss.

"Call me Minsook," she said, smiling as she shook his hand.

"Okay, Minsook?"

"You said it right," she replied.

"Chicken Wing been in today?" Adrienne cracked.

Minsook smiled and asked, "Why do you call him that?"

Aaron watched Miss Adrienne tell Minsook the story of why her cousin was called Chicken Wing. She found it hilarious, even imitating Miss Adrienne's flapping elbow to make sure she had it right. Aaron could hardly believe Mr. Josh had pulled a gun on somebody. Minsook's father Hyung-Ju came into the store while they were talking.

Aaron found himself being introduced to the store owner. "Hey, man," Hyung-Ju said to him. "You like pickles, too?" Aaron nodded. Funny, his cousin Cowboy had told him Koreans didn't like black people. Maybe it was different in LA because these two sure appeared to be nigger lovers. Mr. Hyung-Ju even let him have his pickle on the house.

After a few more minutes of her bantering with them, they left. Minsook looked at Miss Adrienne and flapped her arm. Aaron figured Chicken Wing was in for a hard time when she saw him again.

Riding to Morehouse, he decided to ask about what Cowboy had said. "Miss Adrienne, I thought Koreans don't like black people. They sure act like they like you. And your cousin."

"Sweetie, who told you that?"

"My cousin Cowboy—"

"Who?" she cut him off before he could go on.

"My cousin Al," he answered, knowing she wanted his real name.

She frowned. "Aaron, don't get caught up in that kind of thinking. That's like them saying young black men all steal."

"Ain't that what they think?"

"Didn't they just give you a pickle?"

"Yeah, but that's because I was with you. If I had gone in there by myself, they would have followed me all around the store."

They rode in silence for a moment. She pulled into what must have been the Morehouse campus and parked her car. Instead of getting out, she sat for what felt like a long time. Aaron squirmed. "You okay, Miss Adrienne?"

"Aaron, has any Korean ever followed you around a store?"

"Yes ma'am," he said, a touch of bite in his voice.

"Why do you think they did that?"

"'Cause I'm black."

"'Cause you're black, huh?"

"Hey, Miss Adrienne, why you taking up for them? They do follow us around."

"So Mr. Hyung-Ju and Minsook followed you around the store? Funny, Aaron, I missed that."

"Ah, come on, Miss Adrienne. Okay, not them, but you know what I mean. You go in their stores and you can feel their eyes on you."

"Well, if they didn't follow you, can you really say all Koreans follow you?"

"Nah, I guess not."

"Look, Aaron, I don't want you doing the same thing to them you accuse them of doing to us. Or what white people do to them and us."

"What's that?" he asked.

"I don't want you to stereotype them. Sweetie, don't take Mr. Hyung-Ju and Minsook and judge them by the fact they are Korean. Judge them by who you see as an individual. Can you do that for me?"

"So you saying every Korean I meet, you want me to get to know them before I judge 'em?"

"Exactly!"

Part II

In my Father's house are many mansions: if it were not so, I would have told you. I go to prepare a place for you. And if I go and prepare a place for you, I will come again, and receive you unto myself; that where I am, there ye may be also.

—John 14:2–3 (KJV)

Chapter 1

The Bluff

"Hey man, pull up, up there, Jay," Big Dad said, pointing at the group of cats standing about halfway up the block. Josh eased up the street, slowing to a stop as three guys rushed over to the passenger side window. Dad rolled it down. A short guy with a head full of nappy hair and no front teeth held out a hand full of sacks. "Got them dimes, bro."

Dad looked past him to Miami. Miami jostled around the other cat saying, "Man, Shorty got them kibbles and bits. You don't want that shit, man. I got them boulders."

Dad said, "Let me see what you holdin', Miami." They were some fat dimes. Dad looked at Josh. "What you think, man?"

Josh handed him five twenties. "Get ten, Dad."

"Y'all gonna like that, bro. That's that fire." Dad exchanged the money with him, and they pulled off. Josh saw another car pulling up behind them and Miami flagged it down. Josh turned and swung down another street, eyes searching for the police. They didn't roll through here much, but you never knew.

Josh rolled up the block, making a right. He made another right heading back out of the Bluff. A girl was parading down the side of the road looking like she might walk right in front of the car. Josh slowed down, not wanting to hit her. Not with a pocketful of Miami's boulders.

"Damn, Jay. Ain't that Beanie?" Dad said. Josh took a closer look at the girl.

"What you think?"

"Pull over, man, and let's get her."

Josh pulled up beside her. The girl leaned over and asked, "Y'all want some company?"

"Damn, Beanie, you don't recognize me," Dad cracked.

"Oh hey, baby," she responded.

"Git in," Dad commanded. She slid over Dad's lap into the middle of the front seat. Josh drove down the block to the shotgun house where she stayed. Now they didn't have to drive back across town to bump or turn around and ride back when they finished these sacks and were jonesing for some more; besides, Beanie could suck a bone through a water hose.

They'd met Beanie one night out on the cocaine trail. She was actually their second pickup that night. The first one hadn't gone too well. The girl they picked up off the corner took them to the room she lived in to get them both off. Dad wanted to get down. Josh was already past the point he wanted anything other than a blow job when he was getting high.

Dad handed her a hit and whipped out as she put the rock on a plate on a table. She took one look at him, picked the rock back up, and said, "Here, you too big. I don't want your dope. You ain't gettin' ready to break my body down like that."

Josh almost fell on the floor laughing. Dad was mad as hell. Josh started to go ahead and do a transaction with her anyway, but decided he couldn't do his boy like that. As they were getting back in the car, Dad kept saying, "Hey man, that shit ain't funny. Sorry-ass ho."

Josh laughed at him even more. Then they saw a fat ass walking and pulled over. Josh would always be glad he chose to be a good friend that night 'cause Beanie could do shit with her mouth he'd never even heard of, much less seen.

Josh had hit some dope so strong it made you check to see if you spotted your pants. Coke made your nature rise. In your head, anyway, because after while you couldn't get it up anymore when you started bumping. Cats would lie about how they hooked up with their girl and had all kinds of freaky sex while hitting the bowl. Josh used to believe them. He'd get jealous every now and then because the fellas made it sound like they were sho' 'nuff freaking. Niggers were lying though.

The one thing Josh didn't want was a girl who hit. Watching Hakeem and Duck had taught him that. When he met Duck, she had been pregnant with Lucky. She looked down her nose at Keem and his junkie friends. Duck had liked him because this was before Josh had started hitting. Keem eventually turned him out on the pipe, but he and Duck were tight by then. Keem started her freebasing so she would leave him alone. At the time, he was moving fifty pounds of that redbud a week. He could afford the $2,000 an ounce of cocaine cost in those days. Duck had taken to the pipe and was hitting like a pro in no time at all. Keem had told him later it was the worst mistake he ever made.

Josh's mind drifted back into the present. He needed to quit reminiscing 'cause you always had to pay attention in these streets. You could get caught slippin' and that would be a bad thing. Beanie rubbed his groin while they rode down to the rooming house where she lived. You could tell she had been bumping for a minute. She had lost a lot of weight. Smoking cocaine was the best diet plan going. They went to her room and set up to hit.

Yeah, Beanie was right on T. She wasn't his girl, and she could always make you rise to the occasion no matter how much cocaine you smoked. And these days Josh smoked a lot.

He watched her hit. Every time Josh saw her bump, he swore Beanie was coming. Something about the way she shuddered and gasped, blowing that cocaine smoke out of her nose. She came over to him and motioned for him to lie on his back. He got down and put his hands behind his head, watching her unzip his pants.

Chapter 2

IGFAW

Dear Adrienne,

Thank you so much for querying us with your project. Unfortunately, we did not feel it was the right fit for our agency. While we are unable to comment personally on every query, please know we did give your work our full consideration. Thanks for thinking of our agency, and we wish you nothing but the best in your writing career.

Sincerely,
Juliana

And it had been such a good weekend. She'd hung out in San Antonio with her ballplayer. He'd catered to her love of history by taking her to the Alamo. He'd even introduced her to a couple of his teammates who were kind enough to autograph a basketball for her brother Emmett. Yeah, she'd had a blast.

Only to have her Sunday ruined by this form letter. She wondered if they had even read her book proposal. How could they not see the value in what she had to say? Why didn't they at least want to see a manuscript to make a proper assessment? All her hard work summarily rejected with a "good luck" that felt contrived, phony. She felt a swell of hurt capped by anger wash over her.

She wondered for a second if God was getting her for running around on Reggie. *Stop it, Adrienne.*

"You all right, girl?" her line sister asked.

"I've felt better. Boy, Chelle, I guess I was expecting a little more than a form letter."

Michelle nodded. "You sure you don't want me to stay with you? I know how much this means to you."

"Chelle, go. I'll be all right. I probably need some alone time right now." Michelle had a hot date. Adrienne reached over and squeezed her hand. "Go on, please."

Chelle looked at her before getting up to head out the door. "When are we going to find you a church?"

"Chelle, I'll be all right."

"Do I need to call Alonso?"

Adrienne stuck her tongue out at her and told her, "Don't you dare."

Chelle left. She sat staring at the letter reading and rereading it for several more minutes. *Reggie would get a kick out of this.* And maybe for the first time, she saw clearly what everyone had been telling her. If her first thought was he would gloat over this situation, it was time to cut him loose. And she knew that he would gloat.

Kicking it with the NBA had been fun. The sex was off the chain, but all she could stand was a couple of days of hearing him break verbs. To be sure, her ballplayer was into her. He wanted her to come live with him in Indianapolis after the season. It would be nice to be close to home, but her need to make a better world for her people precluded her ever settling down with him. He wasn't deep enough for her. He listened to what she had to say, but was tone-deaf to the meaning of her words.

The phone rang. She sighed, wondering who it might be. She debated answering before letting it go to voice mail. A male voice started speaking, sounded like her brother Skip. The words blurred in her mind as she mulled over the rejection letter. *Anyway just checking with you* came through voice mail. It was Josh. This was the first time he had called her at home.

She picked up and said, "Hello."

"Hey, Paladin, I was thinking about ya and I figured I'd give you a holler."

"Well, hello, Mr. Josh Gibson. I'm glad you called. I haven't had a chance to tell you how much I enjoyed the black history program. I thought it was really good."

"Yeah, well, we want to make sure we don't contribute to the miseducation of the Negro."

"So are you a history buff?"

"Why, you ask, because I've read ole Carter G?"

"No, silly. It's not just that. It's more so the history lesson you gave me about black Atlanta."

"I want you to love my hometown the same way I do. Besides, you seem to like history, too."

"So have you actually read *The Mis-Education of the Negro*?"

"You a trip. Have you read it?"

She laughed. "You didn't answer my question. Anybody can call out a book title."

"Oh, so it's like that? 'In this effort to imitate, however, these "educated people" are sincere. They hope to make the Negro conform quickly to the standard of the whites and thus remove the pretext for the barriers between the races. They do not realize, however, that even if the Negroes do successfully imitate the whites, nothing new has thereby been accomplished. You simply have a larger number of persons doing what others have been doing. The unusual gifts of the race have not thereby been developed, and an unwilling world, therefore, continues to wonder what the Negro is good for—'"

"Okay, so you read it."

"Sure have. It's the Bible. It's the whole basis for the education for our children at EDCO. We want them to know things like the movement didn't just free black people. It freed America."

"Preach it, Mr. Gibson."

"So what are we going to call yours, *The Re-education of the Negro*?"

Adrienne gripped the phone a little harder. Her foot tapped on the linoleum. "I don't know. I guess I have to find somebody willing to publish it first."

"So you really are writing a book, huh? I was wondering, my naïve one."

"Why'd you call me naïve?"

"'Cause you think you can fix black people. If that ain't naïve, I don't know what is."

"You know, whatever points you might have earned, you sure are blowing them fast."

"Oh, so you admit I earned a couple?"

"I didn't say that."

"You thought it, though."

She giggled. "You are something else."

"I try to be. Look, I can call you naïve 'cause I'm the same way. We both know all you can do is love black people, because they can sure try your spirit. And I want to do what those people in the movement did for me. Clear a better path for the children coming behind me."

"Do you have any kids?"

"Now see, you 'bout to lose some points. My mother used always tell me, 'Boy, don't you bring me anything to rock.' And I was scared of Regina Gibson. She did not play. Besides, if I had kids, you would have seen them hanging 'round the school."

"I was just wondering. You seem to love children."

"I do. Besides, uh, something happened a few years ago that makes me want to do right by kids."

"You want to talk about it?"

"Maybe some time. Not right now, though."

"You sound sad. It must have been bad."

"Hey, let's talk about your book. When you gonna finish writing it?"

"Wellll, I already did a draft, and guess what? I got my first rejection letter."

"I'm sorry. When did you get it? I know you said you were going out of town for a few days."

"It was here when I got home today."

"Something told me to call you. I mean, I started to a couple of times before, but I just really felt like I ought to today. How you feel?"

"I'm not happy about it."

"They don't know what they're missing. You got some good stuff."

"Evidently they didn't feel that way. Thanks, though. You're sweet to say it's good."

"I'm not trying to be sweet. I'm telling the truth. I really admire you. You've got something special in your mind. I wish I was as smart as you."

She squirmed in the chair. "You're smart. And it has nothing to do with smart. It's just something God showed me."

"You sure are religious."

"Does it bother you? I mean, I don't mean to wear it on my sleeve around you, but it's something about you that makes me want to praise the Lord."

"Probably 'cause you talking to the devil."

"You sure are down on yourself."

"Not really, but don't misunderstand. I've done some really evil shit."

"Do you have to curse so much?"

"You think I curse a lot?"

"I do."

"Damn." They both laughed.

"So do you know of a good Baptist church?" As much as he seemed to know about Atlanta, she figured she'd ask.

"Yeah, my boy has a church. Why, you looking for somewhere to attend?"

"I am. I promised my dad. Besides, I need to hear the word."

"Have I not commanded thee? Be strong and of good courage; be not afraid, neither be thou dismayed: for the Lord thy God is with thee whithersoever thou goest."

"Wow, Joshua 1:9. Thank you. I didn't know how much I needed to hear that until you just said it."

"Sister Kate, if you gonna fix black people, you better pack plenty of courage and faith. I'll take you to my boy's church. You want to go?"

"We'll see."

"Your favorite answer. Uh, so you down with IGFAW?"

"What is IGFAW?"

"I Give Five a Week. You are going to tell the parents about it the last week of school. We're going to ask them to give up lunch one day a week and give the money to an HBCU. Genna came up with it and she'll kill me for telling you, but I figure you need some cheering up. And so you'll know, people believe in you even if you were dumb enough to think some white folks would publish a book on how to help niggers. In the immortal words of Richard Pryor, if you dreamed some sh—something like that, you need to wake up and apologize."

"So you and Genna just decided I'm going to pitch this to the parents," she said ignoring his jab at her.

"How 'bout, 'Josh I think it's a great idea'?"

"Okay, Josh, I think it's a great idea. Now, once again, you two decided I'm going to pitch this?"

"Who else? It's your idea, Miss 'invest black, sell mainstream.' We're just putting your ideas into action. I mean, how else are we going to get rid of affirmative action?"

"Okay, you get some points for that one."

"That's what I'm talking about!"

"Don't get any ideas. You have to work hard to get a piece of the pie."

"Pie? You got some pie?"

"No you didn't!" *I never thought I would be laughing like this right now.*

"Yeah, Paladin. We really do want to do the IGFAW thing, though."

They talked for two more hours. He asked what took her to San Antonio. Didn't figure it was his business. She told him she was at a conference. She described every detail of the Alamo to him, surprised at his interest in it. They agreed to meet for church the following Sunday. She threw the letter in the trash on her way down the hall to bed after she got off the phone. Or rather, she threw it *at* the trash. *I'll get it in the morning. What a weekend!*

Chapter 3

Polaris

Josh tapped two breath mints out of their container. He popped them in his mouth and lit a cigarette. Sitting here in the darkness, he mulled over his conversation with Adrienne. Shaun would get a big kick out of seeing him walk through the doors of his church next week. *I must really like you.* He was worried about her. They barely knew each other, but he could sense sadness in her spirit. It was like looking in the mirror. But church, he could already hear Genna and Faith laughing.

He got up and went outside. Standing on his front walkway, he stared up at the night. He wondered where Polaris twinkled in the March sky. He walked down to the courtyard and looked to the northeast. Clouds obscured his view of the North Star. He sighed.

He thought of slaves traversing the Underground Railroad using Polaris as their guide, moving ever northward toward freedom. On nights like tonight, after binging on cocaine, he sought out Polaris, seeking guidance to a north where he could live free of his demons. He'd broken another pipe this morning. He couldn't go to sleep because it kept calling him—*Josh, Josh*—demanding to be fed. He'd broken several these last few months, suspecting their incessant cries in the night fueled his cravings for his mistress.

It had been rough all day. No matter how much cocaine he smoked lately, it was never enough. Shattering the Pyrex cylinder did no good; his unsatisfied cravings continued unabated.

It was in this frame he conceded to his hankering to hear Adrienne's voice. When her answering machine clicked on, he felt a powerful urge to smoke rise within. Her voice interrupting the message was a relief. Their conversation quelled the urge. He enjoyed their bantering, finding himself quoting the Bible to her. *Get a grip, Jay.*

He thought about the night of the program. The Mariner had taken them to dinner at The Sun Dial afterward. Genna, Daniel, Aaron, Adrienne, Josh, and the Mariner had all broken bread together. Adrienne ordered escargot and invited Josh to share. Aaron had asked "What's escargot?" When Adrienne had replied—snails—Aaron had gasped.

"Snails? Damn, Mr. Josh, you gonna eat those?" Josh had cut his eyes at Aaron, trying to calm him down.

Daniel had laughed and chimed in. "You want some, Aaron?"

"Man, that's some white-boy food," Aaron had blurted out.

Josh had been sitting between Adrienne and Aaron. He had patted him on his arm trying to quiet Aaron. The Mariner had signaled to their waiter and said to Aaron, "Food for white boys and Negroes with class," and ordered a plate for himself. Adrienne had snuck him a look of gratitude.

She had ignored Aaron the rest of dinner. Josh laughed at the memory of how hurt Aaron was after a while. She had gone into great detail with the Mariner about the calculus of assimilation. Aaron had tried to cut in several times seeking her attention, but she hadn't given him any more of an answer than a curt yes or no. Josh and Genna had smiled at each other.

Finally, Adrienne had turned to Aaron and asked him if he had seen what Len Bias had done earlier that day. Josh appreciated her for that. Aaron loved Len Bias. Said he was going to be the best player ever. Josh couldn't imagine anyone better than Jabbar, but Bias was his boy, too. He loved the way he stalked the court, soaring above, around, and over his opponents. She soon had Aaron deep in conversation. The Mariner had cracked him after dinner, saying, "Aaron, we're going to have to teach you some class, doc. Come on, I'll run you home and we can talk."

Adrienne had insisted on driving to dinner, so Josh and Aaron had ridden with her. After dinner, she had driven Josh back to Decatur, where they sat in the school's parking lot talking for hours. He got that nagging feeling of déjà vu again when they said had goodbye that night. Josh drifted back into the present. Polaris peeked out from behind the clouds, twinkling in the Georgia sky. *What a weekend.* Josh smiled and walked back up the steps.

Chapter 4

Helen the Miracle Worker

Josh heard the doorbell. He took a last look at the mirror. He couldn't believe he was going to church. He straightened his tie. The bell rang again. He rushed to the door to answer it.

When he opened the door, Adrienne stood there smiling, dressed in a simple black dress with a royal-blue sweater draped over her shoulders. "Hi," was all he could get out.

"You ready?"

"Ah, sure," Josh stammered.

"Well, sir, let's go then," she said as she turned to go down the stairs. Josh followed. She brought to mind Helen of Troy, the mythical face that launched a thousand ships. *I would have boarded one of those vessels if Helen had her cheekbones.* "Did you say something?" she asked as they hit the bottom of the stairs. Josh stammered no. *Damn, I was thinking out loud.*

He escorted her to the door, opening it for her. She got in and paused momentarily. She planted her left leg on the pavement, her dress hiked up far enough for him to get a good, long look at her thigh. She looked at him saying, "Why thank you, Mr. Gibson. You are such a gentleman. This is a nice complex. Have you lived here long?"

"Ah, about four years," he stammered again.

"You didn't show me this neighborhood when we did our tour."

"I didn't, did I?" he answered.

She gracefully lifted her leg, pulling it into the car, and leaned her head out, saying impatiently, "Ready?"

Josh muttered yeah and walked around to the passenger side. He hopped in the car. "You sure you don't want me to drive?"

"No, it's the least I could do."

"Okay, well go up the hill and make a right when you get to the end of the driveway."

Riding through the hills and inclines of Southwest Atlanta, silence cloaked their pilgrimage, only occasionally interrupted by Josh giving directions. He wondered how it would feel to sit in a pew again. He hadn't done so since Regina's funeral.

Shaun's church was a white brick building with a roof in bad need of repair. Once black, it was now graying like a late-afternoon winter sky. Here and there Josh noticed shingles struggling to maintain their coverage of the congregants sitting in the pews. He would have been fine in the back, but he followed Adrienne to a seat on the third row.

The choir began to sing "Pass Me Not, O Gentle Savior" right after they were seated, and memories of going to church with Regina during the dark days after Genna's accident flowed into his mind. Church had provided a salve for his aching heart as he worried about his baby sister and whether she would lose her leg. He had prayed and prayed for her to keep it. And she had. He had believed in God strongly in those days. Later, life would cause his faith to shrivel. Anger would fill the void.

She sang along, unconcerned about her inability to carry a tune. She was a terrible singer. He laughed at her. She elbowed him as if she knew he was laughing at her voice, but she kept right on, undaunted by his chuckles.

Shaun entered, taking his place in the pulpit. Josh saw a gleam of recognition in Shaun's eyes as he prepared to lead the service. Genna and family slid in beside them. She and Adrienne exchanged glances as she settled in. Genna placed her hand on her heart and whispered to Adrienne, "It's a miracle." Josh pretended to ignore them.

Shaun gave a powerful sermon about the need to be a good and faithful servant. He preached about how too often people asked what God would do for them instead of asking what they could do for God. Adrienne bounced up and down on the pew, clapping and saying amen as Shaun went on about the importance of faith in the face of adversity, belief in a better day no matter what sorrow this day brought. Watching her, he felt a tug in his heart. *Where have you been all my life?*

Shaun told them as good Christians, their duty was not to judge but to love, saying the God he served didn't make mistakes and that they needed to embrace his handiwork. Adrienne reached over and squeezed Josh's hand. He saw Genna look over at Adrienne's hand covering his, a look of approval on her face.

He closed by saying no matter what awful afflictions visited their lives, they needed to remember that no matter how many tears fell through the night, faith would bring joy in the morning. Josh shifted in his seat.

Finally, the service was over. Brittany and Larry gave him a hug, glad to see him at church. Daniel looked at Adrienne and said, "I don't know how you got him here, but let me shake your hand."

Genna said, "Soror, you just don't know." She looked at Josh and said, "You know Momma's somewhere grinning, right?" Adrienne smiled and looked at Josh.

Shaun popped over. "Jay Gibson, my brother. Now this is a sight that brings joy to my morning." He reached over and shook Josh's hand. "And who is this young lady doing the Lord's work getting you through the doors of a church?" Josh introduced them. He held Adrienne's hand in his hands, repeating Genna's refrain. "You are a miracle worker."

They chatted for a few more minutes and it was time to go. On the way back home, he asked her, "So how do you reconcile this loving God with what has happened to our people? Don't you think God has fucked us over?" Anger surged in his voice.

She looked at him out of the corner of her eye. "Josh, you know what your problem is? You want to make God your size. I don't want a God I spell with a little *g*. I worship a big-G God. And I admit it isn't always easy, but listening to you, I'm glad I made that choice. And faith is a choice."

"You didn't answer my question," he replied, exasperation creeping into his voice.

"Not that I think it will do any good, but your problem is you can't conceive of something bigger than you. There's a lot of bad in this world, but it's like my Uncle Howard told me when my brother died. You can't understand the mind of God because yours isn't big enough. He reminded me all of us come into this world kicking and screaming, expelled from the comfort of our mother's womb. He told me he never met anyone who wanted to go back, and maybe death's like that. Maybe it's the better part of our journey. No matter what you suffer through in this world, accept God knows best and, more importantly, He knows the other side of what comes after life."

"That's bullshit."

"I'm not trying to change your mind. And why are you so angry?"

Josh looked out the window. "I'm going to tell you something. You'll probably put me out the car, but I'm going to tell you anyway." He felt the car slow. She swung into Adams Park, cruising past the pond at the entrance around to the swimming pool before parking. She cut the car off and turned her head, facing him.

"Okay, I'm listening."

The tone in her voice almost made him lose his nerve. "I don't know, maybe I shouldn't tell you." She leaned over looked him in the eye and smiled. "What?" he asked.

Suddenly he knew where he knew her from. For a moment, he was back in Keem's kitchen that night somewhere in the seventies, sitting in a chair, pulling on a pipe and trying to get it. He'd tried freebasing three or four times before that night without any luck. Keem kept telling him he was pulling the dope wrong. He could hear Keem saying, "Think up, Jay, you got to think up, man." Black-assed Shine was standing there hectoring for a bump.

"Man, Keem, that nigger can't hit that shit. Let me git one, man."

Keem had ignored him, saying, "Think up, Jay, think up." Finally, he stopped pulling, not really feeling anything.

He lied and told Keem, "I got it, man."

Keem shook his head. "Let Shine git one and then we gonna git this shit right, Jay." Shine sat down and took a turn. As he blew the smoke out, the force of the hit made him quiver.

"Come on, Jay. Your turn, man." Josh sat in the chair again. Keem put up a bomb hit. Josh pulled, thinking up. Suddenly, a cocaine-laced warhead detonated his mind.

He trembled from the power of the high. His eyes felt like they were trying to jump out of their sockets.

"Shit, Keem that nigger got that motherfucker. Look at him, man. It fucked him up!"

Keem nodded. "Yeah, you got that, Jay."

They hit for hours. No drug he'd ever tried hit him like this, and he'd had them all. After a while, he started to feel paranoid. He went in the next room and sat at the dining room table. It was dark. Soothing. Suddenly a girl was sitting across from him. *Where did you come from?* He remembered thinking. She was pretty, with long brown hair falling to her shoulders. She smiled at him. He couldn't quite make out her face. He felt her saying everything would be all right. Then she was gone, or at least until this moment; because Adrienne was the girl who had been sitting with him at the table that long-ago night. She leaned over toward him the same way.

He babbled. "Look, slim, I smoke cocaine, okay? A lot of cocaine." Wordlessly, she stared at him. "I have for a long time. A few years ago I was with a friend of mine we call Big Dad. Dad and I were trying to buy a quarter ounce. The guy we usually copped from was out of place. So we got with this girl named Keisha. She hooked us up.

"I shoulda known something was wrong 'cause she let us taste some out of a try bag, but she wouldn't let me taste the bag she sold us. She sold us a quarter of bullshit, some flour. That was crazy. I mean, she should have known better. So we went and made three Molotov cocktails. We took 'em back to her crib. I snuck up to the front of the house she was renting, lit them, and threw 'em through her front window. The house went up like some newspaper soaked in lighter fluid." He hesitated and looked out the window again, sure this would be the end of their friendship.

But something insisted he unburden himself to her, probably the recognition of that long-ago premonition come to life.

"I figured nobody could live in that fire. We took off. I felt bad, but in the streets I run there's a saying—you got to be true to the game. She lied to the game, and that's the price you pay."

"Are you saying you killed her and you don't care?" Adrienne responded, anger in her voice.

He stared straight ahead, looking out the windshield to the pond he used to love hanging around when he was a teenager. "I guess I am, but that's neither here nor there."

"What?" she snapped.

"Yeah, I called my boy Slim the next morning. He came on and said, 'Man, did you hear about Keisha and her kids?' I was like, 'Kids? They were over at her mother's, Slim.' 'Nah, man, she must have got 'em 'cause somebody torched the three of them last night.' He told me they were all dead. I told him what happened. He tried to make me feel better saying she should have known better."

"Oh, Josh."

"Yeah, I murdered those children. I still can't believe it. I can hardly live with myself. I have nightmares about it all the time. Sometimes I wish I was dead. And if I could trade my life for theirs, I would." He clasped his hands together, staring down at them, embarrassed by what he'd told her.

They sat in silence for a long while. Finally, she started the car. Aretha Franklin came on the radio singing "I Say a Little Prayer." She unbuckled her seatbelt, leaned over, and hugged him. "I'm sorry. I am so sorry." She drove him home. In his mind he revisited the many nights he'd sat in his living room, .38 in hand, trying to work up the nerve to put it in his mouth and pull the trigger. Today he was glad he'd given the gun to Dad.

She parked. "So you really have done some evil shit." Her words stung, but the sadness in her eyes hinted she felt sorry for him. He could only nod his head. "I'm going to my Aunt Leah's for dinner. Are you going to be all right?"

"I'll be okay," he told her, getting out and making the long walk up the steps.

Chapter 5

Miss Fix-It

Aunt Leah answered the door. Adrienne walked in and gave her a hug. "So how'd you enjoy service? You think you found you a church home?"

Adrienne smiled down at her. "Yes ma'am."

"Hey, baby girl. How you doing?"

"Hey, Uncle Howard," Adrienne squealed. Her aunt and uncle were quite the handsome couple. Aunt Leah was about four ten; the color of good dirt. Uncle Howard was a six-foot-two alabaster brother. His wavy hair signified the Confederate general's blood mingled in with his slave and former slave ancestors.

"Yeah, Aunt Leah, I really enjoyed service. I think I'm going back. Maybe I can get you to come with me," Adrienne teased, knowing her aunt was firmly AME.

"So did you go with Josh?"

"Yes ma'am."

"You should have brought him to dinner."

"He wasn't feeling well."

"That's too bad. He probably needs a good meal. Howard, Adrienne's dating Lawrence and Regina Gibson's son. You remember him. Josh?"

"I think I do."

Adrienne cut in. "I am not dating him, Aunt Leah. He just told me he knew where a good church is. So we went together, that's all."

"Sounds like something's up. Y'all going to church together," Uncle Howard said.

Adrienne frowned slightly, answering, "No, Uncle Howard. I mean, he's okay, but I don't know about dating him."

Uncle Howard looked at her. "Okay, whatever you say. But do I need to call Alonso? He told us to watch over you."

"Come on, help me set the table, baby." Aunt Leah beckoned for Adrienne to follow her. Uncle Howard went into the family room and sat down to watch television.

Soon they were sitting together eating. They gossiped about the goings-on in their lives. Aunt Leah served ice cream for dessert—black walnut, which she knew was her niece's favorite. After dessert, she and Aunt Leah cleaned the table and moved to the kitchen to finish cleaning up. Uncle Howard went back to his television.

"So who is this girl Sue your cousin keeps talking about?"

"Not Sue, Aunt Leah, it's Minsook. She's Korean."

"Lord, he always did like those yellow girls." They both cracked up. "I guess he got it honest 'cause I love me some yellow boys." She placed her left hand on her lips, raised her eyebrows, and looked around the corner at Uncle Howard. Adrienne laughed again.

"I told him you wouldn't mind."

"Well, I'd rather he dated black women. Lord, that's my child, but he's a little odd. I don't know how the sister girls take him."

"Jewel always liked him."

"She did. Well, at least Sue ain't white."

"He said you'd say that. And it's Minsook, Auntie."

Aunt Leah pulled on a cigarette. "I suppose the good Lord says you should forgive. But baby, I can't forget the look on that man's face back in Mississippi. I try to forgive, but I don't want my sons bringing a white girl home."

Aunt Leah had grown up in Chicago. She had been born in a small Mississippi town. Her family had moved when she was nine or ten after a local man was lynched for what she always called the crime of being a Negro. What stuck with her was the look on his face. She'd said his lifeless eyes seemed to be asking, "Why y'all do this to me?" Adrienne could never get used to how many black families had a story like that in their past. She thought about Josh's grandfather.

"Yeah, I guess the good Lord does say you have to forgive." Adrienne said.

"So what's on your mind, baby?"

"Oh, I was thinking about something Josh told me. You were right. He does use drugs."

"Wash those dishes for me, baby. He told you that?"

"Yes ma'am." Adrienne ran the dishwater.

"You sure y'all not dating?"

"No, Aunt Leah. He's had a rough life. I feel sorry for him."

"Well, at least you didn't say you got a boyfriend. How is old Arrogant Ass?"

"He's okay. I broke up with him last Sunday night."

"Thank you, Jesus," Leah said punctuating her words with an exaggerated look skyward. "What happened?"

"I realized you and Daddy were right. We aren't on the same path."

"You sure Mr. Gibson doesn't have anything to do with this?"

"No, Aunt Leah. We're friends."

"And y'all going to church together."

Adrienne playfully reproached her aunt. "*No*, Aunt Leah. Plus, he needs the good Lord."

"Adrienne, you remember something for me, okay?"

"What's that?"

"Baby, I know you. You see something broken, you want to fix it. I remember that time you brought home that bird with the broken wing at Ada Mae's. I can still hear you fussing because we wouldn't let you take care of it. It's hard to fix a grown man."

"Yes ma'am."

"Be careful washing those dishes. You're spilling water on yourself."

Chapter 6

Gravity

Josh and Adrienne's friendship blossomed. She was constantly spending time at the school. They talked on the phone for hours. But she would not let him visit her or drive her anywhere. They ate lunch together once or twice a week. Spots like This is It or The Beautiful Restaurant or, on occasion, downtown somewhere, like Dailey's.

She invited him to meet her at Vickery's one Friday afternoon after class for dinner. She wanted to talk over her coming presentation at their end-of-year program. Anxious about what to say, she wanted to get feedback from Josh. She knew she wanted to take this chance to explain to parents the strong need for black organizations. Working at a black college and consulting with a black school reinforced what she had learned in her great-aunt and uncle's store as a girl. What she had seen in the Jew Man's store during summers when she visited Atlanta. What she saw in Hyung-Ju's store whenever she visited.

People who controlled their own destiny were better off in America. They had talked several times about the tiredness of the ideas of black conservatives. How they were parrots incapable of developing original ideas that might better the black community. Instead, all they did was mimic white conservatives who argued for equality of opportunity or that racism no longer existed. And though she could not bring herself to believe racism was black people's primary problem, she could also see racism was like gravity. She told Josh one night on the phone there were four elemental forces in the universe—the strong force, the weak force, the electromagnetic force, and gravity.

Surprisingly, gravity was the weakest of the four. It was the most influential not because of its strength, but because it was it was everywhere and it was always attractive. Racism—or as she preferred, the racial discount on black people's humanity—was similar in that it was everywhere in American society, and it always attached itself to black people. Oh, some places it might not be as strong as it was in others, but it was always there. So it held enormous influence over black life.

The strong force was like education. The better educated you were, the better your chances. The Yale professor had convinced her of that. And that black people were better off not going to Yale, because the gravitational pull there was frighteningly powerful. She noticed how the black people at New Haven were made to feel insecure about their intellectual right to be there, no matter how educated they were. Yet black conservatives refused to even picture HBCUs as a vehicle for the pursuit of black learning. They were too drawn to white supremacy. Reggie had always been uncomfortable with these discussions; her ballplayer, unconcerned, since either way, he was getting paid. But Josh egged her on.

The weak force was like experience in the workplace. Even though the argument by political hacks, including black conservatives, was that blacks were given jobs they weren't qualified for, her own life had taught her that black people in the real world needed better qualifications. Because who wanted to be seen hiring a black person who failed? Even Reggie struggled with the idea of how his credentials would not open the same doors. The ballplayer, like the Irish athletes of their assimilation era, benefited from a reverse stereotyping where everybody wanted a buck on their team because they were so damned good at playing ball.

The electromagnetic force she likened to personality. Some people were simply more likable than others. But racism forced black people to work so much harder at appearing likeable. Black people couldn't appear angry. Black people couldn't be too aggressive.

Josh told her she had come up with a missile that would allow black people to propel themselves out of the grasp of racism's influence. She appreciated him for that. He told her she'd made him realize affirmative action promoted white supremacy with its inference that black people were incapable of progressing without access to white institutions. That it was a solution created for a time when law-based discrimination was the norm. It actually slowed the change in attitudes needed for black people to achieve equality.

She complained of her frustration with black conservatives and why they didn't argue for black business formation or, better yet, start black businesses, or why they would not seek to fund HBCUs and promote them as a better alternative to matriculation at white schools. Because, he shot back, they were white supremacists, so it would never occur to them to promote black organizations as a better choice.

They agreed in a changing America, HBCUs would have to change with the times. She pointed out Catholic schools like Notre Dame had successfully transitioned into nationally recognized centers of higher learning as Catholics of various ethnic backgrounds reached full assimilation. Reggie had never listened, so he could not make her laugh at her frustrations like Josh. She still asked herself in the dark of night before she drifted off to sleep how she was able to overlook his violent past. She considered what Aunt Leah had said about her liking to fix what she saw as broken.

Chapter 7

Lenox Road

Josh watched her striding down Crescent Avenue. She was always late when they got together. And he always enjoyed watching her walk. On the balls of her feet, eyes straight ahead, head held high like she was on a mission. She burst through the door. Seeing him at the bar, she walked over waving, "Hi, Mr. Gibson, how are you?"

"What's up, Miss Johnson?" Today she walked right into his arms, giving him a big hug. "Boy, we're in a good mood. Something good happen?"

"Not really, nothing other than it's a pretty day and the weekend's here."

The waitress led them out on the porch. They talked for a few minutes. Then the waitress came back to take their order. They ate and talked and talked and ate until it was almost seven o'clock. She looked at her watch. "I guess I'd better be going."

"You know, we never did discuss the program," Josh reminded her.

"Well, call me later."

"Do you have to go?"

"I've got papers to grade."

"You always have papers to grade."

"Duty calls."

"Damn, don't answer."

She smiled and got up. "Come on, walk me to the car." She opened her pocketbook and pulled out her purse. "I'll pay today. You always do. It's my turn." She placed $25 on the table and beckoned for him to come with her. They walked down the street together.

"Hey," Josh said. "If it's your turn to pay, then let's take a ride. It's my turn to drive."

"Where are we going?"

"How about clubbing? We can have a couple of drinks. You can still get home early and then I'll call you."

"Josh, you don't need to drink and drive."

"Why not?"

"It's against the law, that's why."

"Only if you get caught. Come on, ride with me."

"I don't think so," she replied. By now they were standing next to her car. Josh was parked about half a block down the street.

"Come on, hop in. I'll drop you at your car." He came around and opened the door for her, always angling to catch a flash of those beautiful legs of hers. She slipped in quickly, depriving him of even a fleeting glance. Disappointed, he walked around and got in.

"You got the whole weekend to grade those papers."

She smiled at him. "I don't know, I got a lot of papers."

"Just give 'em all an A and be done with it."

"Why?"

"'Cause I want to spend some more time with you, that's why. I like you."

"Well, I guess the papers can wait a little while longer. I'm sure my classes would appreciate your suggestion, but I wouldn't deny them the pleasure of knowing how well they did."

He saw the outline of her thighs pressing against her skirt, entranced by how big and firm her legs were, seemingly pushing right through the fabric to say, *Hello Josh, how you doing?* He wanted to ask her if they could come out to play.

"You want to come over to my apartment for a little while? We can talk there. I'm sure my roommate won't mind."

"Sounds like a plan. I'll follow you over there. Buckhead, right?"

She cranked her car up, pulling off the curve and heading down the street right past his jalopy. She kept going driving out onto West Peachtree. "You passed my car!"

"I know."

She kept riding, turning onto 17th Street, heading on to I-85. She looked at him out the corner of her eye as she gunned the engine. He wasn't sure what to make of this, but he guessed he'd roll with it.

"I'm kidnapping you," she said in a husky voice.

"Okaaaay," was all he could get out.

"Actually, Genna told me never to ride with you, or at least not until November. Something about your license being suspended for a year. Should I even ask you if that's true? Or were we just gonna ride out and get arrested together? I guess that's your idea of a good time, huh?"

"Well shit, if you knew, why you didn't just say so? Instead bullshittin' me around like you didn't know!"

"Wait a minute! Don't talk to me like that. You know you're wrong. Acting like a little kid . . . I don't know who you think I am, but you don't talk to me any kind of way!" Her voice seemed to rise another decibel with every word. Her eyes were blazing. "I don't want to go to jail! And I don't want you locked up, either. At least not until I get the rest of my money!"

It was time for them to split their sides laughing. She was still laughing as she pulled off the Buford Highway exit and headed toward Lenox Road. She sure could whip this car. He liked the way she handled him, first setting him up with the kidnapping crack, then blasting him, and finally making a crack about their developing business relationship. He was going to get Genna for telling though. He hated snitches, even if they were his little sister.

"And don't get mad at Genna. She's only trying to look out for her big brother."

"Damn, what else did she tell you about me?"

"I can't tell you that. It's our little secret. It's a girl thing!"

"I got your girl thing!" He looked over at her and smiled. She was smiling too, eyes on the road. He wanted to reach over and kiss her, but wasn't sure how she would react. He just looked at her again.

"Is it anything else I need to know?" she asked.

"Well, I smoke like a chimney. I want six kids. Hell, I want to rule the world."

"She told me you smoke. She didn't have to, though. I can smell the smoke on your clothes. Besides, you got a pack of cigarettes in your shirt pocket. I can't believe you smoke so much, though. One of my brothers smokes a pack a day, and he can't go an hour without a cigarette. And let me see . . . that's right, you smoke cocaine."

Rattled, he could only say, "Yeah, I do."

"What about the kids?"

For a moment he thought she was talking about Keisha's brood. Then he realized she was talking about the school. "What about 'em?" He sounded a little more annoyed than he wanted to let on.

"Genna says they love you. Don't you care about how they would feel about you getting high? I mean, it is illegal. You take your name serious, huh?"

"They'll never know. I only get high on the weekends. You're right, though. I do worry about what they would think."

She'd struck a nerve asking about his kids. Sometimes he'd get really depressed about how fucked up it would be if word ever got about the skeletons rattling around in his closet. He used to be pretty sure he could control his hitting. Lately, he wasn't so positive.

"Why don't you stop?" She eased out the words really gently, a whisper, but they resonated. "I mean, I can't say I understand since I never really took to getting that kind of high. I understand you got a good thing going with that school, though. Genna and the couple who introduced us raved about you, how you could get up and have those kids hanging on your every word, how everybody calls you the 'pied piper' 'cause those kids will follow you anywhere. That's a gift from God and you shouldn't fritter it away—how do you say it—hitting."

He wanted to say *Fuck God*, but he let it ride. He knew she'd find a way to turn it on him. She had already ruined his plans to get high later on tonight. She might have him in church again on Sunday if he let fly with that comment. He watched Lenox Road breeze by, reminiscing about how it used to be a quiet, tree-lined street before developers ruined it with all the apartments they were throwing up.

"I'm not sure I can." *Where the hell did that come from?* "I'm going to cut back though; you saying I'm going to be dead at thirty-five from partying?"

She smiled like she was enjoying some private joke. Darkness started to pull a curtain in front of the setting sun, bringing a chill to the air. She was even prettier in the ballet being played out between the dying sunlight and the inexorable march of darkness. The glint of the sunlight's remains lit up her face even as the darkness shadowed her dark, wavy hair.

"I'm hoping you'll live," she paused before completing her thought, "a long, full life."

They rode in silence up to Peachtree, where she turned right at the light, heading in the direction of Oglethorpe College. A vision of Guy Lafleur gliding down the ice toward some Stanley Cup glory flashed through his mind. They rolled through another traffic light and turned into a complex. She pulled around to the back. "Well, here we are, Mr. Gibson."

They were at her apartment. When they reached her door, she asked him to wait outside for a second while she checked to see if her roommate was decent. She came back and signaled for him to come in. He could swear she had a funny look on her face. They walked through the living room into the kitchen, where she invited him to have a seat at the table.

"I have to return a phone call. Make yourself at home. I'll be back in a few minutes. Oh, hold on a sec." She opened a cabinet and produced an ashtray. She sat it on the table. "Just in case you want to take a smoke. Only one, though. And cigarettes only! I'll be back."

She's a handful, he chuckled to himself. He figured it had to be a guy she was calling, judging from the way she was making him all comfy. He was surprised she had an ashtray. He was sure she didn't smoke. Did her roommate smoke? But then the ashtray would have been out on the table already. Somebody here was considerate. He sat there for what seemed like thirty minutes before she bent around the corner. Her roommate never did come out.

"Sorry to keep you waiting."

"That's okay," he replied. He reached over and patted her hand in reassurance. Just then, he heard house shoes shuffling on the floor. It was her roommate. Adrienne introduced them. Her roommate's name was Michelle. They were friends from college—line sisters, in fact.

He couldn't resist a crack about how Deltas were the superior sorority.

"Who?" Adrienne replied.

Her and her roommate reached over the table and high-fived.

"1908, that year was great. I'm going to have to work with you. You don't have any manners or taste."

"Girl, why are you fooling with him?" Michelle cracked.

"Do I know you?" he shot back.

"His sister's a soror. Otherwise, Chelle, I don't know. He's a Morehouse man, too, so you just know he's full of himself."

"Oh, so you took Morehouse 101?"

"What is Morehouse 101?"

"You know, that class in arrogance all y'all take. How you say it . . . 'I'm a Morehouse man.'" Michelle stepped back from the table and stuck her chest and chin out.

He laughed and said, "You got me confused with some of those other brothers. I ain't like that. Besides, I don't need Morehouse to be arrogant. Just being myself is reason enough for me."

"You hear him, don't you, girl? You sound like you might have had a double dose,"

Michelle cracked.

"I guess I can't help but feel superior to a Fiskite. I mean, we did close y'all's football program down."

Adrienne jumped in, "What do you mean, you closed our football program down?"

He got all dramatic for this next bit of commentary, doing his best Grantland Rice imitation. "It was a cold, gray November day in the early eighties when the Fisk eleven took the field against what must have seemed like the Morehouse eleven hundred. Charging across the field at Lakewood Stadium, the men of Morehouse visited upon the blue-and-gold-clad invaders like some biblical plague. Fans who saw the tragedy would ask later, 'Was that Attila and his Huns? Had Genghis Khan and his Mongol hordes resurfaced?' Charging across the plains of Lakewood to rout the Bulldogs fifty-nine to nothing, it was a horde all right—a horde of maroon-and-white-clad tigers who had laid waste to the brave but overwhelmed troops from Nashville."

"Girl, no he didn't!" Michelle whooped.

"Ah, excuse you, do I need to let you see my MARTA schedule?" Adrienne cracked.

"You mean you ain't driving and got the nerve to come in here talking that kind of trash? You all right, Josh Gibson, but my girl is serious about that bus schedule. It's a stop right down the block. Adrienne, let me go get ready." She laughed and shook her head as she went back in the back.

"Let me put my ashtray up. Here I am trying to be nice, and you step up in my apartment talking trash!" She grabbed the ashtray off the table and put it right back in the cabinet. "MARTA stops running about twelve, I believe. You hurry up and you can probably catch a bus in the next couple of minutes."

After Michelle left, they talked all night. She teased him again about dropping him at the bus stop before running him downtown to his car.

Chapter 8

Sarah Smith

"Hand me that bucket of nails, Josh," Faith said over her shoulder.

"Here you go," Josh responded, placing the bucket in Faith's hand.

"You sure are hanging out with your girl a lot these days."

Josh turned his back to wipe some mud on the wall he was sheet rocking. "Who, Ramona?" *Whap*, Faith slapped him on the back of his head. Josh laughed, not bothering to rub his stinging head.

Faith chuckled. "You know who I'm talking about."

"We hang out some. She's cool."

"Cool, huh. And what about Sarah?

Josh frowned. "Sarah's okay. We talked Thursday night. Her and ole Felton seem to be doing real well."

"Wait a minute. What did you call her—Sarah? You mean she isn't the esteemed Miss Smith or the black girl with the white name? Ain't that nothing."

"The hell you talking 'bout, Faith? That's her name, ain't it?"

"Look at me, Tin Man." Josh turned to face her. "Now, you the one who never called the girl by her name. Everybody else was fine with Sarah. It was you who came up with a new nickname for her every week. And what was your favorite? Oh yeah, that damn Sarah. But now she's just plain Sarah."

He threw his hands up. "What? I still care about her. She moved on. She found somebody who treats her right. I love her, Faith. What's wrong with me wanting her to be happy? And since she's seeing somebody else, I think a little more informality is in order."

"Josh Gibson, you ain't shit. And this new girl, what's her name again?"

"You talking about Kate?"

"See, there you go. Let me git your oil can."

"Why you always say that?"

"Tin Man, if I told you once, I told you a thousand times. You ain't got no heart. You don't bleed blood. You bleed oil. And this new girl's got you squeaking."

"Just 'cause I called her Kate?"

"Josh, what's the girl's name?"

"That's for me to know and you to find out."

"Can't say her name, can you?"

"And I was going to invite you to a program we're having at the school. Give you a chance to meet her."

"When, Josh?"

"In a couple of weeks. It's for the end of school. We figured we'd introduce her to the parents."

"You let me know. I sure want to meet Sister Kate. Anybody who can make you forget Sarah must be something else."

"I haven't forgotten her, Faith."

"After while, after while. But Genna says you might have met your match this time."

"You and Hopalong can kiss my ass."

"Lean over so I can oil you, Tin Man."

Chapter 9

Have You Eaten Today?

"Hey, Minsook. Hey, Hyung-Ju," Adrienne called out to them as they walked through the door of the store. Minsook looked at Chicken Wing, smiled, and flapped her arm.

"Hi, Chicken Wing," she said, smiling slightly.

Chicken Wing bobbed his head up and down saying, "I'm going to get you, Adrienne. Every time I come in here now, she flaps her arm like that."

Adrienne shrugged. "What did I do?"

"You know what you did."

Adrienne played him off, asking for a pickle. She knew he secretly got a kick out of Minsook flapping her arm. Hyung-Ju greeted her with "Have you eaten today?"

Adrienne smiled at him, flattered by what he said. "Yes I have, Hyung-Ju, and how about you?" He nodded.

Hyung-Ju had told her things were so bad in Korea after the war when he was growing up it was customary to greet people by asking if they had eaten today. Food was that scarce. So she took it as a great honor he would greet her in this way. Hyung-Ju had also given her a bookmark made from a piece of Korean paper money sealed inside a sheet of plastic. The bill showed a Korean man in what appeared to be a royal gown.

"How's Aaron?" he asked.

"He's doing fine, Hyung-Ju. I'll bring him by next week." They were an odd pair, the Korean man with daughters but no sons and the young black man with a mother but no father, but they had hit it off immediately. She brought Aaron by every Tuesday. Hyung-Ju wanted him to work in the store when school ended.

"So, Hyung-Ju, I want Minsook to come to a program at the school Aaron attends. Would it be okay?"

Hyung-Ju looked at Chicken Wing and then at Minsook. He considered her request for a moment. "Of course, I know it means a lot to you."

"Thank you, Hyung-Ju. Minsook, would you like to come? I need the moral support. And I want to use the store as an example." Minsook nodded. "Hyung-Ju, you can come too if you want." Hyung-Ju politely turned her down. Adrienne knew he would not leave the store. It was his duty to his customers and to his family. She sensed he preferred a world where he could greet people with a simple hello.

Chapter 10

Guy LaFleur

Genna surveyed the conference room. She made sure every chair was lined up just so. It was rare that anything at EDCO met her exacting standards, but Saturday, May eighteenth, was proving to be the rare day she could be pleased with how everything was going. Well, almost everything.

"Come here, Aaron. You look good, sweetie, but let Miss Genna straighten your tie." She pulled it tight, accenting the dimple which matched the ones in his cheeks.

"Thanks, Miss Genna," he said.

"Did Miss Adrienne tell you Hyung-Ju changed his mind and said he'd come?"

"Yes ma'am, she did." Hyung-Ju was coming with Minsook. He was leaving the store with his wife and youngest daughter. It meant a lot to Aaron. Somehow, Adrienne had convinced him to come. Genna watched her walk in the room. Adrienne didn't see her, so Genna watched her for a moment. She sure was glad this soror had popped into their lives. Adrienne was the finishing touch the school, Aaron, and, most of all, Josh had needed. Genna could tell by the way she stood with her hands clasped in front of her skirt that Adrienne was nervous. Her aunt and uncle were coming along with

CW. Genna knew she wanted to do well in front of her family. Adrienne's eyes were wandering around the room.

Genna had sent Josh to the store so he wouldn't be here when Adrienne arrived. She wanted her to miss him. Josh hadn't come to work drunk once in the past five months. Genna suspected his friendship with Adrienne had a lot to do with it. Sure, he still drank at night, but this was a good start. Uncle James had commented earlier on how Josh was doing a lot better. Even Aaron had noticed a change. She still held her breath and prayed. It was good to see him happy again.

For three years, this school had been educating colored folks. Uncle James had told her a few minutes ago how proud he was of them. He told her they were too young to realize there was no way a black private school could work this well, which was why they had done such a fantastic job. He had told her he was glad she didn't have to carry Josh so much anymore.

Genna looked down at her flats and smiled. "Adrienne," she called out, "Hey, girl, how you doing?"

Adrienne walked over to her and they hugged. "I'm scared," Adrienne whispered, holding her hand up with her fingers crossed.

Genna laughed. "You'll be okay." Adrienne's eyes searched the room again. Genna said, "Josh will be here in a minute. I sent him to the store. When are you bringing him back to church?"

"Hey, Miss Adrienne," Aaron exclaimed, popping over to give her a hug. "You sure look nice tonight."

Adrienne told him, "So do you, sweetie. Miss Genna wants to know when I'm going to bring Mr. Josh back to church. I want you to help me with that cause."

"How, Miss Adrienne? You know how he is about church. You were lucky to get him there once."

"You'll see. Just play along when he comes in, okay?"

"Yes ma'am."

Genna watched Josh come into the room. He saw them and came over. She noticed Adrienne's face flush.

"Hey, Guy, what's up?"

"Lord, why are you calling her by a French man's name?" Genna asked.

Adrienne cut in. "Genna, girl, he has a hundred nicknames for me. One day I'm Kate, the next I'm Guy or Carter G. The one name he doesn't call me anymore is Adrienne."

"Well, I understand Carter G and I'm not going to touch Kate, but why Guy? I mean, like the ski pole?"

"Nah, Genna," Josh cut in, "Like Guy Lafleur, the hockey player for the Montreal Canadians. *Sports Illustrated* had an article about him called 'To Pick a Golden Flower.' The article said when the Canadians saw Lafleur, they knew he would be the cornerstone of their franchise. He was the rock on which five Stanley Cup championships were built. She's our golden flower, so I call her Guy. And we're going to build a championship franchise around her. Isn't that right, Guy?"

Adrienne shook her head, laughed, and said, "Genna, what am I going to do with him?" Adrienne glanced around the room, eying Aaron, who now stood talking to Ronald. She waved to him, catching his attention. Aaron walked back over to where they were standing. Adrienne looked at Josh and said, "Aaron's going to church with me next Sunday." Josh looked at Aaron, and Adrienne winked at Aaron. Genna laughed under her breath, already knowing what was coming next.

"How you gonna take him and not invite me? What's up with that, Aaron? When you start going to church anyway? Your own mother can't even get you to go. Where is Miss Mickey, anyway?"

"She's coming, Mr. Josh. I hadn't told her I'm going yet. I thought you could help me do that," Aaron said, a twinkle in his eye. At that moment, CW walked in with Minsook, Hyung-Ju, and his parents. Genna asked Aaron to help her get folks seated. The room was starting to fill.

Chapter 11

Put Five on It

Adrienne sat next to Josh, trying not to bite her lip too hard. Noticing her nervousness, he touched her hand. Genna was in the middle of introducing her to the gathering. There must have been close to one hundred and fifty people in the room, or at least enough that folks were nearly stacked on top of one another. But it wasn't the size of the crowd making her edgy. Standing in front of the lectern on a daily basis had made her comfortable talking to crowds. No, the problem was the people in the audience and how much some of them meant to her. This was the first time she had ever spoken to an audience containing her aunt and uncle. And she wondered how they would all react to what she had to say. Black people believed in the sacred cows she was about to slay, even if they were the wrong answers to the questions bedeviling their community. Ever since Norman, it only really boiled down to one question for her: Why don't we love each other? She wondered if this question mattered to the audience the way it did to her.

Oh well, show time. She got up, striding earnestly to the podium. She looked at Josh and almost burst out laughing at him sitting there, his face scrunched up like he was straining. *You are a fool.* He'd told her last night if she got nervous, she could look at him and pretend he was squatting in the woods taking a crap. She clasped the podium and thanked the audience for taking time out of their busy lives to hear what she proposed to add to the school's curriculum. Taking a deep breath, she got started.

"Josh and Genna asked me to talk to you for a few minutes tonight about a program they want to introduce next fall. I immediately agreed. It's a plan that touches my heart, and I hope when I'm finished, you will feel the same way. My only question was, why me? Josh informed me that like everybody else around here, I have to earn my keep." She smiled at him. "Genna, I don't know how you put up with him, girl." Genna smiled and nodded.

"Seriously, though, he told me I was the right person because I was the inspiration for this idea. And it would give me an opportunity to share with you why I want to incorporate my research into your children's curriculum. So if I can bore you for just a few minutes, I want to tell you about the school's plan to raise money for HBCUs. We are going to call it I Give Five a Week. What we are asking is for all our families to give five dollars a week. Aaron, would you please?"

Aaron walked up and handed her a five-dollar bill off a stack of papers. She discreetly placed it on the podium and waited as he handed each person a flyer outlining the program.

"I used to spend the summers here as a girl after my mother died. One of the great pleasures of my childhood was to work in my Great-Uncle Enoch and Great-Aunt Ada Mae's store in a little town an hour east of here. My aunt used to always tell me you have to make people feel comfortable giving you their money. Make 'em feel like they got something of value in return. So I'm going to try to make you see the value in our modest little plan.

"I'm sure at least some of you are asking, Why give my money to an HBCU? Isn't the time passing where we need our own schools? If my child can go to Harvard, is Hampton really good enough? If Stanford beckons, I reckon I don't really need to consider Fisk; if Sarah Lawrence wants my daughter, is Spelman the right call? Well, that's your decision. But I still ask you to support our schools.

"We forget our history too easily. We forget the March on Washington commemorated the one-hundredth anniversary of the Emancipation Proclamation. How our parents and grandparents knew the one hundred years of affliction we endured following slavery continued to deny us our birthright as citizens of this great country. The people who stood in DC that sweltering August day in '63 knew segregation, not slavery, was our problem at that point in time.

"I think of the civil rights movement as the black journey across the ocean to America. Our circumstances up to that moment were unique to us and the Native Americans. What we confront now is a generic process called Americanization, where we make the transition from black people to black Americans to Americans of black descent to Americans.

"There's an old fable about the wind and the sun. They have a contest to see who can make a man coming up the street take his coat off in an attempt to prove who is stronger. The wind goes first and blows and blows and blows. The man pulls his coat closer and closer. The wind gives up. And the sun turns up the heat so high the man takes off his coat, his hat, and his shirt.

"We are the wind desperately seeking to blow away the racism in which mainstream America cloaks itself twenty-something years after the movement. We had to be the wind to blow away the dark clouds of slavery and segregation that cast a shadow of despair over us for so long. There was no choice. Social agitation and political activism were the winds of change required to complete our journey from *in* America to *of* America." She looked at Hyung-Ju, smiled, and continued.

"We need to be the sun."

"Who among us would choose to stand shivering in the wind when we could enjoy the warmth of the sun? Instead of blowing the ill winds of integration, we should recognize what we are doing is assimilating. The winds of controversy we sow when we foment for school busing and agitate for affirming discrimination programs cause mainstream America to wrap itself tighter in the cloak of racist attitudes.

"Why embrace the idea 'What's white is what's right, and if it's black, we need to throw it back'? And isn't that what we do when we insist on white jobs for ourselves, white schools for our kids, and white neighborhoods for our families? So we huff and puff and try to blow white supremacy down through political agitation and social activism. We need to be the sun.

"What's wrong with opening a black business? What's wrong with going to a black school? What's wrong with life in a black neighborhood? We need to feel supreme in our love of our blackness. We are of America as well as in America now and should consider a new approach. We have finished integrating ourselves into America. We need to assimilate. And we have to choose to do it right.

"Inadvertently, we chose the Irish path to assimilation. It works. Jack Kennedy and Ronald Reagan prove that the Irish are assimilated and accepted wholeheartedly by America. But the winds of political activism and social agitation they blew unto these shores broke down the

Irish family, it split the Irish community, and it led to an assimilation process that lasted over one hundred years.

"A great captain in our journey to America once talked of how one hundred years after emancipation, we remained an exile in our own home. Well, twenty-two years after the March on Washington, do we really want to choose the slowest path to full-fledged participation in America? We need to be the sun.

"Do we choose the Jewish path where we all come forward together in an efficient computation of the calculus of assimilation, where we plot a minimization curve that rapidly reduces our differences with the mainstream, or do we plot the Irish course, a course that leads to a decelerated pace of minimization; the costs being a breakdown in our family structure, a breaking up of our community, and far too many burials of our children? It's our choice. You can have the wind. I want to be the sun.

"Racism is a given. How we approach it is what we get to decide. Do we continue to be the wind? Do we continue to push for access to institutions who don't want us, or do we build our own? And if we feel racism is institutional, what better way to fight it than with our own institutions? It's an ill wind that never changes. I want to be the sun.

"I am afraid we forge a path where we leave our men no choice but to abandon their children. At one time in America, it was a cliché that an orphan was Irish. Do we want this to be what happens in our community? The Irish were the wind, and their men were stripped of their manhood. Any man wants to support his children. A poorly considered approach to oppression denies them that chance. History teaches us denied that opportunity he leaves. Our men need us to be the sun.

"While the Irish blew their winds of change through political activism and social agitation, Jewish people arrived here and chose a different path. They warmed the American spirit with their economic self-reliance followed by educational self-development. Is it better to, say, one day have a black president, or is it better to be prescient enough to change our present so our future is filled with black institutions where even mainstream America might want to join in? I prefer the Jewish path. You can have the winds of political controversy. I want to be the sun.

"I say we should invest in black institutions and black people, in that order. When John David Rockefeller, a business genius and the richest private citizen in the history of the world, decided he wanted to invest in our people, he invested in our educational institutions—not in individuals, in institutions, and if it was good enough for old JD, it's good enough for me."

She picked up the five-dollar bill and held it high.

"So I got five on it. And I will be the sun.

"The strengths we incorporated in our culture were needed to become a part of America. We must turn away from those strengths. They are the strength of the wind, and it is time we become the sun. We must shine brightly with the determination to be economically self-reliant. We need to revel in our blackness.

"Instead of being happy with being the first darkie attorney at Skadden Arps, instead of being satisfied with being the first coon accountant at IBM, we need to work on being the last—the last generation of black people to feel the deprivation of spirit, the impoverishment of psyche our people know too well.

"We need to build an IBM, not work for one. We need to partner with Skadden Arps, not try to make partner there. We don't need to send our daughters to the Seven Sisters to be sanitized; we need to send them to Spelman to find their soul. We don't need to send our children to Yale Law School to become doubting Thomases of their race; we need to send them to Howard Law School so they can become legal lions like Justice Thurgood Marshall.

"Because if those doubting Thomases and affirmative-action babies would take the time to just look in their hearts, deep inside, I'm sure they would find black is more, much more, than a color. It is a state of mind. Be black and be proud.

"And in my mind, being black has always been a reason to be proud. When I got to Fisk, I looked to my left and saw black achievers; I looked to my right and saw black achievers. I looked back into my past on that campus and saw black achievement. I looked forward toward my future on that campus and saw black achievement. Fisk taught me no matter what obstacles fell in my path, I could be an achiever, too. I take that back—I *would* be an achiever. This is the black America I grew up in.

"Yet we turn our backs on all that is good about black America, marking it as inferior, then wonder why mainstream America feels the same. Paschal's was where the civil rights movement ate breakfast. It is where black visitors to Atlanta looked forward to staying in the days before we could go to the Hilton. But now we're too good for the black hotel. We have to stay in the white one. We need to celebrate ourselves.

"Why do we have to go Princeton for affirmation? King was a Morehouse man, Marshall was a Howard man, DuBois was a Fisk man, and Washington was a Hampton and a Tuskegee man. Strong, principled, beautiful black men, the kind of man I as a black woman want to see more of. If HBCUs were good enough to produce these giants, why do we turn our backs on them? What's wrong with black Ivy? I got five on it.

"To be sure, all assimilating groups struggle through the process of Americanization, because it is simply the nature of America, but no group has a greater need for a rapid rate of assimilation than black people. We have suffered enough.

"Political agitation and social activism did the needed work of breaking the back of Jim Crow. But continuing on the same path will only break our hearts. People who don't have anything can't afford to work for somebody else. We need to create wealth because political power won't feed our children. Only productive wealth will do that job. And I don't mean buying a house, I mean building a business. This is the only way to make up for all we have suffered. Make money to seed the growth of our communities.

"It's time to be the sun. Like the sun, we need to switch to a strategy of fusion to create the energy to drive progress for all black people. Fusion comprised of economic self-reliance and educational self-development. Don't bus my children to somebody else's neighborhood. I want the black people who raised me to educate mine. We need to invest in our institutions.

"We had to be the wind. It's our time to be the sun. I built this country. I love this country. I am this country. Black is beautiful. Good dirt is black dirt, and that's where I want to plant a seed—in black dirt. I got five on it.

"The blacker the berry, the sweeter the juice, is what I have heard. And I'm here to tell you there can be no sweeter place than the one where you set the pace. Good black institutions, strong black institutions. A place where you don't have to worry about being the black one—where you're just one. And we can certainly invite our white brothers and sisters to work there, teach there, and matriculate there. Everybody ought to be able to join in that fun. I got five on it.

"A strong cup of coffee is a black cup of coffee. Our greatest strength lies not in a talented tenth or being like fingers on a hand. Our strength lies in the blood of our ancestors coursing through our veins. We need to strengthen what is ours. We need to invest in what belongs to us. I know we don't have much. But can't we all put five on it?

"Why affirm discrimination? Our schools are a gift—a gift our community should support in loving memory of the brave many who were strong enough, sweet enough, good enough, to stand up and say, We've had enough!

"I got five on it."

Chapter 12

Film Study

"Daughter, those were some impressive words you strung together last week. And you're a young woman."

Adrienne glanced up from her beef roast and said, "Thank you, Uncle James."

Josh cracked, "Call him Mariner."

Genna smiled at the gathering around her dinner table. Daniel, her kids, Uncle James, Aaron, Adrienne, and her brother, as Shaun would say, reviewing game films from last week. Even the pain in her back couldn't take away from this moment. *Momma sure would be happy.* "Adrienne, don't listen to Josh. He's trouble."

"Adrienne, don't listen to either one of them. They're both slick," the Mariner interjected. "One more so than the other," he said, looking at Genna as he spoke. "Ain't that right, Daniel?"

"Uncle James, I got to live with her." The table broke into laughter.

"Brittany, Larry, see how smart your daddy is," Genna said.

The Mariner looked at Adrienne. "You know they're not going to listen, right?"

She looked back at him. "Yeah, but I still have to try."

"Well, I tell you what, dear. I'm going to help you. This is what we'll do. I'm going to write a check for five thousand dollars tomorrow, just so I can say I put the first five on it. Then in the fall when we have the first gathering, I going to write another check and present it to the school and say I got five on it. Black people are sight people. We gonna show 'em so they can go out and tell it. Maybe we can get some rhythm to this thing."

Adrienne picked up a napkin and wiped her mouth. "Thank you, old great and mighty Ancient Mariner."

"Daughter, you been hanging around my nephew too much. Like Genna said, he's trouble."

"He sure is, but my Aunt Leah says he's my kind of trouble."

Genna could see Adrienne brush her hand across Josh's knee under the table as she spoke. *Get him, soror.*

The Mariner chuckled. "Adrienne, Casanova once said, 'Tell a smart woman she's beautiful, and a beautiful woman she's smart.' I don't know what he could have told you."

Genna said, "He calls us slick. You see where we get it from."

"Genna, you want to get your thirsty old uncle a drink?"

"I sure will, Uncle James. I see you changing the subject."

Adrienne glanced at Josh. "Well, Uncle James, you taught this one well. Monday I got home from work and there were twelve beautiful roses waiting on me. The note on them wasn't signed, but I immediately knew who sent them because it read, 'From a member of your fan club. Boy, Saturday night, you sure were live.' Unless, of course, you sent them, because old nephew here won't own up to it."

Genna cracked, "Josh, tell the truth and shame the devil." She snapped her finger, "Oh that's right, you are the devil."

Josh cracked back, "Hey, why don't you just hop along to the kitchen and bring that drink?"

Adrienne popped him on the arm. "Don't talk to my soror that way!"

"Can't keep your hands off me, huh?"

"No you didn't," Adrienne retorted and popped him again.

Genna smiled to herself as she walked to the kitchen.

Chapter 13

Like a Monster

"Hand me that brush, Tin Man." Josh passed the brush to Faith." Your girl is something else."

"What girl?"

"Oh you gonna be that Josh today," Faith chuckled as she put down the brush and stared at him. "Josh, it ain't nothing wrong with you liking her. She ain't going nowhere. Even though we both know you sho' gonna try to push her away."

"First of all, I don't know who you talking about. And even if I did, why would I try to push her away?"

"'Cause your ass is crazy. Don't try to play me. What's her name, Audrey, Annie?"

"Hey I like that—Audrey Anne."

"Boy, what am I going to do with you?

"I know you didn't think you were going to trick me into saying Adrienne with that weak move. Audrey Anne, that's funny. I'm gonna use that one, though."

"Josh, don't do her like you did Sarah."

"Nah, you ain't trying to act like you like her. I'm surprised you ain't calling her grand. What's up with that?"

"She's good for you, baby. Not like Sarah."

"Why you always talk about her? Sarah's nice."

"Yes, she is. And that was her problem. How many times I got to tell you? You need somebody who'll get on your Tin Man ass. And Sarah wouldn't or couldn't do that. This girl will put her foot in your ass."

Josh raised his hand to his mouth and pretended to yawn.

"You keep on. I bet you ain't gonna make her wait to get some like the black girl with the white name."

"Hell is you talking about. Stay outta my damn business. We just friends and business partners. Besides, for all you know, we might already have got our sexual healing. A gentleman doesn't discuss such matters."

"And where is a gentleman?"

"Okay, you got that one, Miss Christian. You like her?"

"She's straight. If I didn't have my hands full with Ramona, I might have to give you a run for your money. Those titties look bite-sized. That's what I love."

"Down low, Faith."

"Boy, you think you can handle all that? She don't come with no instruction manual."

"Fuck you."

"I told you, Tin Man, anytime you think you ready, I got something for ya. But I gonna cut you some slack 'cause you got your hands full right about now."

"She is fine."

"Yeah she is, but that ain't what I'm talking about, Josh." Faith looked him up and down. "You smart and you devilish, but that girl ain't no joke. She had me ready to get back on the stroll so I could put five on it. All that shit she was talking. That girl can pimp like a monster. You watch yourself or you might be out there pulling your pants leg up, hollering you got five on it." They both cracked up.

"You mark my word, though, Tin Man—that girl's gonna make you know your heart."

Chapter 14

True to the Game

Josh rode up Lenox Road digesting the late fall nip in the Atlanta air. This was his favorite time of the year. Most people loved spring. But fall was his time, his spirit buoyed by the darkness falling upon the city like his quilt when he drew it over his head before he drifted off to sleep.

The only drawback in the last few years had been his dreams of tiny matchsticks skittering around his apartment, wailing *Josh, Josh, save me please*. But this year felt different. This November evening, he had his license back and he was going to pick up Adrienne.

There she stood! He pulled into the front of her complex. He hopped out, walked around his car, and said, "Would mademoiselle like a taxi?" She smiled at him.

"Depends on whether or not kind sir has his proper papers."

He pulled out his wallet, removing his driver's license to give her for inspection. "Does this meet mademoiselle's approval?"

She held it up to the light of the street lamp, squinting as if to focus better on what the plastic card in her hand said. "Kind sir, you seem to have your papers in order."

He bowed before opening the door for her. She slowly slid in, her legs peeking out from under her skirt and teasing him mercilessly, daring him to touch them. She looked up. "Are you coming?" Then "Oh," before she smoothed her skirt, blanketing those fat, pretty thighs. He sighed.

He strode back around the car, getting in and driving off.

"You know I'm never driving again, right?" she chided. He nodded. "I wanted to get that straight." He could only chuckle. Once it was established she knew he was not legal to drive, she had driven them everywhere whenever they had been together. He'd spent countless nights on her sofa after they yakked with each other for endless hours. She had even spent the night at his apartment twice; him on the sofa and her in his bed. Michelle told her after one particularly long overnight session she was going to have to have a long talk with that boy. Shaun loved her. She had him in church two or three Sundays a month recently. And his clothes were getting tight from overdosing on her Aunt Leah's good cooking.

Late in the summer, she had told him about the NBA. It hurt his feelings. He knew she was frustrated with his inability to make a move on her. He got it because he couldn't explain why he hadn't even tried to kiss her. And those legs beckoned to him every chance they got. He could almost hear them saying, *Josh, come over and play with us.* Something about her froze him, or maybe it was something about him.

Faith kept giving him a hard time. She'd tell him, "You must be one hell of a nigger for her to keep hanging around your trifling ass, and you won't even give her a sniff of what it's like." They kept getting closer and closer, though. He told himself now that he could drive again, nature would take its course. He was hoping it would be tonight. They were having a ball together so far. They planned on shopping tonight, starting at Rich's in Lenox Square.

He knew from experience with Sarah this might take a while. Sure enough, she grabbed six or seven skirts to try on. She modeled them for him in her stockings, showing off an exquisite pair of feet, quizzing him about what he liked. Finally, she came out in a brown skirt with pockets on the side.

He was surprised because he thought she was a little young for this particular piece. She walked up to him and whirled around. "What do you think?" she asked. Before he could answer, she turned so her back was facing him, put her hands in the pockets, and stood on her tiptoes. She glanced over her shoulder. "You like?" she asked. All he could do was nod yes. She asked, smiling, "You all right?" He muttered yes. They finally picked two skirts and three blouses. Afterwards, they decided to go for pizza at a little shop in the Disco Kroger Plaza.

They were happily splitting a pie when he decided to look in the thrift store two doors down to see if a hat he wanted to buy was still there, but it was gone. He dawdled in the store for a couple of minutes talking to the clerk before coming back. Adrienne had a strange smile on her face. Josh asked her if she was okay.

She replied, "Yes. Do you see the guy sitting over there?" She cut her eyes toward a well-dressed, middle-aged white gentleman.

Josh said, "Yeah, what about him?"

"That girl at the table next to him came over after you left and said he gave her fifty dollars to ask me my name."

"He did what?" Josh said. He could hear his voice rising.

She put her hand on his arm leaning toward him. "It's nothing, Josh. I told her I didn't want to give him my name.

I told her I'm here with my boyfriend. She said I should talk to him because if he was giving fifty dollars for my name, it was no telling how much he might give me if I talked to him."

Josh got up, staring hard at the man. The guy had been watching them. He turned his head. He felt Adrienne touching his hand. He walked over to the guy's table. As he approached, he stared down the girl who got the fifty for coming to the table. She looked down at her plate. He sat down at the man's table.

He looked at Adrienne. He turned to the man and asked him, "You want to know her name? It's Adrienne. That's A-D-R-I-E-N-N-E, motherfucker." He punched the guy in the nose as hard as he could as he spat out the second *e* in her name.

Blood shot out of the guy's nose. Before he could grab it, Josh was all over him, knocking him out the chair, stomping him in his face. Then when the guy covered his head with his hands, he kicked him in his ribs, his chest, his legs, and finally in his ass two or three times. He felt Adrienne pulling him away, pleading with him to stop.

He glared at the girl as Adrienne continued to pull him away. "You better put that fifty on his doctor bills." He let her pull him out the door, not wanting to run, knowing the people in the shop would be a lot slower to call the police if he acted like he didn't give a fuck. He broke free and opened the door. "I'll come back and burn this motherfucker to the ground."

He walked to the car. He got in, not looking forward to her rage. Her eyes flashed with fear and anger. He backed the car down the street so the clerk standing outside the store couldn't see his tag. He hoped his girl in the thrift store didn't give a good description of him. He whipped the car around and raced out of the parking lot down Piedmont to Habersham, never once looking her way. Suddenly, she was screaming at him. "What is wrong with you? Are you crazy?"

He didn't say a word, knowing he deserved her anger. Yet he was unwavering in his belief that the guy had asked for what he had given him. Hell, cats like Hakeem would have shot the dude in the foot, no questions asked.

"Say something!" she screamed as he made the right on West Paces and rode past the governor's mansion. He figured silence was the only way to go, as mad as she was. "Josh, I live in this neighborhood. How can I ever go in there to eat again after what you just did? You could go to jail. Don't you think the police are going to be looking for you?"

"Fuck the police. He ain't gonna disrespect me like that and get away with that shit. He saw us together. Plus, you ain't for sale. What, he thinks he can pull a wad of money and just do what he wants to and not get his ass kicked?"

She took a deep breath. "You are crazy. You can't just go around beating up people because they do something you don't like. I can't stand you! I told you my brother died about some dumb shit just like what you just did. Take me home!"

"Damn, Adrienne, calm down," he pleaded. "Can't you see my side of it?" He tried another angle, seeing his current tactic wasn't working. "Look, just 'cause he's white and he's got a little money doesn't mean he can buy you. I wasn't going to let him treat you like that." He regretted the comment before it got out of his mouth.

"So because he's white, you think it's all right for you to kick his face in like that? That's insane. Take me home, you asshole. Take me home, Josh. I mean it. If you're not going to take me home, let me out and I'll call Chelle."

"Damn, Adrienne, why you got to get so fucking mad? I'm sorry I kicked his ass. Do you feel better now?"

"No! Take me home." She folded her hands across her waist and berated him all the way up Peachtree, telling him in no uncertain terms how disappointed she was in his behavior, reminding him he was supposed to be setting an example for the children and teenagers that parents entrusted him with five days a week. She asked him how Aaron would feel if he had seen this fine example of how to deal with disrespect.

"He knows how the game is played."

She went ballistic. "How the game is played? I'm sick of you and that game you're always hollering you have to be true to. Hear me good—that damn game cost my brother his life.

You love the game so much? Go out with it, because you can't be true to me if all you care about is the game!" She looked at him hard. "I cannot believe you. I told you what the girl did because I thought you would see it like I did. Something to laugh at because there's no way I would ever look his way. He's too white and too old, and besides, I'm foolishly thinking I've got you.

"I would expect Aaron to act like you did because he's a child. But you are a grown-assed man. Act like it! You say you want those children to represent the race. Is that what you just did? You want them to grow up black and proud. Well I tell you, there's no way you should ever be proud of what you just did. And threatening to burn that store down! Haven't you had enough of fires? You make me sick."

He pulled into the apartment complex. "There's no need for you to park. I can see myself to the door," she said.

"Adrienne," he said.

"What?" she snapped before he could get another word out.

"I'm sorry."

"You're sorry," she said, laughing sarcastically. "You need to go tell that man you left lying on the floor you're sorry. What did you say your grandmother used to tell you? Being black doesn't give you an excuse to fail? It's a reason to try harder? You weren't trying very hard, were you?" She opened the door to get out.

He sighed and placed his left hand on his head. "You want me to call you?"

She got out and leaned down so she could see him. "No, I think we need a break. You give me a month and I'll call you. I don't know, Josh. You told me you have a bad temper, and Lord knows you've told me some stories about it, but I guess I never dreamed I'd see you act like you did today. If I hadn't grabbed you, I'm afraid you might have killed that man—over a question. I've got to think this over."

"Adrienne," he said plaintively.

"Josh, leave me alone. How could you? We were having such a good time. I thought . . ." she turned and walked away. He sat there watching her climb the steps to her apartment. She fumbled for her keys in her pocketbook, never looking his way. Then she opened her door and went inside. Josh stopped to buy a quart of gin on the way home.

Chapter 15

Bonnie and Clyde, Interrupted

Adrienne slammed the door as she walked into the kitchen. Michelle was sitting at the table on the phone. She cupped the receiver. "Are you okay?"

Adrienne said, "I'm sorry, Chelle," and burst into tears.

"Adrienne, what's wrong?" Michelle said into the phone, "Let me call you back." She stood up and walked over to her roommate. "What's wrong, Adrienne?"

"Ooooh, that damn Josh Gibson."

"Lord, Adrienne, what did he do?"

"We were eating pizza. Josh went to look at some hat and a guy gave a girl fifty dollars to ask me my name while he was gone. When Josh came back, I told him and he beat the guy senseless."

"Oh Adrienne, I'm sorry," Chelle said and took her in her arms. She thought about it for a second. "Meek, mild Josh, the one who won't touch you, put his hands all over some guy for asking your name?" Adrienne nodded against Michelle's shoulder. "Let's go get him."

Adrienne laughed and stepped back. "You are crazy."

"I'm the crazy one? You been going out with a man for almost a year and can't even get a kiss. Oh yeah, I'm crazy."

Adrienne replied, "It hasn't been almost a year!"

"Oh yeah, then what's January to November? Don't forget, you the one who asked, 'Chelle, do you think he's gay?'"

Adrienne laughed again. "You know what? I ought to go and get him and beat him down."

"Girl, you must really like him. And one thing's for sure—you got to know he likes you."

"Yeah, Chelle, he tried to tell me he wasn't going to let some white man disrespect me like that."

"Wait a minute. He beat up a white man in Buckhead?"

"Yeah, Chelle. Got all loud on him. He spelled my name for him and then hit the guy in the nose."

Chelle went over to the door and peeked out the curtain. "Girl, go get under the bed, 'cause you going to jail. You can't beat up a white man in Buckhead."

"Hush, Chelle."

"I'm gonna call y'all Bonnie and Clyde. What y'all gonna do next? Rob a bank?"

"We aren't going to do anything. I told him we need a break."

"A break? And he went for that?"

"He'd better. I'm going to wash my face. You go ahead and call your folks back. I'm all right."

Adrienne walked down the hall to the bathroom. Chelle called out to her, "Do you think he's in love with you?" Adrienne didn't answer. Suddenly, she felt really tired. She looked in the mirror. *Is it me?* A lovely face stared back at her. A little more chest would help, but overall she had a really nice body. Reggie and the NBA always raved over her looks. All men did—except for Josh.

Love me? She shook her head and walked down the hall to her bedroom She lay down on her freshly made bed with the new sheets on it and thought, *Damn you, Josh Gibson.*

Chapter 16

The Tin Man Finds a Heart

Josh pulled on his cigarette. He glanced at the empty liquor bottle. A whole quart, a pack of cigarettes, and still sleep would not come. Adrienne's clothes, still packed away in the Rich's bags, sat on the counter next to the sink. He heard footsteps on the stairwell followed by a loud banging on the door. "Woohoo, Josh Gibson, open this door."

He opened the door. "Damn."

The sunlight sent shooting pains through his head. Faith took one look at him and exclaimed, "Josh Gibson, what in the world? I thought you were going out with that girl last night. I thought you might not be here this morning, but damn, boy. What's up, why you looking so rough? She wise up and kick your heartless ass to the curb?"

He could barely get a yes out.

"Josh, no, I was just kidding. Please tell me you didn't do something stupid the damn day you got your driver's license back." He shook his head, unable to speak. "Lord! Josh, baby, what did you do?"

"I fucked up, Faith. I fucked up bad."

She walked over and rapped him on his forehead—hard. "Boy, do I need to go get my gun? What did you do to that girl?"

He backed up. "Damn, Faith, why you hitting me?"

"'Cause your ass needed to be hit and she's too girlified to do it. Now bring your ass in this living room and tell me what happened!"

He told her about the events of the prior evening, about how everything was going so well until they had arrived at the pizza place. He told her how he had stomped the guy and threatened everybody in the place, telling them he would come back and burn it down.

"I ought to pistol-whip your dumb ass. She actually heard you threaten to set the place on fire, knowing your crazy ass was capable of doing it. That's what you get for telling her about all that crazy shit you did in the past."

"Damn, you think that's really what bugged her out?"

"Well yes, that and you kicking the crap out of that dude right in front of her. Of course, that part she probably ate up, but she can't let your dumb ass know that shit soaked her panties. That ain't your business."

Her last comment gave him hope. "You really think she got off on me kicking his ass?"

"Well, up to a point, Josh. She's not an alley bitch, so she's not going to get off on you just beating the shit out somebody—and remember, I've seen how stupid you can get. But I'm sure she appreciated you getting jealous, 'cause you had to be to do something that stupid. Course, I'm sure you're claiming it was a matter of honor."

"Fuck you."

She smiled. "Now that's the Tin Man I know and love. I guess you do have a heart. Lord, I bet you scared the shit out them white folks. Did you buck up and get all loud on 'em?"

"Yeah," was all he said.

Faith giggled. "I know she was tripped out. You been running round here playing grand, not smoking in front of her, opening doors for her. She saw the real Josh last night, didn't she?" Faith cackled at the thought. "I know she's pissed off. She just knew she was gonna get her some last night and here you go and cut the sho' 'nuff fool. She's probably cursing your ass right now." Faith was beside herself with laughter now. "Yeah, she had been planning that for a minute. 'I'm gonna hook up when he gets that license back.' Lord, of all days for you to act a fool. And here I thought you'd be walking round with your chest all puffed out, grinning from ear to ear. Boy, Genna should have told her, can't no woman plan nothing round your crazy ass. Come on, Tin Man, let's go."

Working on the job she had for him soothed his hangover, but not his heartache. Faith kept telling him it would be okay. Adrienne just needed to get over her anger. When he got home, he called Genna, knowing she would find out soon enough. He wanted to be the one to tell her. Any story about him and his temper was going to upset her. She knew as well as Faith how stupid his anger could make him act.

"Hey, sis, what's up?" he said softly into the phone.

"Uh-uh. What's wrong, Josh?"

"Why does something have to be wrong?" he asked.

"You're calling me sis. Something must be wrong."

"Genna, I did something stupid last night." He hesitated, giving her a chance to question what had happened. But all he got was silence. "Adrienne and I were eating a pizza in the Disco Kroger Plaza. I got up and went down the block to check on something, and when I came back, this white guy had insulted her."

"Insulted her how, Josh?

"He paid a girl fifty dollars to ask for her name."

"What did you do, Josh?" Genna asked, anxiousness in her voice.

"I beat him up."

"Josh, no, please don't tell me you acted a fool in front of that girl. Not when y'all are getting along so well."

"Shit, Genna, what was I supposed to do?"

"Josh, I can't believe you. Is she okay?"

"I don't know. She doesn't want to talk to me."

Genna sighed and said, "Well, you can't really blame her, can you? Have you tried to call her?"

"No," Josh replied, "She said she wanted to take a break from me."

"And you're stupid enough to just do that?"

"What do you mean, Genna?"

"Nothing, Josh. You need to turn yourself in."

He felt himself getting angry. "You want me to turn myself in."

"I sure do," Genna replied. "You know the police are looking for you. They can't have you coming to Buckhead beating up white folks. She lives in that neighborhood, Josh. Do you really want the police knocking on her door, or worse, showing up at Morehouse? They'll take her if they can't get you."

"Okay."

"Okay what?"

"I'll turn myself in."

Chapter 17

America's Hard on a Black Man

Monday rolled around. Genna was still mad. She called him three times Sunday to make sure he was serious about turning himself in. She talked to the Mariner, who talked to an attorney. They arranged for Josh to turn himself in on Tuesday. "Why Tuesday?" he asked.

"Because you need to tell Aaron before you go. And don't call Adrienne. You let me handle that. All you'll do is make things worse."

"What are you going to tell her, Genna?"

"That I'm sorry for ever introducing her to my crazy brother." Behind that comment, he knew to leave Hoppy alone.

As soon as they were both at work on Monday, she went and got Aaron.

"Josh, tell him what you did!"

Then she left.

Josh explained what had happened.

Aaron was stunned to hear what had happened. "Damn, Mr. Josh, you really beat the dude down like that? I didn't think you had it in you."

He had to be careful how he presented this to Aaron. He told him he knew it was a mistake, but a young man would in all likelihood miss the point that what he did was a mistake he didn't want Aaron to repeat. Aaron might hear it as an okay to get physical when he felt wronged. Josh told him he was going to turn himself in. Aaron couldn't believe it. He asked Josh why.

"Because what I did was wrong and I have to face the consequences."

"That's bullshit, Mr. Josh. I wish I had been with you. We'd still be kicking on his ass."

Adrienne was right. He had done wrong by these kids. His reaction was normal to kids like Aaron. He had taken the easy way out. The hard thing to do would have been to swallow it or, more appropriately, approach the guy and tell him how uncool it was to pull such a stunt.

"Man, Mr. Josh, the white boy was trying to chump you. Can't you see that? Miss Adrienne's fine. He just figured he'd buy her right out from under you!"

He couldn't disagree with Aaron's assessment, but he also knew he had set a bad example. He had promised himself he was going to show them the right way to do things. He couldn't shake that thought.

"And she got mad at you for kicking his ass? What kind of shit is that?"

"Nah, Aaron, she didn't get mad at me for kicking his ass. She got mad at me for stooping to his level. On some level, she liked what he did, but she also found it insulting he thought she was for sale, especially so cheap. She wanted me to be better than him. I let her down. You feel me?"

"In other words, you saying she probably wanted to kick his ass too, Mr. Josh."

"Yeah, in a way, but she's got too much class for that."

"And it didn't faze you 'cause you ain't got no class."

"You're funny, Aaron."

"Mr. Josh, I'm glad she's your lady and not mine. I couldn't put up with that."

"Put up with what, Aaron?"

"You know, her being right all the time!"

"Just hope you find somebody just like her one day."

"Is she still mad at you?"

"She's not speaking to me."

"And you getting ready to go to jail? Somebody needs to holler at old girl and tell her to give you a break. You want me to call her?"

Josh laughed. "Not right now, Aaron. Let's give her a minute. I do appreciate your offer, though."

"Damn, Mr. Josh, you should have told me. Me and Cowboy could have got you to help us beat up white people at the MARTA station this past weekend."

"Hey man, I told you about that shit."

Aaron laughed. "Nah, Mr. Josh, I ain't doing that anymore. I wish I'd have been there though. We'd have kicked his ass good!"

"Aaron that was stupid what I did. That's why I'm gonna turn myself in. You remember how I always tell you a man's got to be responsible? I acted like a child."

"You sound like Miss Genna."

"I do, don't I? But check this out. I'm gonna deal with it like a man and face up to it. Man, it's like with your dad. America's hard on a black man, but that didn't give him the right to walk on you. He owed you the right to have your dad. I don't care what he was going through. And for the same reason, I didn't have any right to take it out on that man. I don't know what he's like."

"So you want to be the sun?"

"Man, don't bring her up right now. But yeah, I'm trying to be the sun."

"Yeah, Mr. Josh, I'm gonna be the sun too. I want me a little girl so I can be there for her like Hyung-Ju is for Minsook."

"That's the way, bro, that's the way. You like working there?"

"It's okay, but I want my own spot like you and Miss Genna. I'm stacking some paper on the side getting ready for that day."

Chapter 18

Ms. Dinah Washington

Sunlight slowly filled his living room. So many evenings he had sat in this spot seeing the world go dark. This was better. He smiled to himself. Adrienne slept a few feet away in his bed.

He stood and walked to his bedroom and glanced in the door. He watched her sleep; her back was to him, her body gently heaving with each breath. He smiled to himself, singing Dinah Washington's "What a Difference a Day Makes."

He shook his head, still not quite able to get over how the last few weeks had gone. Up until twenty-four hours ago, he was sure she would never speak to him again. Yet there she lay, the two of them finally fully a couple.

Terrified to call her, he'd written a long letter pouring his heart out to her. He told her she was his North Star. That she was somehow pointing the way back to the sweet, kind Josh of his childhood. The Josh he had been before the chill winds of life had blown changes through his world, changes that hardened him and left him impervious to the precious nature of life. He told her she must be an angel who fell from the sky. He told her God had sent her to him. And that he thanked God for her. How he hoped his misdeeds would not permanently assign him to her doghouse.

He let Genna read it. She laughed a few times, nodding her head before looking up to say, "You did good, big brother. I'll give it to her."

He told her he would mail it. She put the letter in her purse saying, "I'll give it to her because somebody needs to let her know you're locked up. I know you won't. Trust me, Josh. I know just what to tell her."

Genna let him spend Thanksgiving in jail. He was so mad he could barely speak to her. She didn't care, telling him it served him right. Besides, Adrienne couldn't believe she was leaving him in jail. She lobbied for her to get him out. Genna told her Josh turned himself in so the police wouldn't come looking for her.

Josh had been locked up once before when he got a DUI. This time around was different. When he got the DUI, it was four a.m. one Saturday morning coming home from Mr. V's Figure Eight, that legendary Campbellton Road night spot. The cop who pulled him over almost acted like he felt sorry for him. Told him, "I guess you gotta hang out sometimes, but you have to be careful." The deputies processed him at the jail and promptly released him on his own recognizance.

This time he spent two weeks upstairs in a cell. Slim and Dad and some other cats who had been down had warned him, "You gotta act hard 'cause somebody's gonna try you." Soon as he got in the cell, some cat with a big, unkempt 'fro, no shirt, no socks, and no shoes cracked him, "What you in for man child support?" "Josh looked him right in the eye and cracked back, "Nah, murder. I shot some cat for asking me a stupid-ass question." No shirt laughed and said, "Hey man, you a trip." They became fast friends after that.

Slim and Dad were right. You couldn't be a punk. He saw a cat get his ass kicked basically because he was light skinned. And nobody felt sorry for him. In fact, somebody took the cat's food right after that. Of course, it helped Slim's cousin Jeter was in at the same time. He was running things and told Josh he had his back. The Mariner always said it was good to have connections. Genna finally got him in early December. The charges had been dropped or no telling how long she would have let him sit there.

The Mariner had come through with a donation of $10 thousand to the white boy to get him to drop the charges. When Josh told Dad, he said, "Shit Jay, ten thousand dollars? Man, I should go stomp that cracker and get that money back! You want me to go pull his tongue out?"

The days dragged by. It seemed like everybody talked to her, but no one would tell him what she said. She came by the office a couple of evenings to chat with Genna after he was gone. Aaron saw her one of those times, dutifully reporting she looked so good it didn't make sense.

He cracked, "Damn, Mr. Josh, if you gonna get locked up every time she gets mad and kicks you to the curb, you might want to stay off her bad side." Aaron and Genna had a big laugh about that comment. The Mariner had lunch with her and Genna one day, but wouldn't tell Josh what they talked about except to let him know she hadn't mentioned his name. He began to sense all hope was lost and wasn't sure if he even wanted to see her under present circumstances.

Amateur night approached with no Adrienne. For once, New Year's didn't feel like a new beginning. No word from her. Faith and Genna both told him it served him right.

New Year's Eve he sat in his kitchen too hurt to drink, chain-smoking cigarettes, when someone knocked on his door. *Adrienne*, he thought, but then he realized it wasn't her knock. Maybe Genna was stopping by with the kids to boost his spirits. *Yeah, that sounds like Brittany's knock.* And of course when he opened the door, there Adrienne stood, even more beautiful than he remembered. "Hey," was all he could get out.

"You've been smoking," she said.

"A little bit. How you been?"

"Good, are you going to ask me in?"

"Oh, yeah, you want to come in?" *Why do you always make me so nervous?* He moved aside to let her in.

"I believe you have some clothes of mine."

He rubbed the top of his head. "I do. Is that why you came by?"

"Actually, I miss you."

He reached out and pulled her to him. He leaned his face against the top of her head before whispering, "I love you."

She looked up into his eyes. He kissed her, and it felt so good he wondered why he hadn't kissed her before. He took her hand and led her to his bedroom. In an instant, it was over.

She popped up and snarled, "Josh Gibson, you get an F. Josh!"

And suddenly all those nerves went away. All the worrying about whether he could please her disappeared when he saw the frustration in her face. He laughed.

"You are not funny," she snapped. He remembered Kool's old line about moments like these, but he thought better of that crack.

He pushed her back down on the bed and began to lightly stroke her body. She began to moan and call his name—a moment he'd never forget. All the love he'd been scared to show her seemed to run down his nerve endings through his hands and fingers onto her body. His tongue followed the paths his fingers were discovering.

They finished. She got up. He told her, "If you're looking for a towel, they're right there in that closet in the hallway." She turned and faced him and began to clap, slowly at first, then building to a thundering crescendo, punctuating the applause with shouts of *bravo, bravo!*

He thought about last night as he walked over and kissed her on the cheek. She smiled but didn't wake up. He went back to the sofa, doing his best imitation of Dinah Washington.

Part III

For of all sad words of tongue or pen,
The saddest are these: "It might have been!"

Excerpted from *Maud Muller*
by John Greenleaf Whittier

Chapter 1

The Saga of Josh and Adrienne

Josh grabbed her around the waist. He loved the feel of her body. He was constantly looking for any excuse to put his hands on her, but this was dead-serious work. He pulled her back toward him. "Look girl, we haven't been married a week. I'm not ready to lose you this quick."

Adrienne squirmed, hitting him in the ribs with an elbow. Laughing, she told him, "Let me go, Josh. I want to get up top." She was determined to climb on the roof of the boat. He was just as determined to keep his tipsy, nonswimmer wife of four days from making the foray up there with the other revelers who were sharing this unique tour of the Bahamas with them. Looking for something a little out of the way to do after two days of hotel food, trinket shopping, and the ever-prevalent motor scooter excursions, they had welcomed the approach of two native women on the beach behind their hotel who handed them a party cruise handbill.

Their hotel had warned them about the party cruise. Insisted it wasn't safe. So, naturally, they considered going. They had slipped down to the dock to check it out and ran into a white guy talking to one of the tour guides. He heartily recommended it to them, exclaiming he had such a ball, he forgot his wallet the day before. He had come down to collect it. The crew was waiting for him so they could return it.

This sounded like Josh's idea of a good time. Surprisingly, the missus was excited about the adventure, too. They joked with the guy for a few minutes, who was on his fifth wedding anniversary from Minnesota. The wife was in their room still trying to recover from the day before. Josh and Adrienne looked at each other, nodding their heads simultaneously in agreement: this was must-do tourism.

So here they were an hour in, him working on his fourth drink and her as drunk as he had ever seen her on three and a half Bahamas Mamas. She looked incredible, dressed in a yellow one-piece bathing suit and a pair of denim shorts. Her hair had lost its argument with the salty air, so she had pinned it up, exposing those magnificent cheekbones of hers. She hadn't stopped laughing since they got on the boat. He was a lucky man and no way was he losing her to the pristine blue Caribbean waters they now rode on.

She playfully fought him for a few more moments before collapsing back on him. They sat down and he grabbed her drink. "You've had enough," he teased her as he gulped down the final swallows in her cup.

"I'm getting up there." She laughed as she made another mad dash for the roof. He grabbed her again and pulled her down onto his lap.

The gay couple they had claimed as island buddies laughed. "You know that's exactly what she wanted you to do?" said one of them. Adrienne pressed her index finger to her lips and made a loud shushing sound in his direction. They all cracked up. She touched Josh's jaw tenderly. Their eyes locked. She mouthed *I love you*.

An old Redd Foxx line came to him. He laughed out loud.

She looked at him and asked, "What's so funny?"

"You drunk," Josh cracked back.

"Don't make me punch you out," she retorted, balling her hand up in a fist she pressed against his jaw.

He took her hand in his. "You're still drunk and you're still not getting on top of this boat. I don't care what you do."

"Yes sir," she slurred.

The crew lifted a cover off the boat's glass bottom, exposing the clear, blue water below. Everybody *oohed* and *aahed* at the fish swimming beneath them. Josh's mind drifted, back to his first trip to Lima last July, his first chance to meet her dad Alonso.

Mr. Johnson was tall and handsome with big, broad shoulders. He saw where she got those cheekbones. His first comment after they shook hands was, "I can die happy now. I finally got to shake the hand of the immortal Josh Gibson." Josh could only laugh. He looked at his daughter and told Josh, "She says you actually live up to that name. Talks about you almost like you're larger than life."

Josh laughed as she said, "Daddy don't tell him that."

"Well, isn't that the way you talk about him?" he said, winking at Josh.

He and Mr. Johnson shared a love of baseball. They chatted about the all-time greats. Mr. Johnson regaled him with stories about the Negro Leagues. He had barnstormed with the Indianapolis Clowns for a couple of years before blowing out his arm.

He thought about what Alonso said as she chatted with their new friends. "She's had a hard go of it in life, what with her mother dying young and what happened to her brother."

Josh told him he knew.

"Well, what she can't tell you is the difference you've made in her life. I'm not sure she knows, but you have. She's crazy about you. You got a good spirit. I wanted to meet you because I wanted to see this man who makes her beam the way she used to before Norman was killed. She never seemed to get over it before you came along. You should have heard how upset she was after you beat that guy up. She called me that night in tears, sure she had run you off. That's not for her to hear."

"I never would have known. She never spoke to me once until she showed up at my door the day she told me we could see each other again. I guess we understand each other. My mom and dad are both dead, and I have a good friend Slim who was murdered a few years ago. He was like a brother to me. I tell you, Mr. Johnson, she sure is smart. I can't get over how brilliant she is. Even when you disagree with her, you have to admire the strength of her arguments."

"Yeah," said Mr. Johnson. "She gets that from her mother. You must be kind of sharp yourself, though, because even when she was a little girl, she always liked the smart boys. I was scared she might wind up with Reggie because of that. Don't get me wrong—he's a good kid. Just not right for her."

Josh nodded.

"Reggie never made her sparkle the way you do. They were too different from each other for my taste, but it didn't do any good for me to tell her that. She had to figure it out on her own," Mr. Johnson said. "She's pretty bullheaded. Reggie didn't really get into her way of thinking. Plus, he wanted her to take a back seat to his ambition. That would be like asking a canary not to sing."

Adrienne tapped him on his shoulder. "Earth to Josh, earth to Josh," she said, snapping him back to the present. "We've been invited to a party," she said.

"Our room at eight," the tall, blonde half of the couple told him. "Adrienne's got the info." He winked at Adrienne and staggered off.

She leaned against Josh as they got off the boat and walked up the dock.

"Rookie," he teased.

"Old pro," she giggled.

Chapter 2

The Best Hatstand in the Bahamas

"Damn," Josh muttered, sitting up and quickly falling back on the bed, groaning. It was already the next morning. "Adrienne, Adrienne, wake up," Josh whispered in her ear.

"Leave me alone, morning person," she moaned.

He laughed and said, "We missed the party."

She pulled a pillow over her head. "I know, I had to throw up in the middle of the night. I'm glad I didn't need your help. You were knocked out."

A little later he convinced her to go downstairs and put some food in her stomach. Her head throbbed from her hangover. Josh escorted her back to their room, swearing he would never let her get that drunk again. Trying to climb on the roof was bad enough, not getting to see her parade around the room with nothing more on than his straw hat prevented him from enjoying a treat that had been a daily ritual since they arrived. Miss Prim-and-Proper, as Faith referred to her, definitely had her raw side.

The Panama hat was a gift from the Mariner, who told him to wear it in good health. A man going to vacation in the tropics needed a good straw hat to complete his ensemble.

The Mariner hadn't indicated a side attraction would be his lovely bride's affection for it. He almost got upset when she commandeered it not long after they settled into their room, but seeing her preferred attire when she adorned it quickly squelched any objections on his part.

She lay down to sleep. Josh stroked her hair for a minute or two, then got up to go outside. "Josh where you going, sweetie?" she asked.

"Out for a walk. I'll be back in a bit."

"Okay, sweetie, wake me up when you get back. It'll be time for your floor show. And don't take my hat."

He laughed and said, "Yes ma'am."

A few minutes later Josh was ambling down the beach behind the hotel, gazing out at the Caribbean. He pulled on a cigarette as he looked out at the horizon. Beaches were different everywhere he'd been. Some were covered by beautiful white sand. In Tampa, he'd been on a beach covered by shells. The beaches near Hampton were more of a beige color. And the waters came in varying sizes crashing against the shore, small- and medium-sized breakers on the Atlantic, towering waves coming home to rest on the beaches of the Pacific.

But the horizon was always the same. No matter which ocean he'd looked out on, it always seemed to stretch just beyond his vision, beckoning, as if calling him to some great adventure beyond the cresting waters. Today it gave him comfort.

He remembered a conversation he had with Gina about two years before she died. She was trying to explain marriage to him. "See, Josh," Gina told him. "Marriage is not about love or even like. It's about being committed to something bigger than you. It was a bunch of times I looked across the table at your daddy and I asked myself,

'Gina what were you thinking?' But baby, I hung in there because I made a commitment, and every time I did I was glad, because he was a good man and my love for him grew stronger every time we got through a tough time."

He broke in saying, "But that sounds too much like work."

Gina had smiled at him and said, "It is work, Josh. It's a labor of love. Josh, love is like the ocean. There's a lot more to it than that little shallow stretch when you first walk in. And marriage is a leap of faith. When you stand on the beach sometimes, look out at the horizon. That's what marriage is—a journey to the horizon. Oh, you'll never get there, but you got to try. You take that person's hand you love and hop into that boat called commitment and set sail.

You ride off into the great unknown, not really knowing what life will bring, or how this person will act when the boat rocks or even when the sailing is smooth, because there really is calm before any storm. As the years pass and the beach fades, the horizon just keeps getting farther and farther away. But if you stay committed to your marriage and your wife does the same, the ocean of love you ride in will get deeper and deeper, baby. Or at least that's how it was with me and your daddy, and that's what I wish for you and Genna. You find a love that grows deeper and deeper just like the ocean, but you got to work to get there."

He sure missed Gina. Genna had told him after the wedding, "You know Momma would have loved Adrienne." He smiled at the memory and took one last drag on his cigarette before he went back to his room to catch the show. Adrienne was sitting on the bed wearing his hat and nothing else when he walked back in the door.

"Mrs. Gibson, what happens if it's somebody other than me who walks through that door?"

"Well, Mr. Gibson," she giggled. "I imagine they'll go home talking about how nice the hat was they saw in room five fifteen. And the hatstand it sat on, of course!"

She stood up and walked over to him, placing the hat on his head. She looked at it and said, "Nah, it looks better on me," and put it back on her head.

He had to agree she was one hell of a hatstand. And being her husband sure felt like a labor of love.

Chapter 3

Shrunken Dreams

Josh sat across from the Mariner. It had been a minute since he'd been to Dailey's. He always enjoyed coming here. They'd both ordered the duck, which they were currently waiting on. He'd been back home a week when the Mariner had hit him up, wanting to chat.

"Look, doctor, I'm going to give you some straight talk like your Uncle Henry gave me when I was your age. First, I want to say congratulations. I've told you before, you got yourself a good one."

Josh nodded, waiting on the *but* he could hear coming. "And I know you're telling yourself you're going to be faithful. Saying, 'I'm not going to cheat.' But you are, so you might as well accept it—"

"Damn, Mariner," Josh cut in. "Just like that—I'm gonna cheat. You can't give me any more credit than that?"

The Mariner looked right through him, chuckling to himself. "Nah, I can't, doctor. You're male and you're going to cheat. You're thinking, 'I got a plate of filet mignon. The eating can't get any better.' And I can look at her and tell your plate is full because not only is she pretty as hell and smart as a whip, she's got just enough alley in her to keep you in check. But think about it like this—you eat that filet mignon today, it's good as hell; you eat tomorrow, it's still swinging; you eat it every day for a month, you wake up one morning thinking, 'Damn, I got a taste for some chicken. Let me see where I can find some on the menu.'"

Josh almost choked on his cigarette laughing. "So damn, Mariner, you're saying she's going to cheat too? Because isn't she going to wake up one day and maybe want pizza rather than that good Southern-fried chicken she's been eating?"

The Mariner shook his head. This was going to be harder than he thought. "Look, doctor. There are women like your girl Faith who change men like they change clothes, and there are women who just want 'em a little different taste every now and then, but most of them are perfectly content to be loyal to their husbands as long as they are taking care of business. A woman like the one you got is only going to run around on you when you don't leave her any other choice. So if she cheats, that shit is on you, doctor!

"Shit, Josh, you think that chicken you serving is that good. Let's be real—she can get some as good or better. That ain't the issue. You treat her so good she doesn't want to, no matter how many fine-ass Negros she runs across in the course of a day. That's why I backed you up so hard when you kicked that white boy's ass. She was wrong to get that mad. That cat disrespected you and he got what was coming. She'll never admit it to you, but she knows he asked for that ass-whipping and she's glad to know you that big of a fool about her. She didn't give a fuck about him. She cares about you and how you feel about her. But I digress. I'll go back to that point in a minute, but I want you to do something for me."

"What's that?" Josh asked.

"Get her used to you being away from her at least some of the time. If you have to go for a walk by yourself every day, do that, so when you do get ready to go snack on that chicken, your filet mignon won't have any reason to suspect you're eating out."

"Damn, I'll think about it, man. I can't believe I ain't even married to her a month and you already telling me I'm going to cheat."

"Yeah, doctor, I know you think you better than that. I can see it in your eyes, but you're human. You ain't no better or worse than anybody else. Women 'bout to come out the woodwork now that you put that ring on your finger. Josh, don't lie to yourself. Women are better than us in that way, son. So accept that and play your role. Respect her and do everything you can to keep her happy. Part of keeping her happy is keeping her secure. I'm trying to school you about making her feel secure. You take that walk. It'll be good for you, and it'll be good for her."

"So you telling me I got to be that cliché, the brother who runs around on his woman? You can't give me any more credit than that?"

"No, I can't."

"Damn, Uncle James, so you think every brother's got to cheat? Why you say that?"

"Josh, it's just the way it is. I thought your Uncle Henry was wrong when he said that. But he was as right as rain."

"So you took that walk?"

"You got sense, you will too."

"So you telling me my dad ran around on your sister and you were okay with that."

"There's an exception to every rule, and your daddy was an exceptional man. But son, you got too much Washington in you. You got to be at least a little bit whorish. You love those streets too much for me to believe anything else."

Josh shook his head.

"Josh, it ain't just black men who cheat. White men cheat, Chinese men cheat, African men cheat—I imagine all kinds of men cheat. Hell, doctor, everybody cheats. Women are just slicker at it. Look at your momma's friend Pam. She's been married to Tic for thirty-something years, and I bet you she's had different a boyfriend for every one of those years."

Josh thought about what the Mariner said. Pam was notorious. But she loved her some Tic and as far as he could tell, Tic was crazy about her. Gina's friend Debra used to whisper to Gina about the house Debra and her boyfriend rented out in Southwest Atlanta for their Thursday-afternoon rendezvous. And both of them were married to other people. Still, this wasn't sitting well with Josh.

"So why do black men run around so much, Mariner, since you giving me the lowdown?"

"Look, doctor. I'm just trying to give you some good advice. I know how much you love that girl. Josh, where I grew up and when I grew up, the world was real small for a black man, way too small for us to have big dreams. That's a hard way to live. Wasn't no growing up to be a big-wheel politician, or aspiring to be a business executive, or any of that other stuff young men want to do with their lives. All you had were three choices, doctor: you could be a great fighter, a great hustler, or a great lover. It ain't a whole lot of cats who like getting punched in the face, and hustling done right is too much for a lot of cats. But damn, Josh, who doesn't love some trim. Even the cats who could fight and hustle wanted to get 'em some. So don't look down on old cats like me. You might not like some of what we do, but you need to understand every man has to find a way to be a man. And that was the only choice most of us had."

"Okay, Mariner, I never heard it put like that before. Still, man, the world is changing."

"It ain't changed that much. You take that walk."

They changed the subject. They ate together, and the Mariner had Josh ready to roll on the floor with some of those stories he was always good for. They got up to leave. The Mariner handed him a hundred-dollar bill as they were walking out the front door.

"What's this for?" Josh asked.

"Doctor, you do something nice for that wife of yours. If you gonna sweat those curls out her head, every now and then you need to give her some money to get her hair fixed."

Josh said, "Thanks, Uncle James," and headed back to EDCO.

Chapter 4

Taking a Walk

Adrienne said to Josh, "Sweetie, that sure smells good."

"We'll be ready to eat in just a few minutes. Sorry I didn't get dinner fixed before you got here. I was tidying up the apartment."

Sometimes, she was almost upset that he never let her cook. The cleaning-up part she was okay with, though. "You know you don't have to cook every day, right? I'll help you."

"I don't cook every day."

"You know what I mean."

"You keep working on that dissertation and that book and you let me take care of you."

"Yes sir," she said. "I think I'll keep you."

"You sure?" Josh replied.

Adrienne considered the last couple of days, knowing why he asked. A few hours ago, she had tossed all of his clothes onto the floor of their living room. He'd spent the night with his mistress, dragging in at ten o'clock, bug-eyed and sad-faced with his white shirt dark with grime. This was the third time in the six months they'd been married he stayed out all night. She'd barely heard of freebasing before she met Josh. She had no idea of the hold smoking cocaine could place on someone.

Genna had insisted she keep their money. Adrienne couldn't understand. Genna had told her, "Because I want you two to stay married, and I figure the first time he spends your rent money on drugs, you'll be ready to leave." She wouldn't do it until Josh insisted, saying the same thing. And now she was glad she had listened, because she was convinced the only reason he stopped and came home was because he ran out of money.

She had heard stories about people stealing from their relatives to get high. But Josh showed no inclination to do so. And he was always so sorry when he messed up. She couldn't stay mad at him. She found herself trying to figure out how to fix him. After all, she loved him. He was a good husband when he wasn't with his mistress. She would have to figure out something.

"You want to go for a walk after we eat?" He insisted they go walking every evening when it was nice out.

"You can go by yourself if you want to, Josh. I'm working."

"No, I want you to come with me. I need you."

"Okay, but only for a few minutes."

Chapter 5

Let's Go Home

It was the jumper he loved. Seeing it soar high above John Sally one Saturday afternoon, then seeing it fall back to earth right through the bottom of the net—*swoosh*—you could imagine the sound staring at the TV screen. The fluid, panther-like forays to the basket, daring any defender to stop him, were impossible to take your eyes off. Throwing down jams with effortless grace and power over men taller, shorter, quicker, faster, and slower—making them look like boys as he ruled the court with the authority of a Roman emperor. But it was the jumper that allowed him to sack the Dean Dome in Carolina and torch the men in blue for thirty-five points in a legendary performance cats talked about with awe in their voice whenever they discussed Len Bias. Cats loved his game so much they were contemplating pulling for the Celtics, the ultimate concession for black men in his generation.

Yeah, cats were salivating at the thought of him running the floor alongside Larry Bird until he got hold of some of that good Wayne Williams. That's what cats called that killer. That Wayne Williams, in honor of the guy accused of killing a bunch of young black men in Atlanta a few years ago. Niggers should have backed off this shit that would leave as you as dead as the Atlanta missing and murdered, but cats all wanted to see if they could survive that high, powerful enough to snatch a talent so sublime there had been talk he would rival Jordan before he ever set foot on an NBA court. And he hadn't even been smoking when he overdosed.

Josh thought about it as he sat in this room at South Atlanta Hospital, trying to get through the hour-and-a-half-long punishment of a Crackheads Together meeting. His mind wandered, seeking refuge from the boredom of listening to junkies struggling with their demons. He rubbed his left ring finger, reminding himself Adrienne had every right to insist he come here after he had sold his wedding band and the beautiful watch she had spent her Christmas savings on for a few sacks.

Those cocaine jitters were gnawing at the insides of his mind, but the great love he felt for her in his heart kept him seated. He told himself it would only be a few more minutes before he could roll out of there. The $80 sitting in his pocket strained against him, demanding to be spent on a few bumps. He glanced at his ring finger again as insurance against the overwhelming desire to get up and go. He reached in his pocket for a cigarette, his third since he got there.

A guy was saying how even though life was unfair, he was glad because, if life was truly fair, he would have been dead, buried, and forgotten a long time ago. Josh said *Amen* under his breath. Somebody else said he'd heard it was some good news and some bad news when he came into these rooms. The good news was he never had to smoke cocaine again. The bad news was smoking cocaine wasn't his problem.

Josh had no desire to stop smoking. He just wanted to stop doing stupid stuff like selling his wedding band. He should have known it was a trick when the guy told him he was putting it into hock for him. He'd gone back three times trying to get the ring and the watch back. All he wound up doing was smoking more cocaine.

When he told Adrienne what he had done, she hadn't said a word for the longest moment before shrieking, "Josh, I worked hard for that money. It's a whole lot of stuff I could have bought with it, but I bought you that watch because I wanted my husband to look good. And our wedding band! What is wrong with you? No, don't tell me. You couldn't help yourself."

So here he sat, listening to junkies drone on about their problems. Somebody told a story about a guy who was upset about his weed habit. Josh dragged on a smoke, tuning out such a dumb story. Who got strung out on weed? He used to smoke a joint every morning when he was at Morehouse. Then the guy said the dude was spending his bus fare on reefer and couldn't get to work. Josh could relate to fucking money up on drugs.

He lit another cigarette, once again considering getting up and leaving. There was no way Adrienne would possibly know he had left. His junkie mind kept urging him to run over to the Bluff and cop a few dimes. He could smoke them up and tell her he had hung around to talk after the meeting. She'd like hearing that.

The meeting was breaking up. They all stood around in a circle, arms over each other's shoulders, and said a prayer. He took his jacket off the back of the chair he sat in and headed out the door. He wondered if they had a good package in the Bluff. Maybe he ought to roll over to Thomasville or Leila Valley to see what was up.

He felt bad for a moment and rubbed his ring finger again. He stood paralyzed by fear of what he knew would happen next. He would ride somewhere, pick up a few sacks, and do even more damage to her. He looked around for a friendly face to talk to, hoping maybe this dope craving would pass. Everyone seemed to have paired off with someone else. Josh shuddered. Perspiration dripped from his underarms down the side of his shirt.

He wished he didn't have to walk out that door. Somehow, if he could just stay in this room, everything would be okay. He wished there were a pay phone in the room so he could call Adrienne and beg her to come get him. There was one down the hall on the way out, but . . .

He dropped his head. He walked through the door. He looked over to an aisle of chairs just outside, only to find himself looking right into the eyes of his wife. He stood speechless, unsure how to handle this moment. The craving rocked him before fading into nothing.

She walked over and reached up to take him in her arms. "I figured you might need me. I wanted to tell you how much I love you. I decided not wait until you got home." He squeezed her tight.

"I love you, too, Adrienne."

"Come on, sweetie. Let me go. It's going to be all right. Let's go home."

Chapter 6

Test Scores

"Aaron, sweetie, I'm with you. I like the black pinstripe. It looks good on you."

Josh interjected, "I still think you ought to get the navy blue." They were shopping for a suit for Aaron since he'd become a regular at Pastor Shaun's church. They wanted him to have a suit to wear at least some Sundays. They knew he wouldn't wear it every Sunday, but both Josh and Adrienne felt he needed one.

Aaron wanted this suit. Josh had learned at Coke that navy or charcoal gray was the way to go. He thought the navy suit looked good on Aaron. "Dang, Mr. Josh," Aaron replied. "That's for white boys. What, you turning into a white supremacist or something on me?" Josh laughed.

Adrienne stepped in to referee. "You know he's right, Josh. That suit does look good on him."

Josh quit arguing, knowing he'd never win after Miss Adrienne gave Aaron such a compliment. "Okay, okay, but I guess Miss Adrienne's paying for it."

"Miss Adrienne" took a quick glance at his left ring finger. "You think so, huh? I'm paying for it."

Aaron said, "Ah, Miss Adrienne, that was an ugly band anyway. See, now you and Mr. Josh can get brand-new ones." He winked at Josh.

Adrienne smiled. "Stay out of this, Aaron. I know you're trying to help him, but he's going to be in the doghouse for a long time behind that stunt." She stared at Josh. "I worked hard for that money. He's lucky Uncle James gave me some money after he found out what happened, because you just know Morehouse ain't kicking any extra my way."

So Josh reached into his pocket, peeling off six crisp one-hundred dollar bills with a flourish and told Aaron to bring him his change. Adrienne rolled her eyes. "Come on, Aaron, you need a shirt, too. He's not getting any change. If there's anything left, I'm going to put it on a new watch."

He loved the way she and Firstborn took to each other. (Faith had hung Aaron with the nickname Firstborn. She said Josh and Adrienne treated him like he was their firstborn son. So, Firstborn he became.) Aaron spent the night two Saturdays a month. They went to church together on those Sundays. They'd sit around, eat, talk trash, and have a great time together. A lot of times Genna, Daniel, and the kids would hang out with them. Occasionally they would babysit to give Genna and Daniel a much-earned night out. Adrienne was a wonder with kids.

On one such Sunday, Shaun said he saw some preacher in him. Aaron didn't want to hear it, though. Faith said he was just starting to smell himself. She told Josh to give him some time and that Shaun might be right. Aaron was already starting to know his way around the Bible. Adrienne teased him about it, saying maybe he could straighten Mr. Josh out.

She knew how much Josh loved Aaron and how much Aaron loved Josh. He was always telling her, "Mr. Josh is my man." Josh still wasn't really feeling God, but if going to church worked for his missus and his boy, then he had no problem going twice a month. Sometimes, recently, he even went on those Sundays when Aaron wasn't around.

They'd had a long talk about him the night before. Adrienne was wrestling with some ideas and how to fit them in her dissertation when he'd said to her, "Look, Adrienne, you know what you were saying about IQ scores being a lagging indicator of assimilation more so than proof of intellect?"

"Right," she had replied.

"Well, don't you think Aaron is a good example of what you're saying? I mean, we both know he's smart, but he's not going to blow away anybody's IQ test."

Josh had been a National Merit semi-finalist in high school. Genna had to tell Adrienne because he hated to talk about how smart he supposedly was. But this was important. He continued. "My grandparents went to college. My parents were both teachers so Genna and I got exposed to a lot. That's why I test so well. You see what I mean."

She said, "Yes, I think I see your point."

She had always told him fully assimilated peoples were those who were overwhelmingly middle class. She argued somewhere in her dissertation that America was both multicultural and culturally pluralistic at the same time—multi on her assimilating margins, plural in her mainstream center. He'd told her, "Baby, you and I are more mainstream than Aaron. So our scores ought to be higher. But that doesn't mean that he isn't smart, he's just unassimilated."

Her dissertation argued any testing done on brown kids should be benchmarked against some upper middle-class mainstream group, that those scores should be compared to the benchmark over a time frame rather than at a given point in time.

She'd said, "That's why I wanted him to get to know Hyung-Ju. So he could see the value of ownership. It's the best way to make your hard work *work*."

Josh had retorted, "I don't know if working for Hyung-Ju was the right idea. That Korean works his ass off." They'd both laughed. And she'd written about Aaron in her draft.

Yeah, he's coming along. And he does look good in that suit.

Chapter 7

Minsook

"Hey Minsook, I gonna lock the door, okay?" Aaron said over his shoulder to her as he walked to the front of the store. It was time to close. Hyung-Ju believed in him enough to go home early every once and a while. Aaron took that as a supreme gesture of trust. He tried to live up to it.

"Okay, Aaron," Minsook responded. She waited until he locked up before removing the money from the register. "Come on; keep me company while I do the count." He watched her walk in the back. She sure is tiny Aaron thought. Minsook and Mr. CW looked almost like Aunt Leah and Uncle Howard. He towered over her the same way. And she hovered over him like Aunt Leah did Uncle Howard.

"You need a ride home?" she asked.

"Nah, my cousin Cowboy is coming by to pick me up. We gonna hang out for a minute." She frowned. "You be careful, Aaron. It can be dangerous out there on a Friday night."

He laughed and asked, "What do you know about the streets?"

"I know it's bad out there. Why do you call him Cowboy? Does he like Westerns? My father loves Westerns."

"Nah, Minsook, when he lived in LA he got shot in the arm by some Venice Crips. He went to the doctor to get his arm checked out. The doctor was working on his arm when his nurse walked in and said, 'You know he doesn't have insurance.' The doctor started to put away his gear. Cowboy looked at him and said, 'Doc, you ain't gonna take the bullet out my arm?' The doctor looked at him and said, 'Son, this ain't no cowboy movie. That arm will be all right.' So now everybody calls him Cowboy. His real name's Alvin."

"What is a Crip, Aaron?"

"It's a black street gang in Los Angeles. It's two big gangs out there; the Crips and the Bloods, they call them. Bloods fight Crips, and Crips fight everybody, even each other."

"Oh," was all she said. They were quiet as she counted out and put the money in the night deposit bag.

"You need us to follow you to the bank?"

"Would you please?" she said in a way that let him know she was relieved to have someone with her when she made the drop.

"You gonna move with Mr. CW?"

"I can't, Aaron."

"Why not, don't you love him?"

She smiled. "It's a little more complicated than that."

"He doesn't want you to come with him?"

"Yes, he wants me to go with him." She hesitated for a moment. "I have to stay with my parents."

"Why?" Aaron shot back, perplexed by her answer.

"I have to stay with my parents, Aaron. They've been really good to me and they need me here."

"Oh, is it some kind of Korean thing?" She smiled and nodded. A tear edged out of her eye. Aaron looked away. He hadn't meant to upset her. Mr. CW was moving to the northeast to work on his PhD in economics, so Aaron had assumed Minsook was going with him. But now he regretted having asked.

"Well, you can go see him sometimes. Miss Adrienne says he's crazy about you. And his mom thinks you're good for him." Aaron wanted to cheer her up. And Miss Leah really did like her.

"Thank you, Aaron. He's says he's coming back to Atlanta when he finishes his degree anyway. He says he's coming back to me. So I should stay here and help my parents."

"See, Minsook? It's no need to get upset. Everything's going to work out." She wiped her eyes.

"I hope so, Aaron." They heard a banging on the window.

"That must be Cowboy. You stay here. I'll let him in and we'll follow you to the bank."

Chapter 8

Firstborn

"Boy, Firstborn is as sharp as a tack," Josh muttered to himself. He had to give it to Aaron, he did look good in that pinstriped suit. Adrienne and Aaron had been right. Josh was proud of him.

He cut his eyes to Adrienne. She was smiling. He knew she was thinking the same thing. He wondered was else was running through her mind as she touched Aaron's face, then took her hands and smoothed her dress. It was a pretty peach one, almost too bright and cheerful for so solemn an occasion, but Aaron did love her in that dress. And today was definitely all about Aaron. She looked at him, pain in her eyes, seeming to want him to give her some answer to this. But he didn't have one.

He took her hand. "Come on, Adrienne," he whispered. *This is too much*, he thought to himself as they looked down at Firstborn. She reached out to touch him again, a river of tears gushing from her beautiful brown eyes, a whimper passing her lips as she felt Aaron's cold, dead face one last time. "He looks so young," she whispered.

The last week had been crazy. Chicken Wing had called last Friday night. Josh thought it was odd when he asked to speak to him. "Hey, Josh man, you got to stay cool, okay? I got something to tell you. Something bad and I couldn't bring myself to tell Adrienne."

"What's up, man?" Josh asked, fearful of what he was getting ready to hear.

"Aaron got shot tonight at the store."

Josh swallowed hard. "What? Is he going to be all right?"

He felt Adrienne tugging at his arm, asking, "What's wrong?"

"Hey Josh, I'm sorry to tell you, man. They killed him."

"No man, you sure?"

"I'm sorry, Josh, but I saw him. He's dead."

"Josh, what's wrong?" she asked again, pleading to know what had happened. "Is it Aaron?" She told him later she had known by the look on his face.

"You still at the store?" Josh asked Chicken Wing. Chicken Wing said something. He told him they were on the way. He looked at Adrienne. "Baby, Aaron's been shot. He's dead."

Panic-stricken, she snatched the phone from his hand. She pleaded with her cousin to tell her he was lying. Then she began to moan. "Oh God, oh God, no, not Aaron, not Aaron, Josh. Please, Josh, please tell me not Aaron." He was afraid she would collapse, but she eventually gathered herself. "We have to call Genna," she told him. Genna was hysterical when they told her. They all rushed to West End.

Chicken Wing stood with Minsook and Hyung-Ju in the parking lot. Two bodies lay there while the Hat Squad (as Atlanta homicide was known, thanks to the fancy fedoras their most elite detectives sported) gathered evidence. Minsook was distraught, her shirt soaked with Aaron's blood. Hyung-Ju's eyes were hollow with sorrow.

Cowboy sat in the back of a police car. He had pulled up just as it was going down. He had administered street justice and shot the killers as they fled the scene. Between sobs, Minsook told them Aaron had gone to the front of the store when he heard knocking. He thought it was Cowboy. Evidently he refused to let them in, and they shot through the glass.

She heard the shots and had run out of the back in time to see Aaron fall to the floor. He had died in her arms. She said she tried to comfort him. He told her to tell his mother he loved her. That he had tried to be a good son.

Standing here in front of his casket at Firstborn's funeral, he could not make himself believe Aaron was gone. He pictured a jump shot raining down from the sky one Saturday afternoon, a young black man with Bias on his Terrapin jersey swaggering back down the court in the inimitable fashion of the young, gifted, and black, dead too young from a self-inflicted wound because some dope dealer didn't care who he destroyed in the process of getting paid. He thought about Slim, brutally murdered like Aaron because of some street stupidity.

Aaron's mother had put an autographed picture of the Terrapin star in the casket. A parent who knew how much Aaron admired Len Bias had gotten him an autograph before Bias had died. Aaron kept it on his dresser in his room.

This was incomprehensible. He gently pulled Adrienne away from the casket, wanting more than anything to be able to go back in time and change this. He wanted to whimper himself, but he had to be strong for his missus.

For some reason that old Rolling Stones tune "Gimme Shelter" played in his mind. He could hear that mournful opening guitar riff by Keith Richards and Mick Jagger belting out an apocalyptic vision of a world gone mad. That's where they lived—in a world gone mad. He heard Merry "Baby Sister" Clayton wailing like a banshee. The song told the story of a coming storm, a storm just a shot away. And in eighties black Atlanta, the storm was always just a shot away.

Chapter 9

A Prayer in Memory of the Kids

Josh's car constantly found its way to the abandoned grocery store in West End. Hyung-Ju had closed shop after the murder. The memories of Aaron were too strong. In spite of that, Josh couldn't stay away, no matter how much it hurt.

Josh would sit there haunted by ghosts. Sometimes it was Slim whispering Jay to him, trying to cheer him up. Sometimes he could feel Aaron. But mostly it was two little kids yelling *Josh, Josh save us*.

He thought about what Faith had said about him being banished to the ninth circle of hell. He used to laugh at her when she told him that. Only now that he was living there, it wasn't so funny anymore. He'd start out sitting in his car, but, unable to sit still any longer, would invariably get out and go inside. He'd go in the building though the back door, where he'd broken the lock one night in a fit of rage and anguish.

There he'd pull out the sacks he'd bought in the Bluff and put up a boulder on the cylinder he smoked out of these days. He'd light the dope with a disposable lighter and pull on the piece of Pyrex. Cocaine paranoia would set in after a couple of hits. Sounds would draw him to the front of the store. He'd peek out the window, sure the police were snooping around trying to figure out who was in the building. Then he'd rush to the back of the store to hide from them.

He'd hide the cylinder in a hole he'd dug in the wall, hoping the police wouldn't see it if they came in. He'd sit on the floor, folding his chin against his knees, staying low so they wouldn't see him. After a while, he would go peeping again. If he was satisfied the police weren't there, he'd bump. The kids would angrily confront him, demanding to know, "Why you'd do it, Josh? Why'd you set us on fire?"

He would clasp his hands behind his head, unable to answer. He wished many a night he'd been caught a long time ago. He thought good deeds would purchase peace of mind for him. Build a school to build young black people so he could push to the back of his mind the horror of what he'd done. He thought God had forgiven him. Instead, that bastard had simply bided his time in waiting to lash out at him.

And it was his fault. Secretly in the depths of his disconsolate heart he knew his killing those kids had led to Aaron's death. Many a night he sat there and prayed to die so he could leave behind this joyless life and give those he loved a chance to find peace in a world free of him. He feared God's ultimate punishment would be to leave him alive while all he cared about suffocated from the pain of suffering through a Josh-filled existence—especially Adrienne.

He loved her so much. He hated her loving him. He hated himself for taking her through so much. She'd been through so many difficulties—her mother, Norman, Aaron, and now, being the wife of a crackhead. He looked up at the ceiling and prayed again. "God, please let me die."

Chapter 10

We Might Not Make It

In the Billy Wilder film *The Apartment*, the character Fran Kubelik says women who date married men shouldn't wear mascara. She could have as easily been talking about the women of cocaine-addicted men. Adrienne thought about this one night as she watched the movie on TV.

There would be stretches where Josh would appear to get better, coming home for two or three weeks straight. But as soon as she began to have hope, he would go off and spend the night in the streets again. Even the school had lost meaning to him since Aaron had died. They had sat in silence one Friday watching Barbara Walters interview Robin Givens and Mike Tyson. Josh had come home from a two-day bender, suit rumpled and shirt dingy. She could barely tolerate his presence.

After hearing from Givens about Tyson's bouts with depression and her travails of life with him, Barbara Walters posed a question: "What would be the worst thing that could happen to the two of you?"

Givens contemplated the question before answering: "It would be that we didn't make it."

"She doesn't love him," Adrienne said bitterly.

Josh said to her, "How do you know she doesn't love that man? She just said the worst thing that could happen is that they didn't make it. Hell, he kicked her ass. What more do you want from her?"

"She doesn't love him," she repeated.

He asked again, "How can you say she doesn't love him? How can you know?"

She turned to him. "I know she doesn't love him, because I love you. And just like him, you're sick. And because you're sick, we might not make it. But if we don't make it and if anyone ever asked me what the worst thing that happened was, I wouldn't say it was 'we didn't make it.' I would say the worst thing that happened was you didn't get well."

Chapter 11

Let Go

Standing there in the hot shower, so hot it felt like it was setting her skin on fire, Adrienne let the water run over her body. Josh had done it again. It was two in the morning. She knew he wouldn't be home until after she left for work in the morning. She had sobbed; big, racking cries loud enough she hoped he could hear. *Why do I love you?*

The bad thing was, she did. And she couldn't seem to stop. So she stayed in the shower until the water ran too cold to stand under. Her heartache told her he would change if he saw her like this. If he saw her tears, he would be so touched he would put the pipe down for good. But of course, he wouldn't come home.

She got out of the shower and dried herself off. Aunt Leah had made her talk to her Uncle Short Boy. For years, heroin and alcohol had dominated Short Boy's life. But he'd changed. She never knew that Short Boy; he was always just the uncle she so loved. The one who showered her with presents and told her she looked just like her mother.

She had thought he would tell her how to get help for Josh. Instead, he had told her she needed help. Said to her, "Adrienne, Josh is making you crazy. Junkies do that to you. You got to get some help for yourself. And if he's ever ready to give up the high cost of low living, he will. But you got to fix yourself. We need you too."

She had been mad at him and Aunt Leah. Alonso had called her after Leah had told him how she was suffering. He'd repeated what Short Boy had said: "Adrienne, your mother had to help herself before I could help myself." He'd told her talk to Pastor Shaun. See what he might suggest.

Shaun had told her that a couple of the mothers of the church had dealt with drug addicts in their life. One had told him she got rid of her husband. Said that drug addicts and gay men were too frustrating for a woman to try to make a go of it with because they both loved something a woman doesn't have to give. The other had told him it was all right to love your junkie, but sometimes you had to let him go. You can let go with love, but sometimes you just have to let go. He had said if she wanted to talk, to let him know when and who. She'd put off that conversation, but she realized now it was time. She'd snapped at one of her students today. That wasn't her. She would call the mother in the morning. She needed to learn how to let go with love.

Chapter 12

Norman Aaron Gibson

Adrienne was ecstatic. She had successfully defended her dissertation. She was going to have a PhD! Her arguments about inclusive and exclusive discrimination hadn't gone over well with her dissertation committee at first. She had almost lost the black conservative when she insisted racism bore a great deal of the blame for what was beginning to happen in the black community. And when she had explained she felt one thing that would help black people would be the legalization of drugs, the entire committee was shocked.

She had told them young black men were no different than the young Italian men who had bloodied the streets of New York during the Prohibition Era in what was called the Castellammarese War. Young men living on society's unassimilated margins had seen no problem with breaking the law if it gave them a chance to accrue wealth and power. What was happening on the streets of America was predictable. The returns on crime were simply too high to resist. Dr. Black Conservative had given her a really hard time.

Her deconstruction of affirmative action had won the day. Her argument that it was a well-meaning mistake that would contribute to the dissolution of the black family had scored points with her primarily conservative committee.

She had spiced up her argument about approach to racism and the attitudes that reinforced the cultural divide with the thought, "Americans and black people themselves only seem to feel black men are competent at doing the three Ds: dribblin', dancin', and slinging dope. And if America wants to believe the three Ds are all the black community is capable of, the black community doesn't have to buy into this attitude." Dr. Black Conservative had almost been drooling after that statement. Three days after her dissertation defense, he had actually tried to hem and haw about them going to eat and talk, saying he wanted to discuss the three Ds in greater detail. She had played him off. She had started to tell Josh, but she had been afraid he might kill him. He hated black conservatives like Cotton Mather hated witches.

And Josh had been drug free for over eight months. She had changed and Short Boy was right. Somehow he had changed. And now her OB/GYN had informed her she was six weeks pregnant. She couldn't wait to get home and tell Josh.

She hoped it was a little nappy-headed boy. It had been fun being the only woman in her house growing up. She figured a house full of men would work. If it was a boy, she wanted to name him Norman Aaron Gibson. She smiled and touched her abdomen as she pulled in the driveway of the house they were renting from Uncle Howard and Aunt Leah. They were going to have to start thinking about a home of their own.

Chapter 13

Hebrews

Faith shook her head. She looked at him with eyes filled with sorrow. "You know she's going to leave you." He tried to argue. Faith put her hand on his shoulder. "Josh, she's going to leave you. Get ready, because she has to and you know it. I'm not saying she won't ever come back, but she's supposed to leave behind the shit you did and you know it."

"Come on, Faith, don't say that. She can't leave me. She can't."

"Yes, she can, and please don't try to go get her to stay when she does."

"What do you mean? I can't talk her out of it?" His voice rose with anxiety as he spoke.

"She's not going to let you talk her out of it. You'll look up one day and she'll be gone. I told you a long time ago, Josh, a woman gets tired. She can take a lot off a man, and Lord knows she took a lot off you, but there just comes a point when she gets tired and she has to move on."

"You mean she doesn't love me anymore," he said, rising up off Faith's bed.

"Josh, that girl will always love you. I've told you that over and over again. She can't help it. I know 'cause I know what she sees in you. You like one of those big summer storms that used to sweep through central Georgia when I was a little bitty girl full of blast and bluster, terrifying and exhilarating all at the same time. A woman's lucky to meet a man like you, much less grab hold to you. She got to ride the Josh tornado. She can't forget that. And you know I've told you that before. Problem is, Tin Man, your hardheaded ass won't listen. But Josh, baby, you can't straighten this one out. Only God and time can do that."

"Fuck God. People always talking 'bout 'God can do this' and 'God can do that.' If he can do so much, then why did he let this happen?"

"Now you know the only reason I'm going to let you get away with saying that is because I know you're hurting, but it ain't God's fault. It's yours for being so damn selfish and you know it."

"Damn, Faith, I mean . . . I thought I was doing the right thing. I haven't been high in almost ten months . . ."

"Josh, everybody's happy about that, but has it ever occurred to you that maybe getting off drugs was just a beginning? That maybe she wants more from you than just that? And Lord knows you took her through a lot with that dope, but can't you see why she would be upset?"

"But Faith, she's calmed down. It ain't easy right now, but we're talking. We're getting along."

"And baby, you always will, but that doesn't mean she's not going to leave. She's just biding her time. When she gets her shit together, she'll be gone so fast it will make your head swim. And you know what? She'll be right."

"And you enjoying this shit, ain't you?"

"Shit, nigger, don't bark at me! You the one who fucked up. I'm trying to get your ass ready for what's coming. Talking shit to me ain't gonna change anything. I'm your girl. Don't you forget that. Lord knows you need a friend right now."

"Hell, Faith, it ain't like I pushed her down a flight of stairs or some crazy shit like that. Why you so sure she's gonna leave?"

"Josh, you must not of saw the way she looked at you in the hospital. Like you were something nasty, something she didn't want to be near."

"Yeah, I saw."

"Well now, Mr. Gibson, has she ever looked at you like that before? All that shit you've done. Has she?"

"Nah, she hadn't, Faith, but I don't know what I'd do if she left me."

Faith shook her head again. "Tell me something. If you didn't want her to be a part of your life, why didn't you just tell her?

Josh thought about the conversation he'd had with Shaun a couple of weeks ago. "Jay, don't be mad at God. You have to keep the faith. He's simply moving in your life to make you a better man."

"By killing my child, by hurting the woman I love?"

"Jay, you know I love the line in Hebrews that says, 'Now faith is the substance of things hoped for, the evidence of things not seen.' You might want to consider it. Faith doesn't mean you don't ever doubt God, because we all do. Nor does God want you to live a doubt-free existence when it comes to him. Doubt is the yeast that leavens faith and allows it to rise within you. Questioning God may drive you away from him, and with the struggles you've gone through, I can understand why you'd turn your back on him.

"But Jay, man, faith is choosing to believe in spite of the bad times. Faith requires you to humble yourself to the point where you truly believe God knows best. On days like this, it's hard to believe God cares, and honestly, bro, it's your choice as to whether you do or not, but all I know is faith sustains me on my bad days, and more importantly, it humbles me on my good ones."

"So you saying it's okay for me to doubt, to be angry with God at this moment?"

"I'm saying, Jay, it's exactly what God expects. Now let's be honest, man. You have culpability in what happened, right?" Shaun looked him in his eyes. "I'm your boy, Jay. The truth is the light. You could say if you hadn't done what you did, she wouldn't have lost the baby."

"Man, I just thought she was stronger than that. I mean, I can see her kicking me to the curb Shaun. I can see that, but I never would have thought she would have lost the baby. And I do feel responsible. It's killing me, man. And Faith swears she'll eventually leave me because of this."

Shaun considered this for a moment. "She may, but know this: she loves you almost too much. The space might be good for her, good for you, because for you to have done what you did, there's something wrong inside you, something you need to fix before the two of you can go on. And Jay, you're not the first Gibson I told to heed the words of Hebrews. She came to me a little over a year ago. She was seeking help because she was convinced you'd never get off drugs. I told her to have faith.

"She started going to a support group for the families of drug addicts. She told me they were teaching her to let go with love. She told me letting go of you felt impossible. She said you had become the very air she breathes. Yeah, she said that about you. I told her it might take stepping away for you to find yourself. She chose to hang in there even though she doubted you could quit. A year later, no matter how things turned out between you, she saw her greatest wish come true—you off drugs. Don't give up on her, don't give up on yourself, and please, my brother, don't give up on God.

"He must love you an awful lot to have brought her into your life. Man, you don't know how lucky you are to have a woman who loves you the way she does. And she is so strong, Josh. It took a lot of strength to deal with you. It'll take all the strength she has to leave, but she is strong enough to go, if that's what she decides to do."

Josh was as scared as he had ever been. They were right. He knew Adrienne well enough to know she was going to leave. And he couldn't blame her.

Chapter 14

Beanie

There were two bad mistakes he'd made he would always wish he could take back. The first was running up to that house and tossing those fire bombs through the front window. No matter how hard he tried, he couldn't forgive himself for that moment. The worst part was living with the guilt of having gotten away with killing three people. Cowboy was doing time for a manslaughter charge, while Josh was still walking around free.

The second was turning into the Bluff that day. He still didn't know why he'd done it. Maybe he missed the streets. He was riding along when suddenly he saw a familiar face. "Hey, Josh baby!" Beanie yelled. "Where the hell you been, boy?" Before he could answer, she was in the car. They talked for a minute. She was disappointed when he explained he had quit hitting. Then she asked about Dad.

He told her Dad had shot some Korean grocer in the face with a .357. Told her Dad had been trying to come down off a high and lifted two bottles of Mad Dog out the guy's store. The Korean ran out behind him, and Dad blasted him and his black security guard. He had heard both the grocer and his guard survived, but he had a hard time believing anybody could get shot in the face with a .357 and live. She shook her head and said, "Yeah, he always was kind of off."

One thing led to another and they screwed, and afterward he gave her fifty dollars for old time's sake. She asked if he wanted to bump. He told her he was done with that.

He felt pretty fucked up afterwards. He had never even thought about screwing anybody else since he and Adrienne had hooked up, and in those dope traps you had all kinds of crack hos throwing themselves at you.

A couple of weeks later, he was taking a leak when his dick felt like it had caught fire. "Damn," he muttered to himself, immediately thinking he might have the clap. And he and Adrienne had been going at it long and strong for a couple of months. She wanted a baby. *Shit* was his next thought. *Please don't let this be happening*, he implored God, the universe, and whoever else might be listening.

Sure enough, he had the clap. It took him two weeks to find the nerve and words to approach her one afternoon when they were preparing to go to dinner. She wanted to go celebrate and tell him some good news.

He told her, "I got something I need to tell you first." He looked at his shoes.

"Josh, are you all right?" She stared at him. "You didn't have a slip, did you?" *Slip*, that's what junkies said when they slipped up and got high again. Yeah, that was what they called it—a slip. He'd slipped all right. And he wished it had been on drugs.

"No, that's not it, Adrienne. I did something really stupid."

"What, Josh? Go ahead and tell me."

He hesitated. "Like I said, I did something really stupid. I don't know why. I was over by the Bluff a couple of months ago. I saw this girl I use to get high with before I met you. We talked and one thing led to another." He could already see her getting mad. "We had sex."

She started to quake with anger. "You had sex, sex with her."

"Adrienne, I got the clap."

"You have the clap? Damn you, Josh Gibson!"

"Calm down, baby, I am so sorry."

"Calm down, calm down, is that all you can say? You stand here and tell me you have the clap and you want me to calm down. You bastard! How dare you. I'm pregnant, Josh! With your baby, and you want me to calm down. I'm pregnant, and you tell me I have the clap and you want me to calm down." She slumped to the floor, her hands wrapped around her waist. She looked up at the ceiling.

He sank to the floor, attempting to hold her. "Get your hands off of me! Get away from me, Josh. I hate you!"

"Adrienne, please baby, I'm sorry."

"Get out! I can't stand you! Get out," she shouted. She sat back on the linoleum, crying. She wailed and wailed, rocking back and forth as she did, each cry breaking his heart.

A month later, she lost the baby. She moved back to Ohio at the end of the semester.

Chapter 15

The North Star

Months passed. Josh didn't know what to do other than try to fix whatever was broken inside of him. He picked up the phone several times to call her, but lost his nerve when it began to ring Alonso's number. Alonso called him one night and asked, "Josh, when you coming to get your wife? She misses you and I had forgotten how rough it is cleaning up behind her."

"She really said she misses me, Mr. Johnson?"

"No, Josh, but she's my daughter. I know she does. Son, whatever you did, you have to figure out how to make her forgive you. You still love her, right?"

"With all my heart, but I don't know how she can forgive me."

"What did you do, cheat on her?"

"Something like that."

"Something like that? Either you did or you didn't. Well, I know she lost the baby and I know she blames you. I'll talk to her about that. But you need to beg her forgiveness. Maybe she'll take you back."

He talked to her once. "Hey, baby," he said hopefully, thrilled to hear her voice even if it was as cold as he could ever imagine.

"Hey," she replied. "What do you want?"

"I wanted to see how you're doing?"

"Fine," she remarked. They talked for a few minutes before she slammed the phone down.

He sent her a telescope for Christmas. He penned a note. *This is for you to find our star. Look at Polaris and hopefully you see a way to forgive me. I am trying to be better. I miss you. I will love you always even if you don't love me anymore.*

He started going to Crackheads Together on a regular basis. One night he talked to a guy everybody looked up to named Marsh. Marsh was an atheist. They closed every meeting with the Lord's Prayer. "Hey Marsh," Josh asked. "If you're an atheist, why do you always recite the Lord's Prayer?"

"It keeps me clean."

Josh sensed this might be someone who could help him.

Josh believed in God, but he still wasn't sure he liked Him. Marsh wasn't asking him to believe. He was insisting Josh get better. Marsh told Josh he didn't have a getting-high problem, he had a living problem. Asked him if he ever recited the junkie prayer. "What?" Josh said.

"You know, please God let me die. A lot of y'all true believers say that when you out of money and have done some really stupid shit."

Josh laughed and said, "Yeah, I have."

Working together, they reached a point where Josh needed to confess the bad he'd done. When Marsh heard about the kids, he told Josh there comes a point where you have to make amends. At first Josh thought he meant he would have to ask forgiveness. Marsh made him look the word up in the dictionary. It meant to make the situation better.

"Some of these people you've hurt, Josh, you don't really have the right to ask their forgiveness. The best thing you can do for your wife is to stay off drugs and work on making yourself a better man. I don't know what to tell you about those kids. That will come to you. And one more thing."

"What?" Josh asked.

"Are you a Christian?

Am I? "I guess I am, Marsh."

"Christians believe in a forgiving God, right?"

"Right," Josh replied.

"Well, if God forgives you for your sins, why don't you?" Josh laughed. He knew where he wanted to start. After a few weeks, he called Sarah.

Chapter 16

Mirror, Mirror, on the Wall

"Boy, you just crazy!"

"Come on, Faith, why you say that? We had lunch together, that's all. Why you raising such a fuss?"

"Uh-huh, I bet it was just lunch. The two of y'all sitting there, you batting those big brown eyes at her. You gonna get enough."

"Look, Faith, it was just lunch between two old friends. How many times do I need to tell you that? We talked. We caught up on each other. You act like you forget how close we used to be."

"I haven't forgot anything! Especially how stupid she used to be about you . . . And why did you have to quit cussin'? Now you got me so I don't want to anymore around your ass. Next thing you'll quit smoking!"

He pulled on his cigarette, chuckling at Faith. They were sitting on her bed, having an animated debate about his lunch adventure with Sarah. As usual, she was in her robe. Like old times, she was raising hell with him about Sarah. And like always, she didn't understand.

"Look, Faith, she's not some two-dollar crack piece. She's Sarah and she means the world to me. I know you find that hard to believe after the way I treated her, but give me some credit. I'm trying to grow up. I wouldn't do that."

"Do what, Josh?"

"Lay down with her. I know you're thinking I'm sniffing around her so I can mess up her and Felton's marriage. You're wrong, Faith. That's the old Josh. Besides, I love Adrienne. I learned my lesson fooling around with Beanie. I wrecked my life for—what do you always say—seven minutes of pleasure. She may never come back, but until she sends me divorce papers, I'm not going out like that anymore."

Faith studied him for a minute. "Josh, if you wanted to lay down with that crack ho Beanie, you could have come to me. I would have hooked you up and you would have gone home grinning. And you wouldn't have caught the clap. You hard headed!"

"Look, Faith, you know I love you, but I've told you a hundred times that would ruin our friendship!"

"Josh Gibson, you full of it. How you know it wouldn't make it better unless you try it?"

He thought, *It's funny how life works*. He mused on how he had gotten to this point. When he quit getting high, he thought that was the answer to his troubles. Turned out the old heads were right. Getting high wasn't his problem— just like they told him. It was him all along.

He couldn't see that until he made the biggest mistake of his life almost a year off drugs. Only the pain from the loss of his wife and child were enough to make him look in the mirror. There he saw both the problem and the solution.

He came to accept the idea that he had to make amends for his past. Making peace with Sarah was the easy part. Coming to grips with the need for him to turn himself in for the murder of Keisha and her kids was hard.

Faith told him he was suffering from wet brain because it's no way he wanted to go to prison for something he had gotten clean away with. She reminded him there's no statute of limitation on murder. When he told her he had a duty to God to turn himself in, she laughed and told him, "If God had wanted your dumb ass behind bars, he would have provided the police with better evidence, thank you."

She went on to say, "I know what you're going through. Remember, I killed somebody too. If you're any kind of human being—and you are—that tears at you at night." Then she asked, "So did you tell her?"

"Tell her what?' Josh responded knowing full well what she meant.

"Tell her what you did, Josh. I know you never had before."

He paused before answering. "Yeah, I told her."

"And what did her grand behind say?"

"She was surprised. She couldn't believe I had done something like that. She said it explained a lot."

"You mean she didn't get up and run from the table?"

"Nah, Faith, she was cool." Cool wasn't exactly what Sarah had been, but that wasn't Faith's business. A look of fear had flashed on Sarah's face when he told her the dark secret behind his nightmares. She had said now she understood him better, but only after a long moment of anguished silence.

Sarah had stroked his hand. For once, she didn't paper over his misdeeds or change the subject. He would always be grateful to her for that. He called her the black girl with the white name for old time's sake. They both laughed. He called her that because Sarah Smith was the name of an elementary school in a white neighborhood in Buckhead. Sarah told him he owed it to Adrienne to let her know what he was contemplating.

Faith rested her hand on his knee. "Josh, you know you need to tell that girl. Quit trying to punish her!"

"What do you mean punish her?"

Too late—he saw her knuckles approaching. She rapped him a good one right upside the head. "You know damn well you trying to punish her for leaving you. And it's your fault she left. See, I know you, Josh. You think, 'Oh, somebody will tell her and she'll feel awful about me turning myself in.' Or you hoping Genna or me or somebody will call her and say, 'You know what Josh is going to do?' and she'll come running to save your trifling butt. You ain't no good, Tin Man. And you swear you trying to change. You might have fooled old grand Sarah, but I am not going for it!"

Josh bent his head down and stared at the floor. Something inside him wanted her to know he was going to sacrifice his life. He wasn't sure about trying to punish her, but he was past tired of living without her. "Josh, pick up the phone and call her. She loves you. Why can't you believe that? She lost your baby. You think she doesn't want another with you? You're crazy. That girl wants to have a slew of little, crazy, nappy-headed boys who act just like you. Maybe you don't need to call her, because she might come back to you."

He laughed. Faith was shaking her head and laughing with him. She stared at him, trying to gauge whether or not the truth of her words had sunk in. "You really think I'm trying to punish her, Faith?"

"Damn you, Josh Gibson, you got so much sense about everything else, but you are as dumb as a rock when it comes to that girl." Then, softly: "Josh, you need to call her."

"I know, Faith, but every time I pick the phone up I can't dial. I just can't bear her rejecting me."

"Well then, baby, write her a note. Do something to get her back. Crawl to that little town in Ohio on your hands and knees and beg her forgiveness, but before you do something stupid, give her a chance. I mean, all you did was kill some black people. It ain't like they gonna really put you in jail for that. Hell, they might give you a medal."

Chapter 17

I Might Get a Medal

"Hey, Josh, I called to see how you're doing."

"Hey, Genna. I'm doing great now that I hear my baby sister's voice. I thought you might not ever talk to me about anything but business again."

"You're still my brother, even if you are crazy."

"I sent Adrienne a note today."

"You did! Well, you're finally acting like you have some sense again, even though you know you need to call her."

"She doesn't want to talk to me."

"Have you gotten that paperwork yet?"

"Nah, why you ask me that?" More fear was creeping in to his voice than he wanted her to hear. "Have you talked to her?"

"As a matter of fact, I have. It's amazing how picking up a phone and dialing a few numbers will give you a chance to talk to someone. You really ought to try it sometimes."

"You sound like Faith."

"I'm sure I do. And we're both right and you're wrong. Josh, she's been offered a job at Howard."

"Howard, huh? That's a nice hookup."

"See that's your problem. 'Nice hookup.' Why don't you call that girl? Josh, please ask her to forgive you."

"Sis, seriously. Do you think she will?"

"Not if she has a lick of sense in her brain."

"Would you?"

"You mean forgive you for cheating on me with that skank?"

"No—for killing our child."

"Ooh, you get on my nerves. You didn't kill that baby. You can be so arrogant and self-centered sometimes. Everything that happens in life doesn't revolve round you. The baby wasn't developing properly. That's why it died. But you were too busy tippy-toeing around her, too scared of how mad she was to ask. How did you kill the baby? She didn't get the clap. Her test was negative. Josh, she would forgive you if you would just give her a chance."

"Damn, Genna, you my sister. Why didn't you tell me?"

"Josh Gibson, don't yell at me. It wasn't my place to tell you. She's your wife. You should have asked!"

"But every time I tried to talk to her about the baby, she'd throw a fit."

"Don't you think she should have? Who are you? You can't be my brother. My brother was raised by Lawrence and Regina Gibson. He wouldn't be whining about 'Oooh, Genna, she's mad at me.' She's supposed to be. That's your job—to get her to forgive you. She'd gladly have a dozen little Gibsons if you'd let her, but you won't let her."

"I begged her to forgive me and I asked her to come home. You think she'll forgive me?"

"Josh, you are stupid! I tell you what. Why don't you call her and ask her?"

"I might."

"Quit lying to yourself. Just know this. She still loves you. She hates you too, but only because she loves you."

"She told you that?"

"No, and if she had, I wouldn't tell you. Brother or no brother, what you did was wrong! You still plan on turning yourself in?"

"Genna, I just want it off my heart. Faith says they might not do anything anyway. That all I did was kill three black people. They might even give me a medal."

"Josh, I know it's tearing you apart, but what about the people who love you? Don't we get any consideration? I don't want to bring your niece and nephew to see you in prison. What about the school? What about those kids? They need you. Do you think Aaron would want you to turn yourself in?" She was crying.

"Come on, sis, that's not fair."

"I don't care, Josh! I hate you did what you did. You haven't been the same ever since you killed those children. But why can't you forgive yourself? Every bit of happiness that comes to you in this life, you mess it up. Are you being fair to Adrienne?"

"This way she can get on with her life."

"And you get to decide that for her. She doesn't get any say? At least tell her what you're going to do. If she's okay with it, I'll leave you alone."

"Okay, Hopalong, I'll give her a chance to get the note and see what she says."

"Don't call me that!"

"I only do that because I love you. You know that."

"You don't love me. What do you know about love? You don't even know how to love yourself." The phone went dead.

Chapter 18

Don't Let the Clock Strike Twelve

Josh thumbed through her notes. It sure was fun being married to a revolutionary. She'd really opened his eyes to some things. Genna told him she'd gotten a nibble or two from literary agents. Glad to know she was still pursuing publication of this radical version of her dissertation. He started reading the last few sections, starting with a section he had inspired:

There are two main issues surrounding drugs—addiction and the illegality of drugs. I am the wife of a drug addict. I cannot describe the pain of having my heart tethered to my husband's afflicted soul, my tremulous spirit despairing another long night of wondering, where are you? I love him.

He skipped a few pages.

The illegality of drugs brings its own set of issues. Like prohibition during the roaring twenties the crack epidemic has driven the returns on crime to stratospheric heights. And like the Roaring Twenties, the go-go eighties have seen a concurrent rise in the nation's murder rate. The war on drugs is a war on the black community. By forcing drugs underground in an era of soaring demand, we have inadvertently encouraged a generation of young men to chase the abnormally high returns on crime drug-dealing makes available to anyone willing to accept crime's risk factors (prison, maiming, and death).

Like the Jewish, Irish, and Italian gangsters who turned the streets of America's cities into twin rivers of tears and blood during Prohibition, the black and Latino gangsters of our time have fought for market share in our nation's open-air drug markets at the business end of a gun. To read of the gangster in early twentieth century America is to read of men who reveled in the financial, psychological, and emotional returns on crime made available to them by the illegality of alcohol. To look at poor black and Latino communities during the browning of America is to see the lethal combination of values in transition and high returns on crime make slinging dope irresistible to many on society's assimilating margins. After a failed war on alcohol, how can we possibly perceive a successful war on drugs?

He skipped a few more pages.

Commentators argue fatherless households are our problem. Black women know how to raise men. It has been a part of our culture for far too long for me to accept this as the problem. Besides, Al Capone and Myer Lansky, two of gangland's most notorious figures, were raised by their dads. They surveyed an America that looked down its nose at the assimilating masses of Italians and Jews and decided selling hooch would afford them the life their fathers' honest labor in America could not. Discrimination against Italians and Jews thwarted their fathers' honest efforts at every turn. Their fathers' example of seeking the American Dream was not the life they would choose to lead.

Commentators imply blacks are genetically inclined to murder and mayhem. Yet James Truslow Adams made the point during the Jewish assimilation era that the Jew did not bring crime to America, America brought crime to the Jew. I would argue that any marginal group member would find the choice of slinging dope like Nicky Barnes or dribbling a basketball like Magic Johnson or dancing like Michael Jackson enticing. Very few are gifted enough to be an athlete or an entertainer, but anyone can yell "Got them dimes?" and pull a trigger.

And these very rational choices made by the disenfranchised lead America to stereotypical conclusions about not a few black people, but the many. I fear these attitudes will harden and increase mainstream America's discounting of black lives. Returns on crime, not risks associated with criminal activity, are what we should focus on. Legalize drugs and eviscerate returns on crime.

The Mafia in America is slowly dying because young Italian men given a broader base of opportunity by assimilation no longer perceive the returns on crime commiserate with the risks involved. History teaches us young black men will one day view crime's risk-return relationship in the same light. Black people must take the lead in the effort to legalize drugs in this country. That is a war worth fighting. It will accelerate the drive for equality.

Josh stopped. This passage always troubled him. He agreed with her, but he could not envision an America where drugs were legal. Finally, he skipped over to his favorite part.

Since we are enamored with the idea of the gangster as a community icon, maybe an old gangland legend can provide the impetus for change. Peter Maas told in his biography The Valachi Papers *of a single night in the nineteen thirties known as the Night of the Sicilian Vespers, when the Young Turks of the American mafia engaged in a nationwide slaughter of the Mustache Petes who controlled the underworld. Men like Lucky Luciano, Vito Genovese, Frank Costello, and their Jewish allies Meyer Lansky and Bugsy Siegel, ordered the murders of these old line leaders to create a more American Mafia. This* modernized entity would dominate the underworld for decades and turn the Young Turks into criminal legends.

What the sons and daughters of segregation need is a black *Night of the Sicilian Vespers*—a movement to modernize our thinking so we might develop a more efficient assimilation curve. Leadership, not theory, is what we require. New leadership must necessarily eliminate the old and put in place new ideas that would minimize the impact of racism in our lives to the point it is no longer relevant.

This leadership must cast aside the hate in the words of the Honorable Elijah Muhammad and adhere to the teachings of his Message to the Blackman in America—*Respect your sister, respect your brother, educate your children, love and rely on yourself so we might live in a better black community. In fact, we must realize no matter how good it feels to be self-righteous, no matter how warranted hatred and anger may feel they will not solve our problems. Self-love, not hating others is where our focus must lie. We must set a new agenda for us as a people.*

Our social agenda should focus on

1) *Self-discipline:*
   a. *Self-destructive behavior patterns must be eliminated*
   b. *The cultural ideal must center around achievement*
2) *Redefining the educational ideal in our community*
   a. *The educated must regain their status as community icon*
   b. *Family emphasis on learning (trips to the library, home study, etc.)*
   c. *Emphasis on equitable distribution of educational assets (2-4-6-8 we don't need to integrate)*

3) *Redefine hero (the hard worker over the slick mack daddy, the scholar over the dope dealer, the business owner over the corporate executive)*

4) *Recognition of community niches—black problems are no longer monolithic in scope*
   a. *Class-based problems*
   b. *Individual considerations—gender, sexual preference, physical and/or mental disability*
   c. *Stage of life considerations—what we are striving for determines the discrimination we face*

5) *Emphasis on cultural heritage over race—black is more than just a color, it is a state of mind*

Our economic agenda must revolve around:
   1) *Savings—economic self-reliance begins with savings*
      a. *Invest black, sell mainstream campaigns*
      b. *Reduce consumption*
   2) *Economic solidarity*
      a. *Start family businesses*
      b. *Emphasize science and engineering—creative products and services grow large businesses*
      c. *Engage the sun (engineer storable solar and the piston displacement to burn it efficiently—remember how old JD made his fortune in energy)*
      d. *Support HBCUs even if you didn't attend one (put five on it)*

We must begin to deemphasize political activism. Political activism's confrontational nature leads to inefficient assimilation due to attitudes hardened by battles over ideas like affirmative action. However, we should:

1) Vote—this is the cornerstone of American political power and should not be ignored
   a. Vote locally
   b. Leverage our votes by forming multiracial and multicultural coalitions based on mutual need
2) Become political independents—assimilating peoples should be pragmatic, not dogmatic
3) Localize our political interests
4) Hold black politicians accountable—don't complain about white politicians who won't do for you if you elect black ones who see no need to do for you

Our new leadership must be:
1) Black trained
2) Bicultural
3) Race people
4) Financially independent
5) Members of the echo generation—the only people who will be bicultural enough to pull this off
6) Suspicious of black racism—two wrongs won't right our situation

The new leadership must build a bridge to the cultural mainstream blacks can cross with pride and a sense of safety. The new leadership must encourage blacks to Americanize. It must do so while respecting our people. It must not disrespect or belittle the burden we bear. It must remember who we are.

We are America's stepchild. Like Cinderella in the fairy tale, we sit in the corner of our cold, damp room in our home trying to fathom why the only mother we have ever known disdains us so much, why she will not let us go to dance at the grand ball of Americana like our stepsisters. We dream of a fairy godmother of governmental salvation interceding on our behalf, we fantasize about a presidential Prince Charming who might invite us to dance the dance of equality so we might know for once how it feels to be the belle of the ball.

Yet no magic wand transforms us, no glass slipper awaits us. We must break out our sewing kit and stitch together a beautiful gown of economic self-reliance fortified by the threads of self-love. Do we hold to our dream of a governmental fairy godmother, our fantasy of a presidential Prince Charming, or do we learn to rely upon ourselves? Which way, black America? Midnight approaches.

Chapter 19

A Letter in the Mail

Alonso Johnson trudged through the spring snow toward his mailbox. On days like this, the damp, cold air caused his joints and muscles to not so gently remind him of the many years spent on the assembly line at the Ford engine plant supporting his brood of nine. He smiled to himself as he reached the box, thinking he would do it all over again for them. It was a father's job to take care of his kids. Especially after his darling Carol had died so young. His only daughter was so much like her mother some days it was hard to look at her.

The box was full today, mostly with bills. He sighed. It would be nice to pull something pleasant out of that box for a change, from amidst the catalogs, junk, and requests for payments that showed up day after day. He thumbed through the mail as he walked back into his front door. Then he saw a letter for Adrienne, from Josh. He frowned. He was unsure whether to give it to her or not.

He liked Josh. A sadness shadowed his only daughter, one most people couldn't see; but he discerned it all too well because she was his heart. When Josh had showed up, the shadow faded. He teased her when they jumped the broom in this western Ohio burg, telling her, "Yeah, baby, I could always tell you liked him hard."

He was so nice and respectful when Alonso met him; he couldn't believe this was the young man who had beaten a guy up for daring to ask his daughter's name. He could still hear her crying when she called to tell him what had happened, having convinced herself she couldn't deal with a man so crazy. He had told her to take a deep breath because the problem was the boy was so crazy about her, he couldn't help himself. Alonso was from the old school. He liked a man who would stand up for his daughter. She laughed and said she knew he was crazy about her, but fooling with him was more than a notion.

She had come home for Thanksgiving while she put him in time-out. And after she had left, Alonso had found a scrap of paper in her bedroom. Danged if she hadn't been doodling different iterations of Adrienne Gibson on it— Adrienne Johnson Gibson, Mrs. Adrienne Gibson, Mrs. Gibson, Adrienne Johnson-Gibson. And he knew she was a goner.

So he was heartbroken when she came home last summer saying her marriage was over. She cried herself to sleep night after night when she first got home, but she refused to tell him what had happened. Whatever happened must have been really bad to drive her away from Atlanta, where she had found all kinds of good things—Morehouse, her PhD, great friends new and old, and, most of all, her Josh. Alonso swore his first name was *my*. Every time she talked about him, she said *my Josh*.

Alonso loved living in Lima and was glad his cousin Jeremiah had convinced him to come here and give it a look all those long years ago. Pittsburgh was where he was from, but this was home. It was where he had met his Carol fresh off the Greyhound from Chicago to visit some relatives who lived down the block. She never went back.

Their little girl wasn't long for Lima, though. He could always tell. Most of her brothers settled here and none of them had left the Midwest. It seemed like she was all over the place—New Haven with Reggie, Nashville at Fisk, and Dallas for a minute during her days as a stewardess, until she found a home in Atlanta with her Josh. Now she was back in Ohio. She had been working at the University of Dayton this year, but he knew she wouldn't be happy until she found her way back to an HBCU. Her chair at Morehouse begged her to stay, but she wouldn't hear it. So he pulled some strings and got her a hookup at Dayton as a visiting professor. Dayton had invited her back, but Howard was offering her a shot at tenure, so she would be off again this summer.

He wasn't sure if this letter needed to reach her hands. He sat at his kitchen table, debating while he waited for her to make the drive home from Dayton. It was nice to have her with him. They always had such fun together from the time she was a little girl. He conceded he would have to give it to her and let her make her choices.

He knew from the way she still stargazed two or three nights a week she still loved her Josh. He couldn't understand why she wandered outside so many chilly fall nights and just stared at the sky. So one night he asked what exactly was she looking for. She turned to him and said, "The North Star, Daddy." When he asked what was so special about the North Star and she said, "Oh, it's just something for one of my workshops," he left it alone. He knew such a cryptic comment meant it was none of his business.

Then the telescope showed up at their door right before Christmas, a present from Josh with a note attached. She read the note, squealed with delight, refusing to wait for Christmas day to open it. Alonso surmised it had something to do with her staring into the western Ohio night sky. He thought Josh must be something to have his daughter staring off into space like that.

She still wouldn't talk to him, though. Alonso told her, "Don't you think the polite thing to do is to call him and tell him you liked his present?"

She snorted back at him, "Who said I like it?"

About a week later, he found the telescope in the trash. He pulled it out of the garbage and put it in the closet in his bedroom just in case she came to regret throwing it away. He found the note Josh attached lying on her dresser one day when he was tidying up her room. Alonso loved her, but his baby girl was a slob.

Right then, she breezed through the door, books in hand. "Hi, Daddy," she said as she walked over and kissed him on the forehead. "What's up?"

"You got some mail."

"What, fan mail from some flounder?" she said smiling, mocking one of her favorite childhood cartoons.

"Well, Rocky, it's not from some flounder, but I'm willing to bet it's fan mail." He handed her the letter. "It's from Josh."

"Okay, Bullwinkle," she said. She turned on her heel and walked to her bedroom. Alonso got up and followed her. She was opening the letter when he walked in.

"Give him a chance, baby."

"Why should I?" she asked, her voice filling with anger.

"Sit down, baby girl." She complied, surprising him. He expected an argument. "Because you love him, Adrienne, and we both know that. Look, I could care less about Josh. But I know you still love him. At least hear him out. If you don't like what he has to say, move on. But if you still care, don't do something you might live to regret."

She got up to storm out of the room. He grabbed her arm. "You might be grown, but I'll still take you over my knee. Now sit down. That's your problem with Josh. You're running from him instead of going home and dealing with your situation. I know you don't like what I'm saying and I don't blame you, but I'm saying it because I love you. You two need to communicate, but he's scared and you're stubborn!"

"Scared? Josh isn't afraid of anything!"

Alonso thought, *There she goes defending him again.* "He told me he's afraid of losing you because he loves you so much and he doesn't want to live without you. I told him he ought to tell you, and he said every time he's away from you more than three or four days, he starts to doubt someone as special as you could really love him. He gets to feeling that way and he just can't pick up that phone, as bad as he wants to hear the sound of your voice."

"Okay, I'll read it with an open mind. I'm still through with him, though."

Alonso smiled and said, "That's all I ask."

Chapter 20

Elba

Alonso got up and left her to read the letter. He had been talking to Josh because he sounded just like him. She didn't know what to do. She still loved him. Of that there could be no doubt. She knew it when they talked a few months ago. Her anger made her curt and cold, but she could hear how sorry he was in his voice. Why did men have to act like that? Why did this man, her man, have to act like that?

She opened the letter.

Now I know how Napoleon must have felt at Elba, banished to a life of exile, separated from his beloved France—a victim of his own misbehavior. Death would have been a kinder punishment. I know because I sit here heartbroken on this desolate isle we once called home, separated from you, a victim of my own misbehaving, and I wish with all my heart I could turn back the hands of time and relive the moment I so cavalierly tossed away my life with you. I would not have invaded Russia; I would have spent my every waking moment with you.

For life without you is a life not worth living, like revisiting the agony of Prometheus bound only to have my heart eaten anew every morning, chewed upon every waking moment by this unbearable life I now live—one where there is no Adrienne. My North Star has slipped behind a cloud; my compass has gone awry. I wander aimlessly along the cold shoreline, the wind blows, whistles through the trees, and Adrienne, Adrienne, Adrienne . . . the branches whisper your name.

I see your face, your loving smile, the glistening light dancing in your beautiful brown eyes. I reach out to touch you, my love; your image disperses, drifting off to the distant reaches of my mind. I miss you, my love. I think of you my precious one; I want to speak French, mi amour, when I think of you simply because it is the language of love and I want only to speak of love when I think of you.

You are my Audrey Anne and no one else can. Touch me in those special little places, fill in those pain-filled spaces. No else can, not like you, my Audrey Anne. You can make my heart sing, you can make my mind race; with just a simple smile, you bring oh so much joy to me, making a simple little face or holding me in an enchanting embrace. Yes, you are my Audrey Anne and no one else can, not like you, my Audrey Anne.

You are my golden flower gliding effortlessly through my heart, scoring at will, crashing against the boards of my mind, wrecking it just for the fun of it. You touch me and I know there is a heaven. You become angry with me, I see the gates of hell. And the day you walked out of my life, the best part of me died and went to find its proper place in the ninth circle of hell, leaving a shell of a man to suffer and contemplate the depth of my loss.

I think back to the first time I saw you. You skipped through the hallways of my mind, snuck through a door marked Do Not Enter; tip-toed down a stairway and stole my heart.

Funny, you don't look like a thief. Then again, I guess you can't take what already belonged to you.

I want you to come home. I know the Midwest is where you grew up, but the South with me is where you belong. There can be nothing or no one there that loves you the way I do, that *needs you the way I do, that wants you the way I do. I miss you so much. Please come home. Please come back to me where you belong.*

I have always been Thoreau's man who walked to the beat of a different drum, staggering through life a little off-center, always just out of step. Then you came into my life and heard my cadence and chose to march in lockstep with me, and my life became one big parade filled with brass bands and wind ensembles and yes, even a concert section where violins strung together sweet music for me to march to.

You left, my North Star, so now I again wander directionless through this life. Where there was once darkness, your smiling, vibrant face shone a special light. Now that you are gone, like the old War tune says, I have once again slipped into darkness. I want you. I need you. I love you. I miss you so much. Please come home, back to me where you belong.

For Elba is such a cold and lonely place. There is no Adrienne here to warm it with her smile. I sit in my undistinguished little hut, contemplating a return to the sunshine. I plot an escape from this terrible place where the birds won't sing, the skies are always gray, and the temperature is always below freezing.

I must leave here. I must know the warmth of your love again. I must escape and return to a life with my beloved France. Return to a life lived in the arms of my Guy, my golden flower, my North Star, my Audrey Anne simply because no one else can; not like you, my Audrey Anne. Please let me become a part of your life again.

I shiver, stand next to a fire that provides no warmth. I rub my hands together, thinking about a time when my world was filled with wonder, dreaming of the girl who rocked my world. I think about the wonders of the world. The seven ancient wonders and the seven modern wonders, and I think of the eighth wonder of the modern world—the Gibson smile. Its glow is as ancient as time, its warmth as old as the sun. I love you. I miss you. I want you. I need you. Please come home.

I kick a pebble on my daily stroll, listen to the ocean, consider how I drove our life together aground, dashing it against the awful sandbars of lust and the stones of apathy for what was so important to me. Tears form an ocean in my eyes to match the stormy seas that constantly wash up on this beach, ever remonstrating me for my crimes. I gather together the wreckage, turning over each piece again and again, ruminating on how to turn these ruined pieces of my life into a better, stronger ocean-going vessel so we might continue on our journey together once again.

This journey, this saga of the Gibsons—Adrienne and Josh—for me is an adventure tale, a love story for the ages, a love story I want to be without end. So I toil with the idea in mind of reconstructing our future so we might set sail toward the horizon once more. I dream of this every day, and it is my hope we will find our way back to one another and my fear you can never forgive my unspeakable breach of your trust. I fully accept the blame if we can no longer be. Please forgive me, my love. Please come home.

Napoleon left Elba, but never made it to Paris. Something about a man named Wellington at a place called Waterloo. Me, I've got to make it to Paris—that's you.

> Or put another way
> I wish I could write love songs
> With lyrics so inspired
> They'd manage to explain
> What joy your presence in my life brings
> I wish I could write love songs
> So often I've tried
> Jotted down poetry
> Beautiful verse

But they would not do
Somehow
They always fall short of my feelings for you
I wish I could write love songs
Typical of how I really care
Trumpeting out beautiful thoughts
Of how great life was with you here
One day I'll write love songs
Sprinkled with many gentle remembrances
Thoughts and smiles
In consideration
And appreciation
Of how many times
I've been amazed
By the incredible happiness
You brought to my daze.
Tu es l'amour de ma vie.

Your modern Bonaparte,
Josh

Chapter 21

Tu Es L'amour de Ma Vie

Tap-tap-tap. Adrienne heard her heel bang the wooden floor in her room. She stared at the pieces of paper she held in her hand. A cavalcade of emotions swirled inside her. Minutes passed as she read and reread Josh's letter. She picked up the phone and dialed.

The phone rang three times and then:

"Hello."

"Hey, Chelle, how you doing girl?"

"Hey Adrienne, what's up, soror? You calling to say you're coming home?"

"Chelle, I am home."

"Adrienne, you're in Ohio where you grew up. Atlanta's your home."

Adrienne chuckled and said, "I'm not studying you. I called to ask you a question."

Michelle replied, "Yes ma'am, what can your bestest friend help with you? Tell you how you need to come and settle things with that man of yours? Adrienne, I saw him a couple of weeks ago and girl, he is miserable without you."

"Hush, Chelle, what does *tu es l'amour de ma vie* mean?"

It took Chelle a moment to think about it. "Ah, let me see, oh yeah, 'you are the love of my life.' You got a new friend?"

"Chelle, I'm still married to Josh. Unlike him, I take my vows serious. Chelle, he wrote me a letter."

"What did he say, Adrienne? Nah girl, if he ended it like that, you get it and read it to me. I know how hot that last letter was. Are we gonna have to stamp a P for pitiful on him again?

Adrienne laughed, realizing why she had called Michelle. "I can't read you his letter!"

"Girl, get that letter and read me what he said. It'll serve that trifling Negro right if you put his business in the street." It took a few minutes, but Chelle convinced her to read it to her.

Reading it aloud affected her even more than reading it to herself. A tremor took hold in her voice as she recited such phrases as the eighth wonder of the modern world—Adrienne's smile. Her heart pounded with emotion as she ended with "Me, I've got to get to Paris, that's you." *And hey, poetry wow.*

Chelle was silent for what seemed like hours after she finished. "Girl, I'm with him—you need to come home. Adrienne, I know he messed up, but that's the man you love on that paper and you know it. He's the nicest man I've ever met. I know he hurt you, but can't you see how much he loves you and how sorry he is? You better come tend those fires before some other biddy snatches him from you."

"Chelle."

"And I'm surprised at you anyway. You sound like you're scared. All I've seen you handle. That's not my bestest friend. You gonna let a man have you trippin' like this? One you got wrapped around your little finger?"

"Chelle."

"Girl, you must not be hearing the same words I was listening to. 'Death would be a kinder punishment'?

Come on Adrienne. You're the one who always tells me to step out on faith. Where is all that now. Why you gone run from that great adventure, that beautiful journey, the saga of Josh and Adrienne? You gone let a crack ho stand in the way of your blessing?

"You the one always tells me, 'Chelle, life is to be enjoyed not endured.' Lord knows you've endured enough. Enjoy that blessing named Josh God sent you."

"Chelle!"

"What, Adrienne?"

"I gotta go!"

"You gonna call that man?"

"Maybe. I want to talk to Genna first."

"She's going to tell you the same thing, Paris."

"Bye, Chelle."

"You call me and I'm like Josh—please come home, back to the South where you belong."

She put down the phone. Her emotions were whipping this way and that. She sat for a few minutes. *The saga of Josh and Adrienne Gibson*, she thought. Her tapping foot made her smile as she thought about how he said she heard his cadence. And she always had.

Still, she was conflicted. She wouldn't take what he did off of anybody. If Reggie had done something so horrible, she wouldn't have thought twice about moving on. Her ball player . . . But this was Josh, Josh Gibson. *Tu es l'amour de ma vie.* She still felt the same way in spite of—or was it because of—all he had taken her through. Yet she still wasn't sure she wanted to travel that road again. *Lord, I'm so tired of going through all this with Josh.*

She said to herself, "You hear my cadence." And it began to sink in. This was Josh, and he was telling her he had been redeemed by this great love he felt for her. He was trying to tell her his North Star had finally led him back to the Josh of before the fire bombing, the Josh he wanted to be.

She knew for sure at that moment he had written her to say goodbye. He wasn't trying to get her to come home. He wanted her to know how much he loved her. He wanted her to know he accepted the blame for wrecking their marriage. He wanted her to be happy. To go on, because his conscience demanded he give himself up.

"Oh, Josh," she gasped, and picked up the phone.

About the Author

Erskine Hawkins Jr. is a native of Birmingham, Alabama, who has lived in Atlanta since he was ten. A third-generation Morehouse man, he loves his alma mater and Atlanta. He is an accountant by trade who also serves as adjunct professor of accounting at two local colleges.